Euphoria

LORRAINE MCLEOD

ACKNOWLEDGMENTS

Thank you to my husband and my family for having less time with me while I've been writing and editing this book.

Special thanks to my editor.

1 - THE PERFECT PLACE

It was the perfect place to wait for a death.

Swathed in night shadows, the Corinthian pillars of St. Georges Hall concealed the man who would spill blood onto the streets of Liverpool.

Across the street, a car horn blasted at a group of drunken girls as they stumbled out in front of the headlights, staggering from one bar to the next.

He returned his attention to the flashing glass fruit above the doorway of 'The Dancing Lime'. A stupid name, suited to the idiot people who went there.

She was inside. Her impending death prickled his bones, worked its way through muscles and tissues to sting his skin, urging him to cross the street, go inside the nightclub, find her.

Wait. His heavy clothes and fedora were not suited to clubbing.

He surrendered to the wave that surged through his body to break into whispers in his ears. Close now. He could almost taste the sweetness; feel the flow of life energy leaving her.

A door crashed open.

She dashed out, tearing at her face and mouth, pulling out clusters of black and pink hair. She vomited on the concrete and kept running. Two young men ran out after her, shouting, calling her back.

She stopped and turned, clawing at her face. Fingers dug into her eyes and poured blood down pale skin.

He reached out from his mind to grab hold of her panic, too see the demons she hallucinated, to feed from her terror. Finally, the mix was right, the success he'd been waiting for. Grohah would be pleased.

Rosy eyes dangled like cherries on her cheeks. Ribbons of skin draped a veil of flesh over her neck. Vital seconds to savor her pain before her shattered mind surrendered her life. Her mouth widened over ruby teeth. From her throat, a scream like a thousand burning rats tore open the night.

Ripples of bliss electrified his nerves. Every sound, all the energy he could pull from the people, the buildings, the vehicles, all blended to the perfect pitch of elation that blazed his body with a heat that did not burn.

Abruptly, his mind cleared. She lay on the ground. Dead.

Wailing sirens approached, jerking the throng out of their daze. Howls and sobs saturated the summer air.

The Baker slid out of the shadows and inhaled the stench of vomit and blood. Power and immortality would soon be his.

The era of Grohah had begun.

2 - AVOIDANCE

"Why the fuck did Jake have to go pull a stunt like that?" Big Don threw his cigarette butt out of the open car window into the warm summer night. "Marchant will kill him for this, and it won't be quick or painless."

It wasn't hard for Finn to figure out that Jake wanted a new life with Kelly before she discovered what he did for a living. When you worked for a gangster, your life expectancy wasn't always that long. A familiar ache nagged in his chest, memories of the life he'd shared with Amy. A future stolen. Can't get sucked down into what *could have been* when trying to stay in character undercover. Finn concentrated on traffic as he made the left turn into Speke Boulevard towards Liverpool's John Lennon airport.

"Damned if I know,' Finn lied, "but if we don't find him, and the coke, we're in the shit too."

"Tell me something I don't fucking know Sherlock."

I'm going to put you and your piece of shit boss in jail, was what Finn wanted to say, but instead replied, "The hummingbird is the only bird that can fly backwards."

3

Big Don's forehead wrinkles dug deep into his skin as he screwed up his eyes. "What the fuck? Are you some kind of bleedin' bird expert?"

"Nope. Read it on the back of a cereal packet."

"Freak. Fuckin' freak you are."

Finn turned slightly and grinned at his sidekick. "Yeah, because if I was normal, I'd be working in a bank instead of hunting down runaway drug dealers."

Don folded his lips into a thin line and nodded. "Point taken."

The retail park was lit up as though everywhere was open for business, but only night crews watched the deserted stores. Turning left into Speke Hall Road, the airport came into view. Anxiety started at his feet and worked its way up to his stomach, where it sat like a firmly fixed sea urchin, quivering, with no intention of moving. He didn't want to go to the airport; in fact, he didn't want to find Jake at all. He hoped he'd gone already, off to some safe place where Marchant couldn't hurt him. Plus, if they did find Jake, Marchant would want them to kill him, and as a cop, Finn didn't want to have to test his loyalty to that degree. Two people had met a bullet from his gun in his career, and both times a part of him died with them.

Don was silent while Finn found a place to park the car. When Big Don went quiet, he was at his most dangerous. Shit. Walking towards the bright lights of the airport entrance, Finn straightened his back and mentally counted to six on each inhale and exhale. They reached the middle of the three entrances. "I don't think he's here." Finn shook his head, pushing open the glass door.

"Quickest way out of the country," Big Don replied while scanning the airport and people. "This place isn't very big, shouldn't take us long to check out."

Finn was inspecting the layout. Trying to buy time for Jake he said, "I'll take the check-in desks on the right, you take the arrivals."

"Why the fuck would he be in the arrivals section?"

"I don't know, hiding maybe? If we don't check everywhere Marchant will be pissed."

Big Don rubbed his neck, twisted his lips to the left and chewed the corner of his mouth, something he did when he was in reluctant agreement. Finn wondered if he ever thought about shaving his hands. If it wasn't for the heavy yellow gold rings he wore, he'd look as though he was wearing fur gloves.

"Fine," Don replied, "But make sure you check out the toilets."

A few people glanced at Big Don as he walked by them, but quickly looked away. Don looked intimidating when he was in a good mood, but now, with simmering anger seeping out of his pores, he oozed poison.

Finn reluctantly turned his attention to the check-in area. *Don't turn up here Jake. I don't want to kill you.*

3 - SWEAT

Jake pulled the peak of his Nike cap down as far as he could without dislodging the short blonde ponytail he'd tucked up inside it. His father was dead on Marchant's orders and he'd be next if he didn't get away fast.

A few minutes past eleven on his watch, and the oversized airport clock told the same time. No sign of Kelly, but more importantly, no sign of Finn or Big Don. But what if Marchant sent someone else after him, knowing he'd be watching for guys he knew? If he let that thought get hold of him, he'd suspect every man in the airport. Shuddering, despite the heat, he went over the escape plan.

In one more hour they could board the plane. Even though it was late Sunday evening, John Lennon Airport was hot and busy, and hopefully the crowds would help hide him. He wiped the moisture from the back of his neck and dried his hand on his grubby shirt. Weren't airports supposed to be air conditioned?

He tapped rubber soles on the tiled floor. *Where was she?*

A row of telephones lined the wall opposite like grey stationary soldiers, reminding him that his cell phone sat dead in the case on his hip; the charger in his bedroom. He was almost on his feet to call Kelly when the arrival of a stocky man moving towards him made him sit back down swiftly.

Crap. Jake looked up from under the peak of his cap. The guy scanned the airport, obviously looking for someone. Sweat trickled under Jake's collar, making his shirt cling to his back. Jake dropped his head, pretending to tie his shoelaces. Maybe he was overheating because he was fretting too much? Have to calm down. Losing control was not an option.

But the stocky guy progressed toward him. Jake fumbled with the laces while tracking the progress of the scruffily clad feet.

Run. Get up and run now, the panicked voice in his head nagged. *Can't. Have to wait for Kelly.*

His back was a tight coil, legs ready to move in an instant. He counted the blue mosaic squares on the gleaming floor as the black Reeboks advanced towards him from the corner of his eye. Dirty black leather loomed large in his vision. Perspiration tickled his face, stung his already sore eyes, but he resisted the urge to wipe it away. It ran down the side of his cheek, dodging between the stubble to drip from his chin to his thigh, the droplet spreading out to join the other stains on the denim.

He still didn't wipe it, and the man still came toward him.

Jake feigned tiredness by leaning over and putting his head on his folded arms, giving him a view of the entrance.

Kelly walked through the doors.

Sports shoes stopped by the side of the metal bench Jake sat on. They seemed out of place with the guy's clothing. Jake could almost feel the hand on his shoulder, hear the voice telling him to get up and come quietly.

He had to risk moving before the hand fell.

Jake sucked in a breath, tilted his body forward, lifted his head.

Kelly started to move hesitantly towards the seated area. She stood out from the crowd, not only because she was so attractive, but because she looked lost. Marchant's men knew what she looked like, if the stocky guy turned around and saw her…

Jake lifted his heels from the floor, raised himself inches from the bench.

"Carol! Over here," the man shouted, and moved off swiftly towards a pair of black stilettos.

Jake sagged, his body slumped. He dipped his head slightly but turned it to the side to see the thickset man take a suitcase from the arm of a well-dressed petite brunette. His breath escaped in a grateful sigh and he sprung from his seat and made directly for Kelly.

The light bounced off Kelly's red curls and her freckled face made her appear younger than her nineteen years. In her short summer dress she looked like a schoolgirl on vacation.

"Kelly," Jake said quietly, slipping his muscular arm around her tiny waist.

She spun around, "Jake!"

"Did you tell anyone where you were going?"

"No. You said not to so I didn't." Pale green eyes were full of unanswered questions. "What's going on?"

Sliding his arm from her waist, he hooked it through hers. Fear scratched at every nerve in his body as he led her towards the check-in.

4 - A NEW DRUG

Dr. Lysa Warner walked down the corridor to meet the boy in the waiting room. The girl he came to the hospital with was dead on arrival. Probably fifteen to sixteen years old, though it was hard to tell when they were so thin — the third victim of an unknown drug. Weary of covering up young faces, sick of seeing the needle marks in their bodies and pumping their stomachs, Lysa pushed open the door. The single occupant, a teenage boy of about seventeen to eighteen, turned his head and looked at her through bloodshot eyes. "Are you Mark? You brought your girlfriend, Tina in?"

Mark stopped fidgeting with the string on his faded blue, cotton hoodie. "Err, yeah, I'm Mark, is she all right, will she be okay?"

"I need to talk to you, somewhere quieter." Lysa beckoned Mark into an empty examination room, flicked on the light and closed the door softly after him.

The florescent glare made the room appear cold, though it was warm in the hospital. The hard vinyl exam bed shone black in the white room, as did the two plastic covered, steel framed chairs. She sat on one and motioned Mark to take the other. She fought tiredness, and wondered what he cared about more, the girl in the mortuary, or getting out of here to get his next fix.

He didn't sit down. Instead he returned to twisting the string on his hood and chewing the end of it. Lysa needed answers. This was no ordinary drug they were dealing with, and this was the first chance she'd had to talk to someone who may have information they could use.

"Please sit down. I need to ask you some questions."

Mark moved to the window and pulled down a slat on the white venetian blind, peering into the darkness outside. He didn't answer. Didn't turn around.

Lysa softened her tone. "Mark, will you please sit down, it's difficult talking to the back of your head."

Mark turned sharply. "Ya wanna tell me she's dead. Want me to sit down so ya can tell me she's dead."

"It would be better if you came over here. There really are some things I need to know."

"I don't need to sit down, just say it, just say she's dead, go on."

"All right," said Lysa. "Tina was dead when the paramedics brought her in, I'm sorry."

"Ya see," he said, "I didn't need to sit down, I'm all right, I'm all right." He went back to the window and again pulled down the slat and peered out.

Although she felt sympathy for Mark, her teenage brother, Robbie, had shown her the futility of trying to help someone who had no desire to help themselves. "Who are you looking for?" Lysa asked.

"It's out there, ya know that don't ya?"

"What's out there? A new drug?"

Continuing to stare out of the window, Mark laughed. Not a nervous or hysterical laugh, in the way Lysa had occasionally known some people to laugh in reaction to bad news. This was different; almost taunting. The blue-tinged faces of three drug victims rotated in her memory as if on a death carousel. Uneasiness seeped into her pores.

"My job is to save people, but I need your help, Mark."

He turned to face her. "Listen lady, ya can buy whatever ya want on the streets, coke, smack, crack, anything." His left eyelid twitched, and for a few seconds he chewed at a scab on his bottom lip, making it bleed. He spat the dead skin onto the floor. "Ya can buy it from almost anyone, ya know?"

"Yes Mark, I know."

"But the new stuff, well ya can't get that just anywhere."

A new drug *was* on the streets. Relief from the confirmation gave way to anxiousness. "What new stuff? Where do you get it?"

He laughed, "If I knew that I'd be on it."

"So Tina was on it?"

Moving away from the window, he finally sat in the chair she'd offered. A whiff of stale cigarette smoke invaded her nostrils as his face came closer. Lysa tolerated the sourness without moving back.

He dropped the laugh and his voice mellowed. "Just the one time. I guess she took too much."

One hit? This stuff could kill with just one hit? Experience taught her he was watching her reactions and was probably scared she would call the police. Fatigue fell away with the urgency to find out more. Lysa reached for his hand, "Mark…"

As if stung, he recoiled with the speed of a snake before it lunges forward to bite. *Mistake, take it slower.* He scratched his head and stared with eyes that only cared about his next fix. She'd seen that look many times, and far closer to home than a hospital waiting room. "What was it? What did Tina take?"

He stopped scratching his head and went back to fiddling with the strings on his hoodie.   Finally, he said, "To tell ya the truth Doc, I don't know what it is. I just know it makes ya feel real good when ya take it."

"Have you taken it?"

"Told you already, Tina had it, she took it last... Thursday I think. Yeah, it was Thursday."

"And you didn't take any?"

"Didn't get a chance. She told me she took it Friday morning but I didn't see her till the night. Didn't even save me any. Said she only had the one hit." He shook his head, "She was kinda edgy and mad at me for even sayin' she should have kept some for me. Then she went off on this crazy high. I tell ya Doc, she was high as an eagle. She was soaring Doc, she was soaring."

"You're sure it was Friday morning she took it?" Lysa made a mental calculation in her head. "Friday morning to Sunday evening… that's about two and a half days ago. Did she take anything else?"

"No Doc, with this new stuff ya don't need anything else. I could've smacked her for taking it all herself. She was high nearly all that time. Now and again she'd come down and go all quiet like for a bit, then she'd be full of energy again. Fuck, did I ever want to get my hands on it. In the club she started seeing stuff, yelling about worms eating her, and saying I was on fire. Then she stopped yelling and ran outside. That's when she really went nuts..." He stopped twisting the string, his hands fixed still in mid-air as if in a photograph. "So much blood Doc, and her eyes…"

Or, *lack* of eyes. By the time the paramedics had picked her up, the girls eyeballs were nothing more than bloody pulp.

As horrific as the girl had looked, getting a lead on this drug would help to prevent further tragedy. Lysa's own eyes itched with dryness from the twelve hour shift, but she now had some insight into the initial effects of the drug. If she could keep Mark talking a little longer she might find out enough to start figuring out what it could be.

"Tina is the third young person to die from an unexplained drug overdose this week, and if we're to have any chance of saving people we need to know more about it."

Mark frowned. Standing, he crossed the tiled floor and moved back to the window. His hand reached for the slat to pull it down, but as his fingers touched the plastic, he turned back to her.

"Can't your lab people find out all that stuff, why do ya need me to tell ya?"

"We need help. Whatever this drug is, it appears to be almost totally absorbed into the body. We ran tests on Tina, but we can't find much to work with. A small trace of cocaine, but not enough to kill someone." Maybe giving him a little information might tempt him to want to know more, give her something in return.

Mark moved away from the blind and made quickly for the door, anxiousness pricked at her skin, raising the fair hair on her arms.

"Wait. You're the only person who may be able to help us at the moment. Is there anything else you can tell me?"

Mark hesitated, his fingers touching the door handle. "I can't tell ya nothing. I sure as hell can't tell ya where she got it because I don't know."

Lysa tried a different tactic to keep him from leaving. "Okay. Can you tell me how to contact Tina's family? Her identification said she was eighteen but I'm thinking it's a fake because she looks a lot younger. If so, maybe the name on the ID was fake too?"

Mark pulled open the door, "She ran away from a kid's home months ago. I don't know much else."

"So she's definitely not eighteen then." Lysa paused, trying not to scare him away. "I really do need to let her family know. I won't involve you in any way if you can give me any more details."

"You swear?"

"Yes, I promise I won't involve you."

He didn't look very reassured. "You'd better not."

"Promise."

"Okay, well yeah... her ID is fake but I don't know her real last name, she never told me."

"But wasn't she your girlfriend?"

"Not really, we only knew each other a couple of weeks. I only came here with her because... well... because there was nobody else."

He was leaving and Lysa's patience dropped to zero with his impending exit. She made a last attempt to prise anything else from him.

"Can you tell me anything more that can help?"

"I told you. I don't know anything else."

Mark left the room, letting the door swing shut behind him. Lysa leapt up and opened it, shouting to him, "Mark wait!"

He stopped and turned his head.

Lysa called. "If you find out who's selling it don't buy any, don't take it." It was a pointless request but she had to try.

The boy shrugged his shoulders and turned away. He shuffled down the corridor until he turned the corner and was out of her vision.

Lysa checked her watch and realized her shift should have finished an hour and a half ago. Best get back to emergency, finish up her paperwork, and officially hand over her shift.

Lysa picked up her car keys, overwhelmed with thoughts of her younger brother, Robbie. Dread filled her stomach and her nerves. Where was he, and could he access this new stuff on the streets?

Reluctantly, she hoped he'd stay on heroin.

5 - AIDING AND ABETTING

Finn didn't notice Jake at first. In fact, if Jake hadn't stood up at precisely the moment Finn was checking out the front row of seats he'd not have recognized him at all. If Big Don saw them, Jake would be finished.

As Jake crossed the room to Kelly, Finn quickly scanned the area for Big Don. He spotted him returning from the arrivals side of the small airport. Alert and on edge, Finn had only seconds to make a decision. He should sneak up on Jake, stick a gun in his back and tell him they were taking him back to Marchant. But, that would mean certain death for Jake, and as they would have to take Kelly with them, she could wind up dead too. The girl had done nothing wrong except fall in love with the wrong guy. She was fresh with life, and as Marchant had already hinted that Finn would be the one to kill Jake, he might expect him to kill Kelly also. His cover and the entire operation would be in danger.

Big Don pushed through the crowd and made eye contact with Finn. Finn quickly nodded in response and turned as if to walk towards the toilets, then feigned a check of the area, while still keeping Jake and Kelly in sight from the corner of his vision. If Big Don suspected him, he could blow the trust he'd earned so far and be further away from gaining the information they needed on the drug smuggling. Amy would have died for nothing.

Relying on his gut instinct and with purpose, Finn turned his back on his target and walked swiftly towards Big Don.

If Big Don looked over Finn's shoulder he'd see them, and want to know why Finn hadn't stopped Jake. Push that thought away, it wasn't going to happen. Blood rushed through Finn's ears like an ocean wave. Footsteps became heavier, as though he wasn't moving fast enough. Crossing the tiles in seconds felt like minutes, and he was about two yards away when Big Don yelled. Finn's heart almost stopped. The shit was going down and he was right in the middle of it.

"Did you see Jake?" Finn asked, dreading the answer.

"No."

Some of the panic left Finn's skin like a heat haze, but fear for Jake still burned in him. "So why did you shout?"

"Some stupid bastard was lookin' at me funny so I glared at him, and he tried to stare me down so I fuckin' yelled at him."

A current of relief coursed through Finn's nerves, but his heart still pounded. "You yell at some guy for staring at you, and yet you call me a freak?"

"Fucked off pretty fast though." A throaty laugh escaped his bull-like thick throat, making fat lips, wobble on his pock marked face.

Moving to the right of Don, and pointing to the men's toilets, Finn said, "I've not checked in there yet." Big Don turned, following the direction of Finn's finger. The check-in desk obscured from his line of vision.

"I'll go, need to take a piss anyway," Don replied. Finn waited until Big Don was inside the room before turning his head to the other side of the airport. Jake and Kelly were nowhere in sight. Hopefully they were now safely in the departure lounge where Finn and Big Don couldn't follow without a ticket and a passport. He could breathe easy for the next hour until they had to report in to Marchant that they'd not been able to find Jake.

6 - DEAD ROT

Sunlight blasted its way into Mark's bedroom, lighting up the heaps of clothes littering the floor. He squinted, hunger pangs gnawed at his belly, and it took a couple of seconds for him to realize where he was. Then he remembered Tina.

He wasn't sure how to feel about her death. He should be upset, but he didn't feel that bad. Maybe his mum's cancer had used up all the stores of grief in his seventeen years. He pushed painful memories away and decided it'd be a good idea to go check Tina's squat and see if she'd hidden any of that new stuff; she might have been lying when she said she didn't have any more. So what if she'd died from it. People died taking all sorts of drugs, she probably just took too much. If he found any, he'd take a little to start with and see how it made him feel. Besides, it was harder to live life than embrace death.

Silence in the house told him his father was out, especially as the bottom stair — where he'd been lying drunk when Mark arrived home — was now vacant. Mark looked around the dirty kitchen and poured a glass of water to cool his dry throat. There was a time when this house was spotless, not a cushion out of place nor a hair on the carpet. His thirst satisfied, Mark dropped his glass into the sink to join the mountain of dishes threatening to spill over the side and onto the floor. Those happy days would never return.

The kitchen clock lied; it was twelve-thirty. It had been deceiving time for about two months, so he ignored it and started off to the squat.

It took only ten minutes to reach the derelict house Tina had lived in, and like his home, it was deserted. He pushed open the front door that was never locked, hardly aware of the sour smell of damp and vomit that permeated the walls of the place. Desire for drugs pushed him on up the rotted staircase, blind to the cockroach that scuttled out of his way as he reached the top. Tina's bedroom door was open. Mark hurried inside and grabbed the tatty plastic carrier bag from the rotting mattress. Ripping it open, he checked through the contents. Stale body odor rose from the garments, but he didn't care; a pair of dirty jeans, faded black cotton shorts, a couple of tee shirts, and one snagged green jumper. Mark felt inside the pockets of the jeans and found only a worn-edged, folded up letter. No money, not even any loose change. Fuck! Now what?

The letter. Maybe it was from someone he could get money from? Scanning it quickly he discovered it was from Tina's mother. Probably been sent to the children's home Tina had run away from as there was no envelope. There was an address at the top of the paper.

Mark stuffed the paper into his pocket and continued his search around the room. Nothing underneath the mattress but a few crumbs. Might as well leave those for the mice. Frustration rubbed at the edges of his skin. He needed his next fix, and without cash he'd have to resort to stealing again. His mother would have hated to know he'd become a thief. At least death saved her that disappointment. He felt around for any loose floorboards. Finding two, he pulled them up easily and was dismayed to find nothing concealed in the black spaces but dirt.

Mark quickly searched the remaining two upstairs rooms. Discovering nothing, he went back downstairs.

The two larger rooms leading from the narrow hallway revealed no more than the upstairs of the house, so Mark finally entered the kitchen. Dust motes played in the shafts of sunlight filtering through the boarded up window. Intermittent rays cast mottled patterns around the dilapidated kitchen as his vision adjusted to the dim light. Mark crossed the floor to pull out a drawer in the kitchen sink. A creak from the front door snapped him into alert and the sound of footsteps in the hallway prompted a tremor of fear, stopping him instantly.

"Christ, do people really fucking live in this filth?"

The deep, gravelly voice chilled Mark's already agitated bones, and fear insisted on escape. The back door to the yard was next to the sink and Mark dashed quickly to the exit. He gripped and twisted the old brass handle only to find it locked. Knots of anxiety added to the nagging hunger of his addiction. His eyes scanned the room, but no key leapt out at him.

A second voice carried through the empty house. Not as deep, but it sounded just as menacing. "Yeah, well junkie girls don't care where they live."

Junkie girl. They were looking for Tina. Nausea threatened to weaken him, but he had to get out. "Well let's look quick, I don't want to spend a fucking second longer in here than I have to."

"Scared of getting your clothes dirty?" his companion mocked.

"You go upstairs, I'll look down here," said Gravel Voice.

Icy panic in Mark's veins raised bumps on clammy skin. He checked from wall to wall, window to hallway, searching for a means of escape. He spotted another door at the far end of the kitchen and made his way to it as quietly as he could. To his relief the handle turned and the door opened. Another door stood about three feet ahead and he pulled it open, eager to be away.

The smell that assaulted his nostrils made him want to retch. He might have been oblivious to the earlier aromas, but this demanded attention. As his eyes adjusted to the dim interior of the small bathroom the sight greeting him made him temporarily forget about the two men in the house.

Slumped in the waterless and grimy bathtub lay the naked body of Liam. Mark knew it was Liam because of the bleached blonde stripe down the middle of his dark brown hair. Everyone had called him the skunk when he had it done and now he deserved the name. Mark swatted at the flies swarming around him, the buzzing of their wings amplified into white noise in his ears. In the sickly heat of the small room, the squirming mass of maggots in Liam's neck made the corpse appear to move.

Rapid waves of nausea insisted his body expel food and bile from his nose and mouth in a violent expression of revulsion. Vomit splashed over his feet, the floor, his clothes, and a sour sweat soaked his clothes and his skin. Mark trembled at the sight of the body in the tub, but when the heavy hand landed on his shoulder he almost lost control of his bladder.

"Hey you. You know where that girl is?" The rasping voice from behind terrified him. *Maybe these guys killed Liam and now they were after Tina?* He wiped his mouth on his sleeve and turned as the man pushed him forward to gain entry to the bathroom.

"Hey..." the man started and then put his free hand over his nose and mouth. "What the fuck is that smell?"

Mark pointed at the bath and as Gravel Voice stepped forward to inspect what was in the room he took his left hand from Mark's shoulder. Stealing the opportunity, Mark squeezed past and stumbled back into the kitchen.

"Jesus fucking Christ!" Gravel Voice yelled. Mark ran through the hallway and out of the front door, trying his best not to puke again. He had enough problems without slipping on vomit while trying to escape.

*** *** ***

"Finn get back down here!"

Finn was already hurrying down the staircase after being alerted by the voices and the bang of a door on the lower floor. As he entered the kitchen, he saw Don's usually ruddy complexion had paled so much that if it wasn't for his thick black hair, he'd look albino. The day was warm, but not yet hot enough for the watery film that glistened on his forehead.

"What's up? I heard talking down here and then someone running off. Why are people so fucking scared? All we want to do is sell some more gear."

"We need to get out. There's a dead fucking body in the bathroom."

"So what's the problem?"

"The problem is that this fucker's throat's been ripped out and there's flies setting up a breeding colony in his carcass."

"Come on Don, you're acting like you've never seen a corpse before." The look of disgust on Don's face amused Finn. This was a new type of reaction for Don.

Big Don nodded in the direction of the bathroom. "You go take a fucking look then! See how long you last in there."

Finn went to look; the smell grew unbearable as he entered the room. Don was right about the stink, and the kid in the bath looked rancid.

Finn hurried back to the kitchen. "Ah Don, you disappoint me, I've never seen you so shook up about a little dead body."

Big Don was heading out in the direction Mark had taken. "Oh sure yeah, but I've not seen them after a few days in a stinking, fucking hot, airless bathroom!"

"Hang on," said Finn following him outside, "If we come back in a week we could have a side business going."

Finn suppressed a smile as Don's eyes narrowed, his fat eyebrows almost met as he glared at Finn.

"Are you fucking nuts? I'm not going back in that dump again."

"We could make a ton of money."

"Sure. How'd you figure that?" he asked.

Finn grinned. "There's a fortune to be made maggot farming."

7 - SAVING A BROTHER

After arriving home at three thirty in the morning, Lysa hadn't slept until over an hour later. Shift work played havoc with sleep patterns, and letting work spill into her private life didn't help. She'd tried working on a small sculpture, but even that didn't help her unwind. The soft tan stone and the female body taking shape brought back the events of the night. The dead girl and her uncaring boyfriend played a funeral dance in her mind. The melody, sorrow.

Eventually she'd gone to bed and dreamt about Robbie.

Dreams came and went but Robbie was the thread that linked them all together. When she finally awoke, the red digitals on the clock read 12:45 p.m., and he was still in her thoughts.

After a quick shower, she made herself a brunch of sausage and egg. Shaking on far too much salt for a doctor who ought to know better, she tucked into her meal. The phone ringing interrupted her.

Trying unsuccessfully to swallow a chunk of sausage, she picked up the receiver. Lysa went into a coughing fit as the caller asked for Doctor Lysa Warner.

"Hell...ahu!..uhg! O."

Eventually the food allowed itself to be swallowed and Lysa recovered.

"Sorry about that," she said, "You caught me eating lunch."

The voice sounded neither impressed nor amused. "Is this, Doctor Lysa Warner?"

"Yes, speaking,"

"This is Sergeant John Friedman of Anchor Street Police Station. We have a Robert Warner here. He says you're his sister."

Fear sprinkled over her and she gripped the receiver tighter.

"Yes that's right, what's happened? Is Robbie okay?"

"Yes, he's fine. Can't say the same for his victims though."

Alarmed, Lysa asked, "What's he done?"

"I'm afraid I can't discuss that over the phone, could you come down? He says you'll take responsibility for him."

"Yes. Yes, I'll be there as soon as I can."

"Right then Doctor, we'll see you shortly."

Lysa said goodbye to the sergeant and hurriedly dressed in a white blouse and a black skirt. She finished it off with black shoes and a black jacket and as she passed the mirror in the hallway she caught a glimpse of herself. She looked as though she'd dressed for a memorial service. Shivering slightly at the thought, she hoped it wasn't an omen for the future.

She turned the key in the alarm and made sure to lock the deadbolt behind her before hurrying down the steps to her car.

Thankfully, the Monday traffic was quieter than usual. The sergeant's comment played over in her mind, *'can't say the same for his victims'*. The blast of a horn from an oncoming Ford Fiesta prompted her foot to slam on the brake, sending a shot of adrenalin through her veins. Breathing deep before moving off again, she tried to concentrate on the road for the rest of the thirty minute journey to the station.

Robbie would have to come to her place. Their mother wouldn't have him back. He'd also exhausted his supply of friends and relatives, abused their trust and stolen from them. She was the only one left he could call.

The building looked more like a mini prison than a police station. Lysa noted the wire grills on the windows and evidence of metal shutters on the entrance. Litter wafted across the dirt that soiled the pavement, not caring where it lay.

Inside, a rather scruffy middle-aged man sat on a scratched plastic chair in the foyer. He seemed half asleep and slumped into his companion; a woman of similar age and dress. The woman elbowed him in his side and with a grunt, he straightened up.

She turned her attention to the desk. A young man was talking to a policeman about his stolen car. It had been found and he wanted to know when he could have it back. He was a stark comparison to the other couple. Dressed in a navy blue Nike tracksuit and matching Nike trainers with a baseball cap perched on his apparently shaven head, he looked like so many other young people in their designer uniforms. Worry turned to impatience as she waited, and the policeman told the Nike guy to take a seat. Cursing, the youth took a seat next to the woman, scraping his chair as he moved it slightly away from the shabby twosome. Lysa moved forward.

"Can I help you Miss?" The policeman at the desk asked. His slightly greying hair stuck to his head like plastic strips, badly in need of a wash.

Sucking in a mouthful of stale air she said, "I believe my brother is here, Sergeant Friedman phoned and asked me to come down."

"And that would be?"

"Robert Warner."

"Address?"

"I don't know if he has one," Lysa replied. "I've not seen him for several months."

He raised his eyebrows and typed Robbie's name into a computer. "Take a seat and I'll have someone come out to see you," he said.

Looking around the small entrance, Lysa could only see one vacant chair. It was next to the half-asleep man. She stood by the wall.

A young policeman emerged from a corridor to the left, and the older man beckoned to him. After a few words, the younger man nodded and disappeared back down the corridor. Moments later, a tall clean shaven man in uniform appeared.

"Doctor Warner?" he asked, looking at Lysa.

"Yes," she replied, walking the short distance back to the counter.

"Sergeant Friedman. Could you come with me please?" He opened up a shelf in the counter and Lysa passed through, following him down a brightly lit corridor. He stopped at a grey door bearing the title "Interview Room 3."

He unlocked the door and switched on the light. She was hit with a Deja vu from the previous night when she had led Mark down a hospital corridor into a small private room such as this.

Dread clouded her mind; fear that one day she'd hear the same news about Robbie she'd given to Mark.

"Please sit down," said the Sergeant.

Her own words echoed in her head.

The room contained only a table with a hard plastic chair at either side. A poster about drug abuse and a help line number hung on the wall above the table. The sergeant took one chair and motioned her to take the other.

Sitting, she asked, "Is Robbie alright, Sergeant Friedman?"

"Yes, but I did tell you that on the telephone."

Relief washed over her, "I know, I just thought..." Lysa shook her head and then saw the questioning look on the sergeant's face. "I had to tell someone that their girlfriend died last night, it was drugs, and knowing Robbie, well..." she tailed off, not wanting to explain any further.

"Well, your brother is very much alive, though he has committed a crime, Doctor Warner."

"What has he done?"

"He broke into an elderly couple's home yesterday morning, and he's only given us your name today. He scared them half to death."

"Are they okay?"

"Yes, surprisingly. The old gent phoned us immediately when he heard the glass breaking in his downstairs room. We arrested your brother very shortly afterwards. There were a few others with him, but they escaped."

"Has he been charged?"

"He's been charged with breaking and entering, but if you're willing to take responsibly for him we can release him on bail."

"I'll take him," said Lysa. "I'll be honest with you Sergeant, Robbie has a drug problem and nobody else in the family wants anything to do with him."

"Hmm, well we have had dealings with Robbie before, but this is his first charge. Are you sure you'll keep control of him?"

"I will."

The sergeant stood. "If you'd like to wait here I'll draw up the necessary papers and we'll have you and Robbie out of here shortly."

Lysa nodded as he went out of the door. What would she do with Robbie? Fifteen-year-old kids were trouble in normal circumstances, but fifteen-year-old kids on heroin were something else entirely.

The last time she'd seen him he'd looked ill and skinny, his once good looking features sunken and grey. She dreaded to see how he looked now.

8 - KEEPING HER SAFE

Kelly emerged from the hotel pool. Her usually tightly curled hair relaxed into soft waves of deep russet. She'd accepted his lies without difficulty; they fell from his tongue as easily as the chlorinated water from her skin.

She caught the towel he threw and wrapped it around her, tucking it in above her breasts, then sat down on his lap and kissed him softly on the lips.

Her wet, warm skin sent arousal signals to every part of him and he returned her kiss a little too strongly for a man in mourning. She brought love and happiness to his life and if he wasn't careful he could lose everything.

She *was* everything.

At least she never lost a parent. It made it easier for her to believe his story about going to France. His inability to share his feelings had been a problem when he had fallen in love with her, but her understanding worked in his favor. Telling her he wanted to get away, and pretend, just for a few days, that his father hadn't died seemed believable. One day soon he intended to tell her the truth, but in doing so, he risked losing her.

That's if Marchant or his men didn't catch up to him first.

"Why don't we hire a car and see some of the city?" Kelly asked.

"I'm not sure I want to drive."

"I don't mind driving, it might let you think about something else for a while." she replied.

Jake shook his head. She'd be disgusted if she knew his only thoughts were of himself and his own problems. But, he had to keep her believing. "You're right; it's probably a good idea. You run up and get changed and we'll go rent a car."

Her smile sent a wave of guilt to his gut, and he watched her disappear inside the hotel. When he was certain she'd be on her way up to their room, he peeled himself from the plastic sun lounger and went into the reception area.

Kelly thought they'd be going back for the funeral on Thursday, but of course they couldn't. Not unless he wanted the plot beside Dad.

He'd have to call Finn. He rummaged in his pockets for change and luckily he had enough for the call. Moving quickly to the payphones located at the rear of the reception area, he had a clear view of the two elevators that serviced the hotel. He dialed an English telephone number. The tone rang out: once, twice, three times.

Jake twisted the wire in his fingers: four times, five times. At last a tired voice answered.

"Yeah, who is it?"

"Finn?"

The voice sharpened. "Who wants to know?"

"Finn, it's Jake, is it safe to talk?"

"Jake! Where the fuck are you? There's all hell about to break loose, the word is you took the coke."

Jake had his eye on the elevators. "I haven't got long, Finn. I didn't take the gear."

"Well, why the hell did you leave? Do you know who took it?"

"Look they killed my old man for it, what do you think they'd do to Kelly? I had to get her out of the way."

"Where are you Jake? We can sort it out if you come back."

Jake hesitated a moment; the doors opened on the elevator to the right, and several holidaymakers spilled out. Kelly wasn't among them. Good.

"No. I'm not coming back, Finn, not until Marchant finds out who really took the gear."

"Jake, you can trust me, I'll sort it out. What about your dad's funeral, will you be there?"

Jake laughed. "Oh yeah, so they can put me in the ground with him?" The doors on the second elevator opened. Kelly's flame-red hair peeked out from behind a short blonde woman. "Got to go, Finn, I'll call you again." Before Finn could reply Jake had put down the phone and was moving towards Kelly across the plush burgundy carpet.

His smile hid his guilt. This charade would have to end soon.

9 - DISSOLVE INTO THE BLACK

Damp seeped through everything around him. Clothes and bed sheets held moisture which aided the musty smell that encompassed the entire room, even though it was a hot summer this year. There was little point in opening his eyes, The Baker knew the layout of the basement down to the last detail, and the only thing that irritated him was the inconvenience of being too short to reach the small windows near the ceiling. They were grimy with years of neglect; even the sun could not penetrate the dirt. Occasionally, he'd have preferred to be able to open them.

The distinctive Whitby Jet band he wore on his thumb was engraved to his own design. He ran his fingers over the symbols and absorbed their power.

It was comfortable on the small bed, and he liked dressing in black, resting on a black sheet, with his head on a black pillowcase. He reminded himself that black is not a color, but the absence of all color. Invisible.

Pride swelled his flesh, and with every breath he knew Grohah was pleased with him. Without lifting his eyelids, he saw black candles sitting in their black holders, positioned either end of the large wooden table, waiting until the time he would light them. On the shiny stainless steel sink, a box of clear plastic food bags rested next to the spotlessly clean gas oven with its baking trays and cooling racks.

He didn't miss his previous life as a celebrated chef. When he'd worked in London he'd had more offers of work than he could ever take and had his own TV show. Compared to what he would have soon, the celebrity life was insignificant.

Dissolve into the blackness, wait for the voice to come, and with it the next set of instructions. He'd followed directions, using his cooking talents to mix up the Euphoria biscuits, as he knew nothing of drug making. A couple of premature deaths due to adding too much of the plant early in his experiments was unfortunate, but not regrettable. The girl from the club though had taken a little too long to die. Although she'd killed a kid on the day she took the drug, her own demise should have been faster. One day sooner would work better than the almost three it had taken. A last fine adjustment to the mix to fix that little problem, and he would be ready for the 2012 Glastonbury music festival.

10 - SIBLINGS

Lysa put the dirty clothes in the washing machine. They smelled of grease and vomit and she washed her hands even before she put the soap in the drawer. As the washing machine hummed into life, Lysa put on the kettle to make coffee. In the bathroom, Robbie soaked in the tub. How the hell was she going to help him?

The cabinets in the kitchen had been falling apart when Lysa bought the flat. Now, new cherry cupboards with straight stainless steel handles held a multitude of dishes and floor to ceiling opaque glass shelving separated the dining table from the living room area. Plants and many of her sculptures sat on the glass. Her fingers softly stroked the sculpture of Robbie swimming. When she'd made that for him, he'd been twelve, healthy, and swimming for the City. It was easy to renovate a kitchen; all you needed was enough money. If only it was as easy to fix her broken brother.

Lysa put two individual frozen entrees for one in the oven for their evening meal. The shock at the sight of Robbie's ribs sticking through his chest and the lack of muscle in his arms when he'd taken off his shirt pained her. Due to her long working hours, it was quicker and easier to buy frozen meals, but Robbie needed real food to get strong. A trip to the supermarket was needed. Her brother was a fifteen year old junkie and as weak as an old man. He would die soon if she couldn't help him.

The comforting fragrance of coffee filled the kitchen as she stirred the cups, and on hearing the soft padding of his bare feet on the hardwood, she smiled as he came into the kitchen. He looked much better than when she'd picked him up. His shoulder length brown hair smelled of apple shampoo rather than grease, and his skin, though tinged with grey, was clean. He wore her bathrobe, which was the smallest size, yet it hung on his thin frame.

A weak smile briefly crossed his face as he sat down and sipped the coffee.

Lysa sat opposite, "What do you want Robbie? Do you want to live or die?"

He shrugged his shoulders.

"That's no answer, Rob. Speaking as a doctor and not your sister, I'm telling you that you've got a few months to live if you carry on the way you are."

Robbie stared deep into the brown liquid.

"Have you taken a H.I.V. test?" she asked.

He raised his eyes from the steaming mug, but said nothing.

She became impatient with his silence, "If you haven't been screened, I'll draw your blood here and take it into work to be checked."

Finally Robbie spoke, his voice soft and quiet. "What's the point Lyse? If I've got HIV I'll die, if I haven't, the smack will kill me."

Those words, so accurately and gently spoken, struck her heart like a hammer blow. Her baby brother spoke with such painful wisdom that she wanted to hold him tight and will his addiction away. If only it was that simple; if only he could give it up because of her willpower alone.

Tears stung her eyes, her previous impatience dissolved. So small, so helpless. She'd let him down so much; everyone had let him down. Her mother, for thinking so much of work and money she had no time for him. Her father, for becoming so overweight his heart couldn't take the strain anymore.

"I can help you, Rob, but only if you want it yourself."

"I wish you could, Lyse, I really wish someone could." He paused, sipping his coffee once more, "but you don't understand how hard it is. My last fix was yesterday, and I want smack. I didn't give the cops your name right away, but then I thought, well it's the only chance I had of getting out and getting a fix."

"So you used me to get out, and as soon as your clothes are washed and dried you'll be off?" she asked.

"That's what I'd planned. All I could think of was getting a fix."

"And now?"

"When I saw you I remembered how much you've tried to help me and I don't want to rob off you, Lyse, really I don't."

"But you will won't you?"

The coffee cup shook slightly in his hands. "Help me, Lyse; I don't know how to do this..." He dissolved into tears and Lysa rushed over and wrapped her arms around him.

They held tightly to each other while they both cried.

11 - NOT LIKE THE MOVIES

Finn swung into the car park. The morning sun hadn't yet become too hot and he was glad to be away from Big Don for a while; the meat head was driving him nuts. He couldn't wait for this assignment to be over. Keeping company with drug dealers wasn't one of the things he enjoyed in life, but he owed it to himself and to Amy. He thought about her smile, the way she used to tease him about how his hair stuck out from behind his ears when it was a fraction of an inch too long.

He parked the car and dialed a number on his cell phone.

As soon as the switchboard answered, he asked to be put through to his boss.

"Anything new to report, Caffrey?"

"Yeah, Boss, the guy Marchant thinks took the drugs contacted me, says he didn't do it. Don't believe him though."

"That's all well and good, but you're supposed to be finding out who's importing the heroin and where."

"I'm working on it, but these people are careful; seven months isn't enough for them to trust me with information like that."

"Well that's your job, Caffrey, and it's about time I started seeing some results. Somebody must trust you by now."

"I'm getting pretty close to this guy Big Don. You know I want answers, Boss, I owe it to Amy."

D.C.I. Needham cut in. "This investigation isn't about Detective Parsons, and you know we have Detectives Ford and Reed looking into her death".

"Yes, Boss, but I have a feeling about this investigation."

"I do understand, Caffrey, but this is about drug importation, not a murder investigation".

"Yes, Boss," Finn repeated. Arguing with Needham was pointless. "Oh, Boss, better send someone in to 81 Queens square, there's a dead kid in a bath."

"Oh great," groaned the D.C.I.

"I'll check in tomorrow, Boss."

"Yeah, you do that."

Finn hung up the phone and dropped it on the passenger seat. He hated this job. He had no social life, and he spent every day, and even some nights, chained to Don the Rottweiler.

He was definitely packing it in for a desk job after this assignment. Undercover work just wasn't like the movies, and the pay wasn't as good either.

12 - ACCIDENTS HAPPEN

Lysa arranged leave by pleading family difficulties so she could stay at home with Robbie. Unfortunately, they couldn't exist on frozen meals, and they needed good food to build his strength. She had to trust him not to steal half her belongings and vanish while she went shopping.

Lysa packed the car with chicken, beef, fish and fresh fruit and vegetables, climbed in the driver's seat and backed out of the car park. She saw the Peugeot a second too late.

The crunch of grinding metal shook the Metro, and Lysa slammed the brake, sending a fast shudder through her body. Sucking in a deep breath, she started to climb out of the car.

The driver of the Peugeot was doing the same thing.

They both reached the rear of their respective vehicles at the same time.

"Oh I'm so sorry!" Lysa said, "Are you okay?" The man was fairly tall, at least six feet. Almost black hair curled around his collar, sticking out a little behind his ears.

"I'm fine," he replied.

"You might need to get checked at the hospital." Moving closer to his car, she saw the huge scrape, right down to the metal. Great, now they'd need to go through insurances. "Looks as though you have some damage," she sighed. "Even if you feel fine, your car isn't."

He shook his head. "It's not too bad, only a dent and a scratch; I've got a mate who can knock it out for me."

"Still, I'm really sorry," Lysa worried. "There's hardly any anything wrong with my car, and just look at yours." Tears pricked her lower eyelids. No, don't start crying. Maybe because of the problems with Robbie, and overwork at the hospital, she'd been tired — not paid enough attention... "Really," she insisted, "Even if your friend can fix the dent, you'll still have to pay for the paint job it will need. I'll give you my insurance details, but we'll have to report it to the police so you can make a claim."

"We don't need to do that," he replied. "It was just as much my fault."

At least he was being nice about the whole thing, but it wasn't fair that he had to pay out, and besides, if she'd not been thinking so much about Robbie, she would have been more careful.

"I have a lot on my mind today, and I'd feel a lot better about this if you'd let me report this and give you my details."

"And then your insurance payments will go up, and for what? A bit of trouble my mate can fix?"

This was true. Insurance was high enough without adding a claim and making it even more expensive."

"Well, okay," she said. "But I'll pay for the repairs."

"You're determined to pay for something, aren't you?"

"Yes. I insist."

"All right then. If I let you pay for the repair, then you let me buy you a coffee at the café in the supermarket."

That would take time, and she needed to get back to Robbie. "I'm in a bit of a hurry, which is probably another reason I backed into you. If we could swap phone numbers you could let me know how much the repairs will be."

"I feel bad about hitting you too," he said. "As you're so determined to pay for my car, the least I can do is to buy you a coffee while we exchange information."

"I really have to get back home," Lysa said.

"Please? I could do with a quick break, and I hope you don't mind me saying, but it would be better to relax for a few minutes before getting back in and driving right away."

He had a point. Normally she'd have been fine to drive after such a little bump, but she was tired and worried, and she hated to admit it, a little shaken. "It's my brother, he's ill. I should get back to him."

"Nothing serious I hope?"

He looked concerned, but she wasn't ready to tell him about such a personal issue. She couldn't lie either. "It could be serious, but I'd rather not talk about it."

"Sorry, I was being nosey. Just one cup?"

The words 'just one cup' reminded Lysa of her Mother. She would say that when she was trying to get you to stay a while longer when visiting. Often, she would go into asking if she'd met a nice doctor yet, to which she usually replied that she met lots of nice doctors every day.

She'd have to trust Robbie a little. If he wanted to run he could be gone already, and she probably should take a few minutes to unwind. Maybe another fifteen minutes would be alright.

"Well okay, I'll just park the car."

Three minutes later, they were sitting in the little cafe.

"I haven't even told you my name. I'm Finn," he said extending a hand to her.

She took his large hand in hers and shook it. It was strong and warm, and she was reluctant to let it go, but she did.

"Lysa," she said, "Lysa Warner."

"Well, Lysa Warner, I'm glad we bumped into each other."

They both laughed at his bad joke, exchanged phone numbers and he promised to let her know what the damage would cost. Lysa pushed a loose strand of hair behind her ear. Her needle-straight blonde hair didn't stay in a ponytail well at the best of times.

'So, Lysa, what is it you do when you're not backing out of supermarket car parks?"

"I'm a doctor at the hospital — emergency at the moment."

Finn put his cup back on the table. "Must be tough dealing with all those drunks on a Friday and Saturday night."

"It can be, but it's what I signed up for. I'm thinking of moving more towards drug rehabilitation, but I have to do more studying first. What do you do for a day job?"

"I have a day and night job; really, I'm in security," he answered.

"Alarms and things?"

He took a sip of his coffee before answering. "Nope, more like looking after people and keeping things in line."

His answer seemed a little evasive, but then maybe in security you had to be, after all, he didn't know her.

"Anyone special in your life, boyfriend perhaps?" he asked.

"Only my brother Robbie, I'm looking after him at the moment, and I really can't stay long; I have to get back to him."

"No handsome doctor chasing you?"

Despite her worry, she laughed. "Now you sound like my mother. She's always asking me when I'm going to settle down with a nice doctor." Hesitating for a moment she added, "There was someone, his name was Tony. We broke off our engagement six months ago."

"I'd say I'm sorry, but then I might never have met you. You might have been off on some tropical honeymoon today instead of in a car park."

"At least you're honest," she replied. "Do you have anyone special?"

His face softened, a slight smile touched his lips and his shoulders sank a little before he spoke. "There was. My fiancée, Amy, died a year ago."

Instinctively she wanted to reach over the table for his hand, but she'd only just met him. "I'm sorry. It must have been a tough time."

"It was, but I'm over the worst. We had a pact with each other, that if one of us died, that we'd never forget, but we would start again when the time was right."

"Was she ill?" As soon as the question left her mouth she wished she hadn't asked. Quickly she said, 'I'm sorry, I'm prying. You don't need to answer that."

"No worries. We were both in the security business, high risk sometimes."

His smile revealed a dimple under his left cheek. Changing the subject she asked, "What else do you do? Any out of work hobbies?"

"Don't really have much time for anything except work right now. We have a bit of a big job going on so I get called away a lot. Once it's finished I might take a holiday somewhere hot with a beach, beer, and a ton of waves."

Lysa grinned. "You like the ocean? It's my favorite subject to sculpt."

"You're a sculptor as well as a doctor?"

"I'm okay, it's relaxing and I really enjoy it. I have a life size piece I'm working on in my studio called *Charlie*, and a smaller piece at home."

"Maybe I could come to see it sometime?"

"Sure, if you really want to." He was so easy to talk to, inviting him to see her work felt fine. "My brother used to like watching me sculpt, until he became sick that is." She checked her watch. A half hour had passed. "I really must get back to Robbie. I can't leave him too long on his own and I've already been here longer than I intended to."

"I'll come with you."

As they walked back to the car park, Lysa wished she had longer. "Thanks for the coffee," she said as they came to a stop next to her car.

"Maybe we could do it again, only something a little stronger next time? I could take you out for a drink, or maybe you'd come and see a movie with me?" He hovered at the back of her vehicle. "I'd understand if you said no, you've only known me half an hour or so."

Should she meet him again? She hesitated for seconds, but her instinct told her to say yes and a smile creased the corners of her mouth. "I'd like that," she said, and then thought of Robbie and the smile dropped.

"Hey don't look so down at the prospect, I'm not that bad am I?"

"It's not that. I'd like to, it's just that Robbie needs me now." Lysa sucked in a breath wondering if she should tell Finn about Robbie's problems. Earlier she hadn't wanted to talk about it, but now her honesty took over. "I won't lie to you, he has a drug problem. He's trying to stay clean but it's going to be difficult."

"I see."

"If you don't want to see me again, I understand. It's not a great point in my favor having a junkie for a brother."

"You're a doctor. Can't you get him on a rehab program?"

"I can, but I have to be sure it's what he wants. There's no point in him taking up a place that could help someone who really wants to get clean."

"I'd still like to see you again. When and if you can."

"Are you sure?" Lysa asked, "It's probably going to be tough going for Robbie, and I might not have a great deal of spare time for a while."

"I'm pretty busy myself at the moment, but maybe we could arrange to spend our not-so-spare time together?" Finn asked.

"I'll have to take it a day at a time," she replied.

"That's okay, I'll call you.'

"If you don't change your mind," she replied.

"I won't. Can't say when we can get together, as I really do have a busy schedule at the moment, but I will call."

Lysa unlocked her car and slipped behind the wheel.

"I'll see you again," he said, leaning on the open door. "Soon."

"I'll look forward to it." He moved back so she could close the door. Finn started back to his Peugeot as she reversed out of the parking space.

Her rear view mirror showed him standing next to his car until she drove away. He waved as she stopped at the entrance before pulling out. She waved back even though he wouldn't be able to see her response.

Given her circumstances, it wasn't the right time to be dating anyone, but he seemed nice, and she could do with something to look forward to. If he did call, maybe she could figure out a way to see him again, and still be able look after Robbie.

13 - CHANGES

It was two days since Jake had phoned Finn. Tomorrow would be Thursday, the day of his father's funeral.

The French sun delivered morning greetings through the hotel windows. Light fell across Kelly's hair, polishing each strand to shine like a newly minted copper penny. What he was about to do was going to hurt or confuse her, but he had no choice. Nothing short of the ceiling collapsing would wake her up before eight a.m., so he'd be able to shower and slip away safely.

Jake slid out of the bed and went into the bathroom. His father's death was a gnawing hole in his chest, raw, bloody and cavernous, but fear for Kelly enabled him to function. If they killed her, he would never survive the pain.

Neatly folded white hotel towels filled the rails next to the shower. He grabbed a hand towel and threw it on the tiles outside the shower. Inside the plastic cubicle, miniature shampoo and conditioner bottles sat on the shelf. If only his life could be as neat as this bathroom. Jake turned on the jets and ramped up the heat. As the water ran over his body, he cursed himself for hooking Marchant up with that freak, The Baker. If he'd walked away, he'd never have become involved and his dad would still be alive. But then, if he himself hadn't nicked the coke... He scrubbed the shampoo roughly into his scalp. It was all his own fault.

He had to go back but he wouldn't put Kelly at risk by taking her with him.

As soon as he'd seen The Baker, he'd known there was something wrong. Dressed all in black, with black hair and a black fedora, he hadn't looked normal, but it was the look in his eyes that confirmed it. He didn't look *at* you, he looked *into* you.

How stupid of him to think he could get out of this life and settle down somewhere with Kelly. He should have known that Marchant would never let him go, even though introducing him to The Baker brought in a new line of income.

Fine needles of spray rinsed the lather from his hair, pushing the foam down his face and back. The bubbles disappeared down the drain as easily as his life would if he didn't manage to sort things out soon.

Jake turned off the water, stepped out of the cubicle, and rubbed himself vigorously with one of the perfectly laundered towels. Catching sight of himself in the mirror, he was proud he'd kept in shape; one of the perks of the job — the use of Marchant's gym for free.

Supplying the addicts with Marchant's heroin, crack, and coke didn't bother him much, it was a way of life, but The Baker's biscuits did weird things to the kids.

The first two kids they'd given them to flipped higher than anyone Jake had ever seen. They'd seen angels, talked to imaginary beings, thought they could do whatever they wanted without any risk.

He'd seen people high. Witnessed the things they did, how they came crashing back down. Saw the cravings. Watched people sink so low they'd do anything. Steal, beg, sell anything, including themselves for a cheap fix. Jake had seen enough of drugs to not be tempted himself, though he was happy to sell it. He was only supplying a demand. If he didn't do it someone else would. Besides, he usually only supplied the local dealers and he never had to deal with the damage his goods caused.

He stopped in the bathroom doorway. She was naked under the bedcovers and his body wanted to join her under the sheets. No. He had to keep to the plan, had to keep her safe. Touching her soft skin, lying in bed sleeping next to her, making love for hours, these things would have to wait. How lucky he was that she'd walked straight in front of his car that night. He could still see her face through the windscreen of the car as he'd stopped inches away from her. Two seconds later, she slumped onto the front of the car and slid down onto the road.

A crowd quickly gathered, all believing he'd hit her. The police arrived and questioned him, only satisfied when one of her friends came forward to say that he hadn't hit her, and she thought someone had spiked Kelly's drink in the students' bar.

Not being able to get her face out of his mind, he'd gone to see her in hospital the next day and thereafter couldn't let her go.

It was for Kelly he'd decided to go straight. Make a new life for them both. With the money he'd make from Marchant's drugs, he could do it.

Hair still damp, he picked up his small bag and left the room, closing the door softly behind him.

At reception he left her a message to say he'd been called away on business, but would be back the day after tomorrow and to wait at the hotel for him.

It was only seven thirty in the morning and he had an hour and a half to kill before the hairdressers in the town opened. He wasted the time in a cafe having breakfast.

Emerging from the hairdresser at ten thirty, he looked a completely different man. His below the shoulder blonde hair was cropped to a dark crew cut. Within half an hour, he was on the train to Calais and was eating lunch on the shuttle at twelve forty-five. Another five hours and he would be in Liverpool.

14 - COUNTING

In the cellar, The Baker sealed up ten biscuits to a bag. Each one he placed carefully in a cardboard box taken from the local supermarket. Every box contained forty bags of biscuits and he was filling his fifty-sixth box.

Some of the new batch had gone to Marchant, and they were already having the desired effect. Now he had to transfer a batch over to another contact he'd made in Leeds. It was unfortunate the first couple of kids had died so quickly before the full effects of the drug could be seen.

Nervous excitement gripped him; the evening to come would be the big test. It was the right time, two days after Marchant had sold the last lot on the streets. The kids had been flying on the first day and now he had the mix right, the real effects would soon kick in.

The riots would start. First here in Liverpool, but within days it would spread to other cities, and then the festival.

When that happened, Grohah would be pleased.

He grinned as he sealed the box. By the end of the year everything would be so different. Soon, Grohah would have his first batch of blood. When the ten thousand death count was realized the new world would begin.

15 - A SECOND WARNING

Mark clutched the letter in his jacket pocket, staring at the house. Knowing he would knock on the door and deliver the news the occupants wouldn't want to hear didn't make it any easier, but there was no one else who could. All the emergency room doctor had known was that her name was Tina. She didn't have any other details to give to the police, so no one would tell her parents. He might be a junkie now, but he used to be a caring person when his Mum was alive, and this was the right thing to do. Drawing in a breath for courage, he walked forward.

It was a nice, respectable house. Tidy pink rose bushes ran the length of the small front garden, with a white painted wrought iron railing sitting on top of the small wall. Matching gates latched across the driveway.

A short balding man in blue overalls worked on a red Volvo inside the open garage.

Mark attempted to straighten his jacket, but he didn't look a lot better, so he zipped it up to hide his crumpled tee shirt. The gate opened silently and Mark moved up the driveway.

The man came out of the garage to greet him. His round flushed face shiny with sweat.

"Can I help you son?" he asked, wiping his hands on his overalls.

Mark didn't want to do this; didn't want to tell this happy smiling man that his daughter was dead.

"You all right lad? Are you looking for someone?"

Mark pulled the crumpled letter out of his pocket and held it out to him. He made an effort to speak as nicely as he could. "Are you Tina's Dad? I'm looking for her parents."

The man scanned the letter, and looking up he said, "Yes, I'm Christina's father, why have you come? Does she need more drug money?"

"No, she doesn't need anything." Mark hesitated. "I just had to come and see you."

Mark turned his head as he heard the front door of the house open and a middle-aged woman walked toward them. She looked like she'd stepped straight out of the perfume section of a department store.

"Who's this, Owen?" she asked.

The man looked questioningly at Mark. "What do you want? What have you got to do with my daughter?"

Mark shuffled his feet, trying to put off what he had to say to them both.

"There...there isn't an easy way to say this," Mark stammered. He couldn't look the couple in the face; instead he stared down at his scuffed trainers.

"Go on, son," the man said quietly.

Mark went for it. "Tina died early hours, Monday morning. It was drugs, but the doctors don't know what type. She died in The Queen's Hospital, in Queen Street, Liverpool."

He looked up now. The woman stared as if she could see through him, then she simply turned without a word and went back inside the house.

The man didn't go immediately after her, instead, he looked at Mark in much the same way the woman had. "Why didn't the police come to tell us? How do I know you're telling the truth?

49

"Because she didn't have any real ID on her, and I didn't know your address until I found a letter ya sent." Mark paused, staring back down at the gravel. "I didn't want to go to the police ya know?"

"Oh right…"

"Ya can call the hospital, or call the police in Liverpool and tell them you're Tina's parents. They'll check and tell ya I'm telling the truth."

"Do you want to come in lad, have a cup of tea? You've travelled a long way to come and tell us. You could have just phoned, if you had the name and address."

Maybe they were in shock, or wanted to keep him there so they could call the police? That was the last thing he needed. More questions, digging around. "I thought it was the kind of news that shouldn't be given over the phone. I wanted to come and tell ya myself. I'll be back off home now." Why did this man seem so calm? But it didn't matter; he had to get away now he'd done what he came to do.

Owen looked gratefully at Mark. "Thank you, lad. Thanks for coming to tell us." He reached into his pocket and pulled out a ten pound note. "Here take this; it must have cost you to come here."

Mark shook his head. "It's okay. I hitched a couple of lifts."

Owen pushed the money at him. "Take it; go on, you look like you could do with a square meal inside you."

Mark took the money. Partly, because he didn't want to offend Owen, but mostly because he needed it.

Mark turned to go back down the driveway, as he reached the gate he turned to look at Tina's father, who still stood cemented to the same spot.

"Hey son, don't spend it on drugs," said the older man. "Don't end up dead like my Christina."

Mark nodded, it was the second time in a few days he'd been warned to stay clear of drugs and maybe one day he'd take the advice, but not today.

He headed back towards the motorway to hitch a lift. The sooner he was home, the sooner he'd get his fix.

16 - DANSE MACABRE

Finn and Big Don sat in the projection room of the old cinema, now a dance club renamed D. Zone. Faces of silent movie stars stared out from the wall where the screen used to be. The area directly in front of Charlie Chaplin and Fay Wray had been transformed into a huge semi-circular stage where new party-goers danced and writhed to music their predecessors would have found incomprehensible. The sloping floor had been transformed into two levels. The highest level contained twin smaller dance areas and drinks bars.

Finn surveyed the club, with its three dance floors, three bars and numerous sweaty dancers.

In the upper level, in the side boxes that had once claimed higher price tickets, low couches lay, for the kids to either make out, or pass out on. The smaller dance floors were situated directly below, and led to a central area containing gleaming metal tables and chairs, a bright contrast to the plush couches in the bays.

Down on the main dancing area, statues of dead and living movie stars paid mute attention to the throng. Up at the back, where Finn stood watching, the room which once housed the projector and its operator had been enlarged to make a lavishly

51

furnished office. The wall which had once contained a central small projection window had been replaced by an entire span of toughened glass.

Finn moved over to sit on a settee, and was joined by Big Don, whose large frame took more than his share of the seating. Their boss, Marchant, lounged on the chair opposite.

Finn hadn't yet been able to pin anything on Marchant; he had too many legitimate businesses. He had to get something on him soon though; this job was starting to really depress him. Gathering evidence was one thing, making it stick was another. Marchant's file was four inches thick and Finn had read through the lot. Marchant had been running the south end of the city for six years, and killed his predecessor with enough savagery never to have to get his hands dirty himself again. The victim's hands and feet had been cut off before he died. Finn had seen the letter kept by the police as evidence, which had been sent to the man's wife, informing her how an ink pen had been filled with her husband's blood, and described how he had been forced to write her a goodbye note after the pen had been placed in his mouth. In excruciating pain, and severely weakened by blood loss, he had done it, then Marchant had pulled out his teeth one by one. Six months later, when the coroner released the body for burial, Marchant--having had the teeth made into a set of dentures -- sent them to his wife days before the funeral.

The victim had been left to bleed to death, but luckily for the suffering man, an old associate with a score to settle had found him and shot him in the head.

These thoughts flickered through Finn's memory as he looked at the man he considered to be one of the most evil he had ever come across.

Photographs of the hands and feet Marchant had hung from lampposts in four parts of the city flew into his mind. Marchant's display sent a powerful and frightening message; he had control of all criminal activity within those boundaries. Anyone ignoring this was given one warning, after that, they wound up as fish food.

Marchant spoke quietly, in a soft voice with only a hint of an Irish accent. "Don," he said, barely moving his lips. His arm rested on the deep turquoise velvet of the chair. The brandy inside the tumbler he held was still, as if it too, was afraid of the man who held it.

Don instantly looked across to the wiry man sitting opposite him.

"Yes, Boss?"

"I want you and Finn to go pick up The Baker, he has a batch ready for us." He paused a moment. "He wants to come into the club to see how the kids react after a couple of days on the stuff." He glanced out of the window to the busy area below and Finn followed his gaze. The club was filling up. Wednesday night half-price drinks had proved popular and the floor was packed. The kids seemed to be dancing more wildly than usual. A couple of girls gyrated on tables near the upper dance floor, a group of lads were cheering them on as they tore off their tops and revealed bare breasts to their audience. Finn switched his attention back to Marchant, who continued to watch for a couple of seconds before turning back to Big Don and Finn. He indicated the girls through the glass. "Maybe he'd be interested in one of them, maybe it's some kind of sex drug he's put in those biscuits."

Don laughed, "Yeah, Boss, the way he looks, he probably has to drug a girl before she'll let him fuck her."

Finn said nothing, but looked back out of the window and waited for Marchant to give them the address. The girls still danced on the tables.

One of them disappeared.

Finn rose from the couch and walked over to the window to look closer. The girl had vanished under the table and there seemed to be several men on top of her.

In an instant, the second girl reached down for one of the lads and yanked him up towards her with strength that seemed unreal for her slim body. Then she dropped him back down.

"There's something going on down there, Boss; I think a girl's being raped," Finn shouted.

Marchant rose from his chair and, followed by Big Don, moved nearer to the window. No noise could be heard in this soundproofed room: no screaming, no music, no singing or stamping of feet.

As Marchant reached the glass, the security staff had already reacted to the disturbance as a large crowd gathered around the tables. The dancing girl suddenly reached down again, and with one arm, pulled up one of her friend's attackers. He immediately started to try to rip off her skirt, but before he could manage even a slight tear, she took his bent head in both her hands and with a quick twist, broke his neck and flung his limp and broken body into the crowd like a discarded beer can.

Security men pulled people away and tried to get to the girl under the heap of bodies. Finn couldn't see her at all, and her friend went back to her frenzied dance.

People started to move back. Some tried to escape the center of the disturbance. It was like watching a horror movie on mute.

Marchant looked on at the scene with a faint trace of amusement on his face while Big Don showed no emotion whatsoever. Violence meant nothing to them, and it sickened Finn. He couldn't blow his cover, but he couldn't let the girl be gang raped in a nightclub. He let out a low breath as the stewards reached the youths, who reminded him more of a pack of hungry lions than humans. As more people scrambled away from the circle, the sight before him made him want to retch.

Music still pounded outside the room, the dance floor continued to heave with sticky dancers, the majority knowing nothing of what was happening outside their own private world.

The only people left in the center of the disturbance were the girl dancing on the table and the girl on the floor with about five or six youths. Suddenly, security men stopped trying to intervene and stood back as a grinning girl emerged from beneath the boys.

She appeared to be wearing a red body stocking, but it was blood that covered her skin. She was naked, her blonde hair matted crimson. She was the only one who moved, the boys lay still. A tangle of half-dressed, skin-shredded corpses.

Slowly, she stood up and lifted one of the bodies, holding him in her two arms above her head. Blood rained down on her from his open neck, drenching her face; her body swaying to the beat of the music in a Danse Macabre. No one moved toward her. Without warning, she threw the boy. The force of the body knocked a steward with arms like an ape into the table behind him. She jumped up to join her friend on the table, shook her tangled hair, and danced to the music Finn couldn't hear.

On the lower dance floor, a girl flew off the stage into the tables, but dashed back up and dived into the crowd. Within seconds, the entire stage was a mass of flailing arms and legs. People ran for the exits. Security men were forced out of their daze and raced to try and break up the fighting.

Flames licked the drapes that hung over the box areas, and a crowd of youths piled wooden chairs around the two girls who were still dancing crazily. The beautiful bar staff fled, and a boy wildly shook a bottle of spirits over the chairs and struck a match. The girls showed no fear as the flames lapped at their legs and they waved their arms over their heads to the music. A band of dancers surrounded the funeral pyre as madly as the flames that grew stronger with each second.

The electricity blew. The only light came from the blaze that tightened its grip with every second. Before Finn could move toward the doors, he was showered with water. The sprinkler systems kicked in.

"Right then boys," said Marchant. "Looks like The Baker will have to wait for the next show, rain stopped play on this one." Finn couldn't see the amusement he knew was on Marchant's face, he could hear a trace of it in his tone.

"Time we left," finished Marchant.

17- RETURNING TO LIVERPOOL

Jake checked into a small hotel on the outskirts of the city center on his arrival back in Liverpool. His fake driver's license informed the landlady he was Geoff Wainwright, and he spent the evening watching TV and the night trying to sleep. Unsuccessfully.

Thursday arrived with the plan of picking up his package and getting it to his contact in Birmingham. Easy. So long as nobody recognized him.

Instead of his usual designer clothes, he dressed in a mid-blue suit and a crisp white shirt, both newly purchased on his arrival home. He knotted a grey satin tie and tried to look serious. He now resembled a business man; someone who was used to dealing with people and getting his own way.

The black leather shoes pinched his feet, but he wouldn't have to wear them long. He could have phoned Finn from the hotel, but decided against it, not convinced he could trust him.

A few minutes to three. The shirt collar irritated his neck and he pulled at it trying to release the heat trapped in the suit and tie. Glancing up and down the street before leaving the hotel, he quickly crossed the road and turned left around the corner to where he'd parked the rental car. Half an hour to pick up the coke, and then another two hours to reach Birmingham.

The green digitals in the rental car read three o'clock, and the radio newscaster blabbered on. Within minutes, his father's coffin would be entering the furnace. The few mourners would be sure to include Finn and Big Don. Marchant would send them to see if he turned up, which was precisely why this was the best time to pick up the drugs. Guilt punched him in the head while grief kicked him in the gut because he wasn't there, but one death in the family was enough for one week. He sent a silent goodbye to the man who had loved him all his life. It took a little less than his estimated half hour to reach the city center and parking was never easy. He tapped the steering wheel impatiently, waiting in the queue to park in Victoria Street. Finally, he was able to feed the meter for an hour's worth of time. Locking up, he walked left toward Dale Street. About halfway along was the building where he'd rented an office. Jake ran up the stone steps and pushed open the heavy carved wood and glass door.

The inside of the building had been renovated; the only remnants of a bygone age being the white painted ornate plaster moldings on the high ceilings. Jake hardly noticed as he entered the elevator and pressed the button for the fourth floor. A smart middle-aged woman stopped it on the third and entered. She smiled at Jake and pressed fourth also.

Great. He had hoped to enter and exit the building without being seen at all, even though it would probably not be possible. They stepped out of the elevator together, the woman entering the office directly opposite, while Jake walked down the corridor to his left. Taking a key from his inside pocket, he opened the door to 34A.

*** *** ***

"Even he's not fucking stupid enough to show up here." Big Don stamped his cigarette into the gravel outside the crematorium.

"It's his old man, though. You think he'd turn up for his funeral." Finn looked around, but there was no sign of Jake. Still, even if he didn't attend the service, surely he would be around somewhere, maybe skulking in the bushes? Finn made a mental note to stop watching so many bad movies.

"You don't know him as well as me," said Big Don. "He's a right bastard; doesn't give a fuck about anyone except himself."

"He's got that girl now though, he must care about her."

"Yeah? He's probably done her in so she can't grass him up," growled Big Don. "Hasn't been seen anywhere for days, has she?"

"Might have taken her with him."

"Well he sure as hell ain't coming here." Big Don headed back towards the car. "He's fucked off for good. He knows better than to show his ugly face around here again."

Finn took a last look around the outside of the crematorium: no cars, and no shadows behind the trees. Don was right, Jake wasn't coming.

"Come on then, let's go pick up The Baker." Finn walked around to the passenger door.

Big Don squeezed into the driver's seat. "Fucking weirdo, he puts the creeps up me, that one."

Finn nodded. "I don't like the way those biscuits make the kids act, the papers said there were thirty two killed in the club last night."

"Marchant could do without kids slaughtering each other in his place. He's gonna tell that fucking nutter he don't want no more gear off him."

"Why do we have to pick him up then? Couldn't we have told him that?"

Big Don pulled the car out of the driveway and out onto the main road. "Don't you know how Marchant works by now? He likes to finish things himself so there ain't no misunderstandings."

"Is he going to kill The Baker then?"

Don smiled. "No, Finn. You're gonna do that for him."

18 - NEW ACQUAINTANCES

Mark knew the dangers of lying wasted on a park bench in this area, but his exhausted body had no intention of helping him move. It was too much effort to open his eyes, even though he was awake. Resting on the hard metal seemed preferable to going home to his alcoholic father and miserable house. Hunger rattled his stomach, but he was too tired to drag himself up to go and find food.

It wouldn't be dark until past ten o'clock, and although the sun had set, the summer sky was still light. A voice with a pronounced English accent invaded his depression.

"Would you like to earn some money?"

Mark lifted his eyelids to see who spoke. In his present state of mind he didn't much care the voice seemed so out of place in the body it came from.

Money was money, no matter who was offering.

"Yeah, I wouldn't mind."

Fighting through the fog in his head, it didn't register how strange the man looked, dressed all in black with a hat on a warm summer evening, but something rapped at the back of his brain and told him to get up, and get away.

"Spend a few days with me, and you can have all the drugs you want. Plus, I'll pay you fifty a day."

Mark forced his body to pull him into a sitting position. "Hey, I'm no rent boy. Ya want one of them, ya can go somewhere else." Shakily, he managed to stand and take a step away.

"No, no, you misunderstand me. I don't want to have sex with you."

"Oh sure, I bet that's what all the pervs say before they rape some kid."

"Please, sit back down and I will explain."

Mark hesitated and warily sat back down, making sure he had at least a foot and a half distance between them.

"Okay, if ya not a perv, what the hell is worth all the drugs I want and fifty quid a day."

"Look at me, my appearance is a little strange, don't you think?"

Mark looked the man over more carefully. Unease stimulated his senses. The guy looked much more than a little strange.

"Well if you know ya look odd, why are ya dressed like that?"

"I have a medical condition. I must cover as much of myself as possible, and whenever I can, I must stay out of the light."

Mark let out an uneasy laugh. "What are ya? A vampire or something?"

"There are no such creatures as vampires, but there are things you know nothing about. Things I can teach you."

"I don't think I want to learn if ya don't mind." Mark was almost ready to leave; this was getting weird.

The man smiled, "I want you to sell drugs for me."

Growling need in Mark's belly started to overrule his mistrust of the stranger. The guy was old, and Mark could handle himself if things became too creepy. Besides, he'd need more drugs soon, and this guy could be his ticket. Still, he didn't want to appear too eager.

"Now ya talking in my language," Mark replied. "But tell me why ya can't sell them yerself?"

"Isn't it obvious?" The man looked down, indicating his clothes.

"Oh yeah, right. Medical condition, though it shouldn't stop ya dealing at night, or having people come to your place."

"I don't want to roam the streets peddling my wares, and I won't have anyone know where I live. I have my reasons, which I'll explain later if you agree to work for me."

"Fifty a day and all the drugs I want? No catch?" It seemed much too good to be true, but it was tempting.

"That's correct."

"And there'll be no funny business, 'cause I'm telling ya now, try anything and I'm off."

"Come with me, my van's over there, you can check it out for yourself, all I have in there are my provisions. Nothing to be alarmed about."

The man stood up and started off towards the van. Mark hesitated a moment before following him and warily checking out the inside of the van. It contained boxes and boxes of biscuits, nothing else. No weed, no smack, and no coke. He checked out the front of the van. No knives, no gun. Still, the oddball could have something hidden in all those black clothes.

"So where's the gear?" he asked.

"You're looking at it."

Mark was puzzled. "Where?"

"In the back, in the boxes."

"But they're full of biscuits."

"Exactly."

Mark went back to the open doors. Leaning inside, he pulled a box toward him and reached in and took out a biscuit. It resembled a chocolate chip cookie without the chocolate chips.

"This is drugs? Ya won't get anyone to buy these."

"But I already have."

This hardly made sense. In the past he'd made biscuits with pot, but he'd never heard of it being sold on the streets like that. Besides, with his accent and dress, this guy didn't look or sound like a drug dealer.

"Who? Who have ya sold this stuff too?"

"Heard of a man by the name of Marchant?"

Mark's face would have paled if he didn't already possess skin that was almost transparent. Every junkie knew who Marchant was. He held the biscuit in his hand. "Ya saying Marchant bought these?" Mark recalled headlines on the newspaper stands about D. Zone burning down.

"You catch on quick. Now do you want to help me or not?"

Mark didn't like the idea of getting involved with a man like Marchant. The two heavies in Tina's squat had been his men. Tina must have got the stuff that killed her from them, but he didn't know why they'd been looking for her. It hurt his brain trying to figure it out, so he stopped thinking about it.

"Look, if ya working for Marchant, I want nothing to do with it. I've lost a couple of friends recently, and I don't wanna join them."

The man laughed. "I don't work for Marchant. I work for someone infinitely more powerful than him. Marchant is but a gnat on the water compared to my mentor."

Mark had almost decided to walk away when the gnawing in the pit of his stomach started again and his skin started to itch.

"Can ya talk fuckin' English?" Mark asked. "Ya promised me some gear, and I'm not taking that stuff if that's what made all those kids in the D. Zone go mental."

The Baker produced a small clear plastic bag from somewhere in his enormous coat. Mark spotted the small quantity of white powder through the transparent wrapping.

"Is this what you want?"

"Is that all you got?"

"I have plenty more when you need it. Do you accept the job?"

Mark reached for the bag, but The Baker moved it just out of his grasp.

"Do you accept the job?" he asked again.

"Sure."

"Then we must shake on it. You can call me Baker. And you are?"

"Mark, Mark Hawthorne."

A pale hand extended to shake on the deal. Mark didn't hesitate. The man's hand was cold, as though it had been in a fridge. It probably should have been blue, but it was a normal pink color. Maybe it was part of the medical condition? Mark ignored the doubts that tapped at the back of his mind like a sculptor chipping at an ice statue.

"Well, Mark Hawthorne, jump in the passenger seat and we'll be going. I want to arrive before midnight." The Baker held out the bag and Mark stuffed it into his pocket immediately. Pulling open the passenger door he climbed up into the vehicle. While snapping shut the seatbelt he asked his new companion, "Where are we going?"

"The Glastonbury music festival. With the summer we're having, it should be a great turnout."

Mark settled back into his seat and took out his prize.

It would be a good journey.

19 - OLD FRIENDS

Rush hour traffic was something Jake hadn't accounted for, but even though the journey to Birmingham took longer than expected, he found a small bed and breakfast easily enough. Calling Kelly from a payphone, he smoothed things over with her for his disappearance.

The noise in the pub was familiar, and he was pleased it was crowded. He sipped his brandy while watching the men at the corner table, waiting for the right moment to approach. There were four of them. Three he knew, one he didn't. The three he knew were mid-thirties to mid-forties, but the other one looked younger. With his new haircut and dressed in a short sleeved green silk shirt and black chinos, Jake was confident they wouldn't recognize him. The black shoes still hurt his feet a little, so while he was sitting down, he edged the back of his heels out of them. The change of image was worth a little discomfort if it prolonged his life expectancy.

He checked his watch-- ten-thirty. They would leave for the club in around an hour. After another ten minutes, he pushed his feet back into his shoes and crossed the room.

"Mind if I join you fellas?" Jake pulled a stool up and sat at the table with them.

"Hey pal; clear off if you know what's good for you." The eldest of the four, a man with greying brown short hair and a pock-marked face, glared at him.

"What's the matter, Lou; no time for an old mate anymore now you're on the up and up?"

"Fuck off. We're no mates of yours." The youngest one-- who Jake now figured was in his early twenties-- stood up and pressed his hands on the table and leaned forward, staring into Jake's face. He reminded Jake of himself at that age, far too arrogant and full of his own importance.

The kid was probably thinking he must be incredibly stupid not to have left their table immediately. It's what Jake would have thought if some jerk had come up to a table where Marchant was sitting with his guys.

Putting his glass on the table, Jake smiled and said, "Don't you know your old mate, Jake, boys?"

Jake enjoyed the looks of puzzlement followed by slow recognition creeping into their faces.
Lou was the first to speak. "Well, I don't fucking believe it!" He laughed loudly and slapped Jake hard on the back. "Bleeding hell, Jake. That's some stunt to pull on a mate. I was just about ready to punch your lights out."
"I could see that, that's why I told you who I was."

As the other two older men joined in the laughter, the younger one sat back down, a guarded expression on his face.

"Somebody after you, Jake lad?" Lou's laugh rose up from the pit of his pot belly. It rumbled around the pub, drowning out the chatter from the surrounding tables. Jake observed that the black spaces, which used to be in Lou's wide mouth, were now filled with gold teeth. His jaw was probably worth a nice bonus for a hit man.

Jake joined in the laughter. "Can't a man have a change of image without you lot jumping to conclusions?"

"Must be a woman then, you got some bird ordering you about now, Jake?"

Jake took the opportunity offered him. "Yeah, she's not that keen on long hair, says short black hair turns her on."

"Does she like it as short as mine then Jake? Maybe you could introduce me."

Jake turned to the man on his left. "Short she likes, Phil. Billiard ball is taking the piss."

Phil rubbed his hand over his shiny head. "Hey, us baldies get plenty of women, you know what they say about us."

"Dream on Phil, I've seen you in the shower," replied Lou.

"I didn't know you two were that close," grinned Jake. "Did you know about this Al?"

Al lit a cigar. "Nope, what those two do is their business." He took a puff and blew thick smoke in Jake's direction. Jake didn't react; the arsehole did it purely because he knew Jake hated cigar smoke. "Now come on lads, I'm talking about when we used to play football a few years back."

"More than a few years back, Lou, it's nine or ten since you took that slug in the knee, and it was a couple before that when we used to play," replied Phil.

"I guess so, maybe fifteen? Still, at least I got the bastard that shot me!"

Another round of laughter filled the table, before Lou spoke again. "Hey, Jake, this is Connor, he's Ken's nephew." Lou indicated the youngest of the group, who sat silently while the others laughed.

Jake offered his hand to Connor. Connor eyed him suspiciously before shaking Jake's hand.

"Sorry to hear about Ken," said Jake. "He was all right."

Connor pulled his hand away. "He was a bastard. He deserved all he got."

Jake noted the hardness in the youngster's eyes; they could have been made from diamonds. He made no argument about the worthiness of Ken, the kid was right. He turned back to Lou. "Going to the club later?"

"Yeah, Collins wants us all in tonight." Lou stopped for a moment, as if hesitant to continue. He then lowered his tone of voice and leaned closer to Jake.

"Hey mate, we've had some weird stuff lately, now don't laugh when I tell you about it."

"Would I laugh, Lou?"

"Yes, you would," Lou grinned, "but I'll tell you anyway."

"Do you think you should be telling this guy anything? Collins wouldn't like it," Connor broke in.

Lou turned to the younger man. "Now you listen here, you were still pukeing over your mother's shoulder when me and Jake here got together, I'd trust this man with my life, so you just keep it shut."

"Collins can make you puke if you're telling people his business," smirked Connor.

Lou reached across Jake to grab Connor's shirt, lifting him half off his seat.

"Come on Lou, leave the kid alone, he's just trying to do the right thing, he doesn't know me from Adam."

Still gripping Connor, Lou turned his face to Jake. "He insulted you and tried to take the piss out of me, I can't allow that, Jake."

Connor's eyes still held their emotionless gaze; if he was scared of Lou, he didn't show it.

"He's just a kid. I've got a proposition for you to put to Collins for me."

Lou let go of Connor's shirt, the boy dropped back to his seat.

"You just watch your lip with me kid, smarter guys than you have tried it and lost."

Connor nodded his head. "Sure."

Satisfied with Connor's response, Lou turned back to Jake. "As I was *saying*," he said, "this weird guy dressed all in black approached us with a deal. At first we laughed in his face, he was offering us drugs baked up as biscuits, but then he, shall we say, *demonstrated* his goods, and by Christ did they have an effect."

Jake interrupted. "Marchant's been using him as well."

The surprise showed in Lou's face. "You mean he's up in Liverpool too?"

"I didn't have a clue he'd been here." Jake replied.

"We sold the stuff on yesterday, he said he'll be back if we want some more." Lou shook his head. "Weird looking bugger though.'

"Yeah I've met the guy," Jake agreed. "We thought he was a nutter till he showed us what the stuff does. He gave us some as a trial first, to see how it went." Jake lowered his voice slightly. "It flew out."

"Not like Marchant though, to buy stuff off some weirdo that turns up on the street," replied Lou, rubbing his fingers over his scarred chin.

"Marchant tried to check him out. No one had anything on this guy, seemed like he came outta nowhere."

"So why'd Marchant buy offa him then?" asked Lou.

Jake leaned back in his chair and smiled. "Who the fuck is Marchant scared of?" he asked.

"Marchant's not scared of anyone!" Lou laughed loud, with Phil and Al joining in. Only Connor stayed silent.

"Exactly!" Jake joined in the laughter. "He had nuthin to lose, and money to make on the deal, and if there's one thing Marchant likes, it's money."

Jake noted Connor sitting quietly. It felt as though the kid absorbed all he saw and heard, storing it away like a camel for future use. This kid could be a dangerous commodity in a few years' time. If he lasted that long.

"But," Jake said, "to the reason I'm down here. I've got some coke for Collins. Do you reckon he can shift it?"

The joviality subsided. Talking deals was money, and money was something they all placed a high importance on.

"Depends how much you want." Lou's face showed no lines of laughter now; his thick white eyebrows drew lower and closer together. Jake watched the upper lids of his eyes grow into hoods to cover the previous amusement.

"Can you get me a meeting with Collins?"

Lou slapped him on the back again as he stood up. "Come with us mate, we're on our way to the club now."

The five men left the pub a little rowdily, and as it wasn't far to the club, they walked rather than hail a cab. Screams and shouts reached their ears seconds before dozens of kids spilled out of a narrow side street and straight into their path.

By the time the men realized the kids were fighting each other, they were caught up in the middle of a riot.

"Fuck this boys, I'm not getting arrested for a load of drugged up loonies, head for the club," shouted Lou above the bedlam.

Jake saw the glint of a blade in Connor's hand.

"Put that away kid,' Jake yelled. "The filth'll be here any minute, they see you with that and you'll be banged up with all these crazies."

Connor paid no attention, and slashed a lad who came towards him brandishing a glass ashtray. It was as though he didn't see or feel the blood spraying over him. The younger man then walked calmly after his companions, knife by his side, ready for use.

Jake wanted out. He hadn't come to Birmingham to wind up in some stupid riot. He tried to follow Lou and the others, but a crowd surrounded him. He used his size to crash through them, trying not to look at their faces. A sudden heat assailed his upper arm. Ignoring it, he carried on through the throng. By the time he was clear, Lou and the others were nowhere to be seen.

Police sirens grew louder as they neared the disturbance. Jake walked quickly, careful not to run and arouse suspicion. Not that the wound on his arm wouldn't do that anyway.

A trail of blood betrayed his path.

20 - THE BOYS ARE BACK

Persistent ringing penetrated Robbie's dreams. It must be Lysa; she must have forgotten her key. Maybe she'd managed to get his blood tested. She'd pulled him through the worst of the withdrawal, wiping up the vomit, and stopping him from disintegrating completely. Still, exhaustion, anxiety and cravings drummed in his brain. Forcing himself out of the bed, he pulled on his shorts before padding down the hallway. As he turned the latch, the door flew in.

His nose hurt so much he was stunned for a second, the force of the door knocking him to the floor.

Laughter filled the hallway. "Mornin' Robbie, mate," grinned a tall freckly youth. "So this is where you bin hidin'."

The three youths pushed past him into the living room. He followed them. How had they tracked him down to Lysa's?

"How'd you get past the door downstairs?" Robbie asked, wiping at his watering eyes.

"Waited 'till some old biddy came out and pushed past her," smirked the freckled one.

"Hey boys, get a load of this," a short boy with blonde tightly curled hair flicked the switches on Lysa's stereo.

"Leave it out, Davo, its Lysa's."

"Yeah, and think how much smack it could get."

"No, I'm not nicking off Lysa, she's the only one left who cares about me." Freckles unplugged the video. "Leave my sister's stuff alone, Mick."

Mick smiled and walked quickly towards him, throwing his arm around Robbie's shoulder. "Now Robbie, mate, we care about you, look what we brought." Mick motioned the smallest of the three over to them. The short lad picked a scab from his shaven head before rummaging in dirty pockets and bringing out an empty syringe and a small bag.

A voice in his head told him to grab the drugs, fast, but love for his sister and all she was trying to do for him fought back. "No," said Robbie, "I'm staying clean, I promised Lysa."

Mick laughed. "And what will your precious sister think when she comes home to find you and half her stuff gone? Will she think you're staying clean then?"

"I'm staying clean and I'm staying here," trying to convince himself as much as his friends. "She'll be back any second, you'd better go."

"She ain't comin' back for ages, we watched 'er go out," said Skinhead. "Bet you're sorry now you told us 'er name. All we 'ad to do was look 'er up in the phone book."

"How'd you know I was out? You lot just left me when the cops turned up, didn't care about me then, did you?"

"Hey, we made *enquiries*," said Davo. "Once we found out your sister bailed you out, we reckoned you'd want us to spring you."

Robbie pushed Mick's arm away from his shoulder and sat on the settee. "Well I don't want to be sprung, so you can all fuck off."

"Now you know you've got to come with us, Rob," Mick sneered. "We can't go away empty handed, look at all the gear your sister's got. We can make enough out of this to get us all down to Glastonbury."

As Mick spoke, Davo went through to Lysa's bedroom. Robbie leapt up from the settee. "Hey keep out of there! Leave

Lysa's things alone." In the few seconds it took for him to reach the bedroom door, Davo was already raiding Lysa's jewelry box.

Mick was behind him, chatting into his ear. "Robbie, mate, you might as well come with us; she'll never believe you didn't turn the place over."

Skinhead pushed past them into the bedroom. He pulled open drawers and tipped them out onto the bed.

"Yes she will, she believes in me!" yelled Robbie. "Get out all of you, just get out!

Skinhead held up various pieces of Lysa's underwear. He found a black lace thong and started rubbing it against his crotch. "Ohhhh ohhhhh fuck me!" he mocked in a feigned orgasm, bringing peals of laughter from Mick and Davo.

A mixture of disgust and panic fought for superiority in Robbie's stomach. "Put that away!" he shouted frantically, jumping over the mess of clothes that was already on the floor. He punched Skinhead in the mouth, forcing him backwards onto the floor beside the bed.

"Hey Rob," complained Skinhead. "You coulda knocked a tooth out."

"I'd be doing you a favor if I did!" Robbie was about to dive on top of Skinhead to deliver another punch when Mick and Davo grabbed him on either side.

"Come on now, Rob, he's only having a laugh," said Mick.

"Yeah," joined in Davo, "he doesn't see real women's undies, ya know, ones that are actually worn by someone and not in a shop window."

"Yes I have!' retorted Skinhead.

"Takin' ya sisters knickers out of the washing machine doesn't count," Mick teased.

"Why can't you all get out and leave me alone? I have a chance to get clean."

Mick laughed. "Sure Rob, how many times have you wanted to get clean before and always gone back to the smack?"

"This time it's different. Lysa pulled me through the last few days without it."

Mick waved a bag under his nose. "Come on Rob, you know you want it, your eye started to twitch, it always does that when you need a fix."

Mick was right, he did want a fix, but he wanted to stay clean too. He hated the eye thing, because after that the jitters came, and Lysa believed in him. The problem was, he didn't believe in himself. He would only bring her more grief if he stayed. Looking around at the damage in her flat, he was defeated. He'd already let her down badly. He was useless, a useless addict.

As Robbie relaxed, Mick and Davo let go of his arms.

Skinhead grabbed a padded stool with wrought iron legs from beside the dresser and ran into the living room. Robbie heard crashing and splintering glass. It had to be the kitchen shelves.

"Come on Rob, time to go." Mick put his arm over his shoulders once again and led Robbie out of the bedroom.

They were right, time to go. He was stupid to ever think he could live a normal life again, be Lysa's little brother again. Make her proud of him.

He shook himself free of Mick, went into the hall, and pulled his jacket from the rack; he couldn't bear to look into the living room to see the damage. Throwing it over his shoulder, he walked out of the front door into the hallway. Tears tried to escape from the back of his eyes as he stepped out into the bright morning sun.

It was hopeless. He'd never be free of the mess he'd got himself in.

21 - HEADLINES

"But he wasn't there, Boss. We searched the whole place. The bastard's gone." Big Don stubbed his cigarette out in the white plastic ashtray. Marchant looked up, unimpressed.

"Your job is to find him, Don, that's what I pay you for—to find people." Marchant's voice never varied in tone.

At the other side of the desk Big Don rubbed his forehead.

Marchant's gaze rested on the wall to the right of them. He admired his display case of combat knives. Some modern, some antique, but all deadly. This wasn't good. Marchant had a peculiar fondness for selecting particular knives to torture or kill specific people. It was in the reports, and it was never pretty.

Marchant returned his attention to Big Don. "Have you read the papers at all today, Don?" he asked. "No, of course you haven't. If you had, you might have more to tell me."

Marchant was talking about the rioting, but he didn't need to read the papers to find out. All the information he needed was at the touch of a phone.

Marchant picked up a folded newspaper, flipped it over to the front page, and pointed. Big Don and Finn read the headline automatically.

DRUG CRAZY KIDS KILL TWO HUNDRED.

The night before, at the time they were looking for The Baker, gangs of kids had gone crazy in three other major cities. There'd been riots in Manchester, Birmingham, and Leeds. In Manchester, it started in a dance club, similar to the incident at Marchant's club two nights earlier. In Birmingham and Leeds, kids had started attacking innocent people walking along the streets. The true figure of the deaths was two hundred and twenty four; that included the kids who had either turned on each other, or killed themselves.

"This," said Marchant indicating the story, "has something to do with our man in black." He paused, "It would seem our supplier has other outlets he hasn't told us about."

Finn and Big Don had searched half of Liverpool the previous night for The Baker, until finally, at three thirty in the morning, they'd given up. After falling into bed for a few hours, Finn had taken a quick shower and waited for Big Don to pick him up.

"Shit Boss, this is the first I've heard of it." Big Don shook his head. "You think that Baker weirdo's done all this?"

"It doesn't take Einstein to work that one out, Don." Marchant leaned forward over the desk. "I want The Baker found, and I want Jake found."

Finn took a step towards the desk. "You think Jake has something to do with this as well?"

Marchant looked up. "Maybe. He disappeared at the same time as a good deal of my merchandise. I don't want any of this," he waved towards the newspaper, "coming back on me. He might have a side-line going with The Baker. It was Jake who put me on to him in the first place." Marchant's voice hardly registered above a whisper.

"Jake's worked for you for years, why would he steal from you?"

Marchant leaned back in his chair, his hands clasped loosely. "You seem eager to defend Jake. Could it have been you, Finn? Did you steal the coke?"

Finn couldn't reveal Jake had called him. Be careful; don't blow seven months' work.

"Of course not, Boss, you can trust me. I just thought Jake was a smart guy that's all. I didn't think he'd be stupid enough to double cross you."

"Yes, that would be very stupid, wouldn't it? The thing is, Finn, you and The Baker both have something in common."

"What's that, Boss?"

"You were both introduced to me by Jake. Now first, Jake disappears, then The Baker vanishes." Marchant paused a moment. "When are you doing a magic act, Finn? You know they say things happen in threes?"

"I'm not going anywhere, Boss. I'll be around as long as you need me."

Crap. Finn had to give Marchant a reason to trust him. He tried to ignore the edginess creeping into his nerves. Can't blow the cover, stay calm.

Marchant's low voice snapped his attention back. "I have a job for you. When you've done it, maybe I'll believe you're loyal."

"Just name it, Boss," replied Finn.

"It would seem," said Marchant, "that for some reason of his own, The Baker wants the kids to cause mayhem. I won't pretend to know what his reason is, but he's used me in his little experiment, and I won't allow anyone to do that."

"What do you want me to do?"

"Ahh now, Finn, maybe you could help me out here. Where do you think The Baker will strike next?"

Finn shrugged his shoulders. "Glasgow, London, any major big city, maybe."

"What about major events, events where there'll be thousands of kids, do you reckon he'd strike there?"

"Depends. If he just wants to get the kids killing each other he might, but if he wants to create chaos all over the country, he'd hit the cities."

"Where're you thinking of, Boss?" asked Big Don.

"Not sure; I don't care what he's up to, but he's not getting away with using my club for his little games." Marchant looked thoughtful, Finn and Big Don stayed silent.

Finally, Marchant spoke. "The Glastonbury Festival starts today. My contact in Birmingham needs some extra supplies to sell down there." He looked at Finn. "You can take it. Make sure it gets there safe."

"Sure Boss, just say where and when."

Marchant took a pen from the desk and wrote an address on a notepad on the desk. He tore off the paper and handed it to Finn. The handwriting was as neat as his voice; he must have received top marks for presentation at school.

Finn read it and put it in his shirt pocket. "Where's the gear you want me to take?"

Marchant smiled. "I don't trust you that much, Finn. Big Don will drop you off home so you can pick up a change of clothes. I want you back here in your own car in an hour and a half." Turning to Big Don he said, "When you've dropped him off, you go and pick up two packets; one coke, one heroin." He reached into his pocket and took out a key he threw to Big Don who caught it and put it quickly in his own pocket.

"Well go on then, get a move on." Marchant waved them out of the office.

Neither Finn nor Don spoke as they descended the green painted spiral staircase to the gym below. The girl behind the desk flashed a perfect smile at Finn as they walked past her to the exit. Her muscled body didn't appeal to him, even though she was a nice-looking girl. With her olive skin and Spanish features, she hardly needed the ton of make-up she wore.

Finn smiled back and followed Big Don outside. It wasn't until they were driving along that Big Don broke the silence.

"What have you done to upset the Boss?"

Finn was on alert. "Fucked if I know. I think he's just getting a bit nervy after what happened in the club. I mean the cops are poking around in the gym as well now."

"Marchant doesn't get nervy. I know him better than anyone, no-one upsets him, he's too clever."

"Well he certainly doesn't trust me. He doesn't even want me knowing where anything's kept."

"He trusts his instincts, and they haven't let him down yet."

"What about your instincts Don, do you trust me?"

Big Don glanced at his companion. His expression revealed nothing, and his reply was silence. They drew up outside Finn's flat. Finn hoped he wouldn't have to live here much longer, he missed his own house with memories of Amy wrapped up safe in its walls. "You didn't answer my question," he said getting out of the car. Walking around the pavement to Big Don, he leaned an arm on the roof, looking in the open window.

"I don't know..." Big Don paused a moment. "Just watch your back, Finn, if you try and get one over on Marchant, it won't work. He'll catch up with Jake and The Baker soon enough, and if you're not who you seem to be, he'll be burying the three of you."

Finn nodded. "Advice taken." He glanced at his watch. "See you back at the gym at half eleven then." Finn turned and went up to his flat. By the time he was inside and looking down onto the street, Big Don had sped away.

Finn packed a sports bag with some casual clothes. He wanted to see Lysa before he left for Birmingham. He'd arranged to cook a meal for her and Robbie in her flat tonight. He didn't want to break their date over the phone, she might think he was just messing her around. Better to go in person, tell her he had a business trip.

Well, it was the truth.

22 - JUGGLING

Finn hoped Lysa would be home. Her voice crackled through the speaker.

"Who is it?"

"Lysa, it's Finn."

"Come up."

She sounded a little strange. Probably the intercom.

When he reached her first floor flat, the door was wide open against the wall. Clothes and household items were thrown around the entrance.

"Lysa!" Finn ran down the hallway to the lounge. She sat red-eyed amongst the debris of her home, holding some broken treasure in her hands. Furniture and other belongings lay around her—none of it was upright. Glass showered the living room and kitchen.

Panic gnawed at his gut, but he couldn't let it take control. "Are you all right? Did someone hurt you?"

She looked up at him; mascara streaked her cheeks black. "I should have known. I shouldn't have put so much faith in him."

"Robbie did this?"

Lysa shook her head. "Probably, but I don't think he'd have made such a mess; he must have had a little help."

Finn looked at his watch. Ten forty-five a.m. He didn't have long to get back to Marchant's gym.

"If he'd just stolen from me," she started. A fat tear escaped her eye and rolled down her cheek. "I could have forgiven him, I could have." He wanted to rush over and hold her, she looked so lost, gazing around her wrecked flat at the empty spaces where it seemed her T.V. and video had been. A double vein of pink wire led to speakers at either side of the left wall, their stereo heart ripped out. Pieces of shelving stuck out of the wall that divided the kitchen from the living room like jagged opaque teeth.

"I'm going to check the other rooms. I'll be back in a few seconds."

She nodded silently and he moved methodically through the flat. Her bedroom was destroyed, picture frames smashed. Underwear hung on various door handles in the bedroom. Toilet paper and towels covered the bathroom floor.

He came back into the living room. "Where do you think he'll be? I'll help you look for him." Life kept getting more complicated. He wanted to stay and help Lysa, but he couldn't afford to lose Marchant's trust and maybe blow the investigation. She was so tiny, swamped in the mess of her wrecked flat. "Do you trust me, Lysa?" he asked.

She wiped her face with the back of her hand. "I've only known you a few days. I think it's a little early to ask questions like that. Look what happened when I trusted my own brother."

"I'm not an addict. You can't put me in that league."

"I don't even know where you live, and what brings you here now anyway? I wasn't supposed to see you until tonight."

Finn squatted down on the floor, and squeezed her left hand. He wanted her to believe in him, but he couldn't tell her the truth, not until the investigation was over. Even though he'd only known her a short time, he didn't want to leave her alone to clear this up. For a second, he wondered if he was trying to save her because he hadn't been able to save Amy. No. Lysa wasn't Amy, and she wasn't in imminent danger. But he did feel she was special and he wanted to help.

"What if I promised you I wouldn't let you down? I called in because I have to go on a business trip to Birmingham and I wanted to tell you in person rather than over the phone."

"You'd better go then." Lysa stared at the blue carpet full of broken glass and books.

"Why don't you come with me? I have to go and pick something up, but I can be back here by twelve. All you have to do is clean yourself up and pack a bag." He smiled at her. "I'll even book us separate rooms just to prove I haven't any ulterior motives."

Lysa shook her head. "I hardly know you. We've not even had a first date and you want me to go to Birmingham with you?"

Finn had to admit, it did seem a bit odd to ask her to go with him. "Okay, I know, I understand you'd probably not normally go off to another city with someone you've only just met, but I hate to leave you here with this chaos and worried about your brother."

She didn't look convinced, but she hadn't said no yet.

"Please. I promise to behave like a perfect gentleman. I know you don't know much about me, and it might seem risky to come away with me, but I promise we'll have single rooms. You can even drive yourself and follow me there."

"Seems silly to take two cars," she replied.

"Then we'll go in mine. Give you time to think."

"Separate rooms?"

"I swear. We won't even book the rooms until we get there."

She sighed at the disarray, and then looked back to him. "I don't feel like cleaning all this up right now, really".

"So it's a yes?"

She nodded. "Okay then, but I want your life story on the way."

"That shouldn't take me long," he smiled. "When we come back, I'll help you clean this place up." The police officer in him kicked in, and although he knew what her reply would be, he had to ask. "Do you want to report this?" His eyebrows rose as he spoke.

"No, I can't really, can I? You go and do what you have to, then pick me up. I'll be ready for twelve."

Finn stood up and offered her his hand to help her, and she took it with her right hand, still clutching something in her left. She moved slowly down the hallway, with Finn following. He saw her catch sight of the underwear on the wardrobe doors. "Just bring what you need," he said. "We'll replace anything else when we get back." He gave her a quick hug and kissed her on the forehead. "I'll be back at twelve. Lock the door after me."

She hugged him back and he felt something hard in his back. As they pulled away from each, other he saw what looked like a grey statue in her hand. He asked, "Can I see?"

Lysa unfurled her fingers to reveal the broken statue of the swimmer Robbie had once been. A smooth arm arched over his head, fingers poised to dive back into the water. The long, lean stretch of his back, but broken now, jagged at the hip, legs lost somewhere in the debris of the room.

"It's Robbie, back when he was twelve. He loved swimming. When we used to go on holiday, we could never get him out of the water." The sadness in her eyes reached out to him.

"Is this one of yours? Did you carve this yourself?"

"Yes, in much happier times."

"He can still turn it around, Lysa. Lots of people do, and he knows he can count on you. When he's ready, he'll come back and you'll be there to help him." He wished he could stay. "I'll be back soon, and when we come back, we'll fix all this up. Lock the door after me."

"But it was only Robbie," she started.

"Humor me, lock the door."

She followed him to the doorway as he walked down the stairs.

"Lock it," he said, looking back over his shoulder.

"Okay, okay." She closed the door and he waited until he heard the lock click into place before heading back to his car.

***   ***   ***

Climbing back up the spiral staircase to Marchant's office Finn worried about bringing Lysa along with him. If she found the drugs, he would either have to tell her who he was or risk losing her. He knocked on Marchant's door.

"Come in."

Marchant sat in his usual chair watching a television which was situated in the corner of the room. A reporter was talking to a longhaired youth of about nineteen. Finn's attention was drawn to the set. The reporter asked the kid why he thought people were rioting.

"Y'see man, it's the olds, the government, they know nothing about us. The politicians, they don't give a crap about us."

"Even if that were true," the reporter replied, "riots and murder aren't the answer. Is it right that there's a new drug on the street? There're reports that an unidentified substance has been found in the bodies of the dead who've been involved in the incidents."

The greasy haired lad laughed. "The name's Euphoria mate. Get it right." His tone changed to one of mocking. "Not an un-i-dent-if-ied substance."

The reporter was unable to hide his discomfort. "So, you're saying that this new drug has a name, and that name is Euphoria?"

"For a suit, you're slow to catch on aren't you?"

"If this drug turns ordinary people into murderers, why take it? Especially as it ultimately appears to kill its users."

"We all gotta go sometime," the lad raised his fist above his head. "The Children of the Revolution!"

Marchant pointed the remote at the set and the screen went black. He turned to Finn. "You ready to go?"

"Sure."

"How are you going to find the address?" asked Marchant.

"I'll buy a street map."

Marchant turned to Big Don. "Give him the gear."

Big Don moved to a cabinet by the door and brought out a small briefcase. He placed it on Marchant's desk and flicked it open. Inside, Finn saw two sealed colored transparent bags; one blue, one green.

"The blue one's the coke, the other's the heroin. You tell Collins that it's good stuff, pure."

"How much do I pick up for it?"

"Ten grand, not a note less." Marchant's lips turned upwards in a half-smile. "You can do that, can't you, Finn? I can trust you with it?"

"Sure you can, Boss."

"Right then, when you get to Birmingham, book yourself in a room somewhere, then call me. I'll have set up a meeting with Collins for you."

"Right. As soon as I have the money, I'll head straight back."

"See that you do," Marchant nodded to Big Don to shut the case, then he added, "Hope you don't get too lonely, Finn, maybe Big Don could fix you up with a girl when you get back." The smile was mocking, but Finn said nothing in reply, turning his attention to Big Don, who appeared to be having trouble with one of the latches on the case. Finally it snapped shut and he handed it to Finn.

"I'll be off then."

"I'll speak to you later, Finn."

Finn left the office, passing the girl at reception on his way out. She didn't see him this time; she was too busy checking would-be body builders into the gym.

Finn's car was parked around the back in one of the reserved spaces. He could call in to the station, but two bags of drugs weren't enough to get Marchant on. He had to find out where he stored everything, and where his supplies came from; that meant winning his trust.

Finn would have to keep the suitcase away from Lysa. If she found out he was carrying drugs, she'd cut him out of her life before he had a chance to really get to know her.

*** *** ***

Blood no longer flowed from the wound in Jake's bandaged arm, and his grumbling belly hurried him to the nearest café. Ordering a lunch of burger and chips, he figured he'd better ring Kelly. She'd be expecting him back, and she may head home if she didn't hear from him. He swilled down a lukewarm cup of coffee, then went out looking for a pay phone. The first two were broken, the third only took phone cards and of course he didn't have one. The bed and breakfast might be a better choice; he'd seen a phone in the hallway.

Finally, he rang the hotel in France, only to be told Miss Winter checked out that morning, but had left a message to say she was going back to England if anyone called for her. Jake frantically rang the airport to see which flight she was on.

They wouldn't give him any passenger information, but the next flight from that location would be landing in Manchester at twelve forty-five.

Jake checked his watch, if she'd made that flight, she would already be on her way back to Liverpool. There was no time to track down Lou and arrange a meeting with Collins. Frustration over not being able to meet Collins was surpassed by fear for Kelly. If Marchant found her…

He hurriedly threw his clothes into his sports bag and checked out of the bed and breakfast. Sick with the knowledge that it would take him at least two hours in the traffic at this time of day, he drove with one thought in his mind. He had to get to her before Marchant did.

23 - BIRMINGHAM BUSTED

This city was even smokier, dirtier, and darker than the one they'd just left. Spaghetti Junction with its twisting concrete bridges and pillars could easily have come from a futuristic science fiction film. He counted his luck to be travelling with Lysa even if he doubted the wisdom of bringing her along.

She wanted to know more about him, so he told her about Amy's death the year before, the night before their engagement party. It still stung a little to talk about her.

"I'll never forget her," he said "but it's time to start living again. I found working long and hard helped."

"Overwork can cause its own problems," she replied. "My ex, Tony, became obsessed with work." A fleeting hint of sadness laced her voice. "People are more important than money."

"People are more important than anything," he added.

"I agree."

They were both quiet for a while, and Finn reflected on what he'd learned about her, letting the experience of newness and excitement take over for a short time. Normal chatter resumed as they neared the city, discussing places to stay, food, and plans for the evening.

They found a nice hotel and booked two rooms. After settling in, they went down to the hotel bar. Lysa talked about Robbie and her worries for him.

Before going for dinner, Finn made an excuse and said he would follow her in. He tried to phone his boss, all lines were busy, which he supposed was to be expected. He then phoned Collins on the number that Marchant had given him.

"Yes," said a gruff voice.

"This is Finn, Marchant sent me from Liverpool."

"Finn? I thought it was Jake he'd sent down."

"Jake? We've been looking for him. Is he in Birmingham?"

"Never mind that, how do I know you're from Marchant? I've never heard of any, Finn. It's always Jake I do business with."

"Yeah well, I've got the gear, not Jake. Ring Marchant, he'll tell you who I am." What was going on? He'd assumed Marchant would have informed Collins that it was he who would be delivering the drugs.

"No, I've already spoken to him. He said he was sending a new bloke down, but when Jake turned up, I thought he must have changed his mind."

So Jake *had* been in Birmingham. Maybe still was. "Mr. Collins, can I ask when you saw Jake? Mr. Marchant is very keen to track him down. We think he did a runner with some of Mr. Marchant's supplies."

The man at the other end of the phone laughed. "Is that so? Well, well. Jake didn't let us in on that tidbit of information." More seriously he said, "We can't make the deal yet, the filth are crawling all over my businesses, it'll have to wait a while. Call Marchant, he can't have missed seeing the news today, he'll know the score."

"Marchant wants the deal done as soon as possible. He needs me back in Liverpool."

"Well Marchant will have to do without you for a few days."

"Do you know where Jake is?" Finn asked. "Mr. Marchant will want me doing something with my time."

"No, the boys met up with him, he offered us a pack of coke. I'd have it except the riots broke out and we've not seen or heard from him since."

"I don't suppose he said where he was staying?" Finn asked hopefully.

"Our Jake's not that stupid, not if he knows Marchant's looking for him. It does explain one thing though."

"What's that?"

"The boys said he had a new haircut, cropped short and dyed black."

"Is that so? If you hear from him would you let me know? Mr. Marchant would be grateful."

Finn relayed his mobile number to Collins. If Marchant got to Jake first he'd be dead. A dead witness was no good at all.

Finn met Lysa in the dining room. She looked gorgeous in a short black silk dress. The shoestring straps revealed lightly tanned skin, and her fair hair lay loosely over her shoulders. At least for the next couple of hours, he was going to forget he was on an assignment; he was just going to be himself.

"I thought you'd run out on me," she said smiling.

"After dragging you down to Birmingham with me? No way."

"I have a lot of baggage. Not everyone wants that."

"I'd have to be crazy to run out on you." What a corny thing to say. How embarrassing. She was looking up at him, smiling. She probably thought he was a right idiot. He eased himself into the chair opposite, hoping he didn't do something even more stupid like pull the cover from the table.

"Sorry. I watch so many bad movies I tend to pick up the dialogue."

"Really? I'll have to recommend some good ones then."

Embarrassment made him concentrate on the menu. She made him feel hopeful again. Amy had been his life, his love since he was eighteen and she seventeen—both in the Police Force, and loving their chosen careers. Except on that rainy November night, with the winds gusting at 70 mph, he'd lost her for good. Now Lysa was here, and even though she looked nothing like Amy, there was something there —something he couldn't quite identify, a kind of a warmth, humor, and depth, things he'd loved about Amy, and it seemed that Lysa shared.

Lysa ordered chicken with salad. Despite concentrating on the menu, Finn hadn't managed to retain anything, so asked for the same.

They talked about everything except Finn's job and Robbie, keeping the conversation light and chatty, not wanting to touch on anything that might spoil the evening. Finally, they were the only people left in the dining room, and the waiter hovered nearby, wanting to clear their plates.

"I think he wants us to leave," said Lysa, her eyes darting to the left without moving her head.

"You could be right. Shall we get a bottle of wine sent up to the room?"

"Whose room?"

Finn hoped he hadn't made a mistake with his suggestion. "Yours, mine, whichever you want. We can sit in the bar if you like."

"No, your room will be fine, then I don't have to kick you out when I'm finished with you," she grinned.

Finn stood and reached out a hand. "So, you're one of these liberated women who use us poor men and then cast us aside when you've had your fun."

"Maybe." She took his hand. They had hardly stepped away from the table when the waiter was clearing away their glasses.

His arm felt good around her slim waist. The nearness of her body as they walked to the bar made him wish he could forget his assignment and spend his time in her company alone.

But he couldn't. Reaching into his pocket, he pulled out his room key.

"Here," he said passing it to Lysa. "You go on up and I'll order the wine."

Reluctantly, he freed her from his arm

"Okay, but don't be too long, or I might go back to my own room."

Her long legs seemed to go on forever as he admired her walking towards the lift. It would be easy to fall in love with her. But, he had to call Marchant.

Finding a quiet corner of the lounge he tapped out the number. Marchant answered almost immediately.

"Boss, it's Finn. Collins won't do the deal yet, too many coppers around."

Marchant spoke quietly as ever. "That was a possibility I suppose."

"If you don't mind me asking Boss, why did you send me down here if you thought he might not do the deal?"

"I don't mind you asking, Finn. Surely you know why."

"Sorry Boss?"

"It's all a matter of trust, Finn, how long can you hang around there with that much gear on you? Aren't you afraid you might be picked up?"

"No. Not really."

"Just why is that?"

For a moment it felt as though Marchant was on to him. It seemed he knew he wouldn't be picked up at all.

"Because the only people who know what I'm carrying are you, Big Don, and Collins."

"What if you were picked up, Finn, would you implicate me?"

"No, Boss. I know better than to do that."

"I hope so, Finn."

Finn let out a slow breath. Marchant was only concerned with his loyalty. He wanted him to sweat, to worry that he might be caught with the gear on him.

"Have you anything else to tell me, Finn?"

"No. I'll wait for Collins's instructions."

"You haven't seen anyone else?"

Did Marchant know Lysa was with him? "Are you sure you haven't anything else to tell me?"

Finn decided to bluff his way through. "No, nothing important."

"I spoke to Collins earlier. I already knew he didn't want to do the deal yet. He told me something else as well, something very interesting."

Damn. Collins must have told him about Jake. If Marchant got to him first, he'd kill him without a doubt. He'd have to tell Marchant he knew about Jake now; it would be another test of loyalty.

"Oh yeah," said Finn. "He said his boys had seen Jake down here, said he'd changed his hair, cropped short and black."

"Why didn't you tell me that before, Finn?"

"Sorry, Boss, forgot all about it. I've had a busy day I'm knackered."

"Well you keep your eyes open for our Jake, and if you see him you tell him that we're keeping his girlfriend comfortable."

"She's turned up too?" The surprise in Finn's voice wasn't faked.

Yes, and Big Don's keeping her company, so if you see him, you tell him I want to see him. Make sure he knows Don is looking after her."

The line went dead. Finn hit his end button and walked over to the bar to pick up the bottle of wine. This was bad. Really fucking bad. It would be no use phoning his superior to go in for her. It would blow Finn's cover, and besides, his boss would never risk a big drugs bust and the chance to put Marchant away for the sake of one girl.

He tried calling anyway, but the lines were still busy.

Finn fought with his emotions in the elevator ride to their room. He felt something for Lysa, something more than attraction, but now Kelly, a girl he hardly knew had to come first. He reached his door as Lysa walked out.

"Hey, I wasn't that long," he said.

Lysa glared at him. "Now I know what you do for a living."

"Lysa, I told you..."

"Bastard!"

Shit. She must have found the drugs, but before he could say anything else she'd slammed her own door behind her.

Finn rushed into his room. Scanning it, he didn't immediately see the briefcase. Moving to the wardrobe he found it open on the floor, obviously fallen from the top. The catch had opened as it hit the floor spilling the contents onto the floor.

"Damn!" he muttered, how the hell could he explain this? The ringing from his phone stopped him going after her.

"Finn," he said into the receiver.

"I want your arse back up here."

It took a second for Finn to figure out exactly which boss required his arse back in Liverpool.

It was Marchant.

"What about Collins?" Finn asked.

"Fuck Collins. Jake's back and you're the only one he'll speak to."

"Why me?"

"Well I really don't know? For some obscure reason he must think he can trust you." Finn caught the distrust in Marchant's voice.

"How do you know he'll only speak to me?"

"Because he called reception in the gym and left me a message. He knows we have Kelly, and says he will only deal with you. Why would that be?"

Finn imagined Lysa packing her bag while he was speaking to Marchant.

"No idea, Boss."

"Leave now, Finn. We'll wait up for you."

Marchant hung up and Finn was left staring at an open briefcase and listening to a silent receiver. He tucked the phone back into his pocket and hurriedly shut the case and shoved it under the bed.

Moments later, he was knocking on Lysa's door. "Lysa I can explain. It really isn't the way it looks."

Lysa didn't answer. He knocked again. "Lysa please, just listen to me for one minute, then, if you want to leave I'll drive you back."

The door opened, Lysa glared at him. "How could you get involved with me and be dealing drugs after I spilled my guts to you about Robbie?"

Finn trusted her, but didn't want to tell her everything yet, not if he didn't have to.

"Look, just come back into the room with me and I'll explain."

Lysa eyed him suspiciously. "I should call the police, any decent person would, and me most of all. I've seen the results that filth brings."

"Please, Lysa, this is important, just come back in and give me one minute, just one, and then you can call the police if you like." He held out his hand. "You can even use my phone."

Lysa came out of the room and closed the door behind her. She kept her key in her hand, but took the phone from him. "One minute," she said.

Finn's mind searched frantically for a cover story, by the time they were both in his room with the door safely shut, he had one.

"Sit down," he said perching himself on the edge of the bed.

"I'd prefer to stand."

Finn drew in a breath. A little lie now would be okay, he'd tell her the truth as soon as he could.

"I'm helping out a friend. He did something really stupid and now his girlfriend is being held in Liverpool by the people who want to find him."

"Go on."

"If I take these drugs back for him, they'll let her go."

"Are all your friends involved in dealing?"

"Of course not, Jake got involved by mistake. He was working for this guy who owns the D. Zone. It's a nightclub."

"I know what it is," Lysa glanced at her watch. "Thirty seconds," she said.

Finn talked faster. "Look they sent him to pick up a package, and when he arrived there were cops all over the place, it was the night the club burnt down. He panicked and ran, and they thought he'd nicked the drugs so they grabbed his girlfriend. Now he has to get the gear back, but he's scared they'll kill him, so he's asked me to take it for him."

94

"So why won't they kill you instead?"

Finn was stuck, if his hastily thought up story was real, why indeed wouldn't they kill him instead?

"I don't know. I suppose they've got no real reason to kill me."

"As you've been with me the whole time we've been here, when did you find time to meet him to collect the case?"

"He left it in the room for me," he lied.

"Minute's up." Lysa turned to go.

"Wait, Lysa, I'm telling you the truth."

"Don't insult my intelligence. I've seen enough liars in the emergency room to know when I'm hearing a tale, and unless you can come up with something better, you can forget I exist."

She was leaving. A few more steps and she'd be at the door, turning the handle.

"Okay, Lysa stop. I'll tell you the truth."

She turned her head. "Oh yes?"

Finn stood and went to the wardrobe. He rummaged around for a few seconds and brought out his identity card.

"I'm working undercover, I'm a cop."

Lysa crossed the room to him. Checking out the card she said, "Right then, I suppose you'd better tell me the truth now."

"Can I tell you while I pack?" he asked. "I'm afraid I have to go back to Liverpool right now.

24 - VIGIL

Jake sat on the flat roof of the launderette. It was cramped behind the air vent, and every now and then he stretched his legs. He watched the gym all night.

He despised the 'body beautifuls' as he called them. The men mostly worked in offices and didn't lift as much as a tin of beans when they were at home. The women were nearly all housewives trying to recapture their youthful bodies. Pity their wrinkled faces couldn't reflect the hard work they put in.

The muscles in Jake's tanned arms were there through hard work and were there to do a job—to beat the other guy to a pulp harder and faster than he could beat you.

After checking Kelly's flat and not finding her, he'd raced to the airport and waited until the last flight from Paris had arrived. Calls to her phone were unanswered and fear nagged that she was on the earlier flight and in Liverpool before him. Racing back to her flat as fast as speed limits would allow, he was just in time to see Big Don shove her into a car. As Jake was driving a rental he'd been able to follow them discreetly to the gym, making sure he kept enough of a distance not to be noticed.

Marchant's men came and went, but Kelly had not been moved, so he phoned Marchant to tell him he'd speak only to Finn.

Jake believed Marchant when he said Finn was out of town, he'd not seen him with Big Don and Kelly so it was probably true. Now he sat and waited, fearful of what Big Don might do.

Jake remembered the young prostitute Big Don had raped and beaten. Even Marchant's hardest men had been disgusted at the things Big Don bragged he'd done to her. Jake prayed that one of those other men would be with Kelly. He couldn't allow himself to think Big Don might be alone with her.

But if he was, and he hurt her, Jake promised himself he would kill him.

25 - THE JOB COMES FIRST

Finn and Lysa stopped first at her flat. The place was exactly as they'd left it. A light pulsed on the answer machine and Lysa hit play. Robbie's voice slurred into the room.

"Ss, sorry, Lyse. I didn't trash the flat. I don't want you thinking I wrecked it after all you done for me." There was a pause and Lysa turned to Finn, saying nothing as Robbie's voice continued.

"I'm a no good waster, Lyse, they're all right. I won't lie to you. I'm high, it's the way it's got to be, Lyse, I'm gonna die to the music, in the sun. Bye, Lyse, love you."

The machine fell silent. It was a couple of seconds before Lysa spoke.

"I know where he is, Finn. I know where he's gone."

"Where do you think he is?"

"I know where he is. He's at the Glastonbury festival. He wanted to go last year, but Mum wouldn't let him." She turned to face him. "I have to go to him, Finn. I have to."

"How do you think you're gonna find him in a crowd that size? Let me get my business up here sorted out and I'll come with you."

"No, Finn, you have to get on with your job and I have to find Robbie."

Her expression and the determination in her voice told him she was not going to be swayed to wait for him. "All right," he said. "At least get some sleep first; we've been up all night. I'll call you as soon as I can."

"Okay, but if I'm not here when you call I'll be on my way south."

Finn reached into his pocket for a pen. Picking up a magazine from the floor, he hastily scribbled down his number. "If I don't catch you before you leave, call me as soon as you arrive at the festival. I'll follow you as fast as I can."

Finn's body ached with lack of sleep, but he had to get to the gym. He didn't want to leave her, but she was right, he had a job to do. "I'm sorry, Lysa, but I have to go. You get some sleep and I'll speak to you soon. Lock up after me."

He bent his head to kiss her, it was meant to be a quick, light goodbye kiss, but she reached her arms up and pulled him close.

That kiss made Finn want to stay more than anything, as their mouths sought each other, he found it hurt in his chest to pull away from her.

But he did, otherwise Kelly Winter could end up dead.

26 - COMING INTO THE LIGHT

As the sun rose over Glastonbury Tor, it was time to come out into the light.

Brown sun-burnt fields were littered with tents of all sizes; large, medium, some big enough only for one. There were countless minibuses, campers and vans, painted in myriad colors, some sprayed with graffiti, and others painted with pictures.

Sweltering Somerset heat was building already, and soon cans of Coca-Cola would be selling at inflated prices — double, sometimes triple their recommended retail price.

The Baker changed from his heavy black clothing into a green shirt and a green pair of jeans. He tied back his long black hair and shaved with a portable battery razor.

Green was the color of renewal.

Yesterday he'd sent Mark out with the biscuits. This batch was perfect. His secret ingredients included the seeds from a rare flower of the family Convolvulaceae, which was once used by the Aztec civilization to induce hallucinations. The more common example of this species of flower could be found in most garden shops, but he'd travelled to Mexico for just the exact one he needed. Little trace of the substance would be found in the human body once the effects had worn off.

The hybrid plant he'd created using Grohah's instructions gave birth to extremely potent seeds. These he had crushed and mixed with a Mexican hallucinogenic mushroom. Finally, combined with a biscuit recipe, the mixture was baked at high temperatures together with a sprinkling of cocaine. In the last five minutes of baking, he smeared the sap from the stem of the plant over the top of the biscuits. This would create chemical changes that at first gave the user a feeling of extreme elation. It wasn't until twenty or so hours later that the hallucinations would take effect. The Baker communicated with Grohah and learned well. Grohah's years in exile had not been wasted. Merging modern drugs with the ancient methods, a powerful combination was created. Fools thought the 2012 prophecy meant the end of the world, when what it really meant was the birth of the era of Grohah.

From Mark's dreams, The Baker took pictures of Tina. She was his real first success, taking a few days longer to die than his first subjects.

He smiled. How easy it had been getting the biscuits out on the streets. Men were greedy.

The time spent buying the additional drugs he needed was well spent. Of course he'd bought far more than he needed, but that had come in useful now to help him control Mark. He sat and studied his sleeping assistant. He'd warned him not to take even a bite of Euphoria, but he could have anything else he wanted. How long would Mark be able to obey? It was time to rouse him. "Mark, get up. I have something to show you."

Mark grunted and turned over in the sleeping bag The Baker had provided.

The Baker shoved him hard with his foot. "Get up, there's something I have to show you."

Mark's eyes opened slowly. "What time is it?"

"The right time."

Mark half sat up, leaning on his elbow. "What the hell does that mean?"

The Baker moved several boxes of biscuits from the side of the van and opened the hatch that would normally contain tools and pulled out a small golden box.

The Baker carefully set it down in front of Mark. "What I am about to show you no one but myself has seen since the ancient Aztec civilization walked the earth."

He opened the box and reached inside.

27 - GETTING OUT ALIVE

Kelly's cheek hurt.

If she could reach up to touch her face, she suspected she'd find it swollen, but the plastic cutting into her wrists behind her back prevented her from trying. Her body ached lying on the hard blue rubber gym mattress, but it was preferable to the concrete floor.

Pain in her face reminded her not to call out. Last time she'd tried that, the big guy, the one they called Big Don, had punched her hard. She'd fallen against the wall, and with her hands bound, she had no means to save herself as she scraped down the wall, leaving some flesh behind. When they'd finally left her alone, they'd tied a rag around her mouth and every time her tongue touched the cloth, it sucked the moisture out of her mouth. Her wrists were covered in moisture that her mouth lacked, but Kelly didn't know if it was blood or sweat that lingered on her skin.

Harsh light from the bare bulb that dangled in the windowless basement room hurt her eyes. It glared down at her, filling the room with constant brightness. Kelly slept on and off, and though she felt it must now be morning she had no real idea of what time it could be.

The sound of multiple footsteps thudding down the concrete stairs outside the room made her turn her head towards the door. It swung open and the well-dressed, quietly spoken man entered. He was flanked by the big guy who'd hit her and another man with dark hair.

"Take that off her mouth and sit her up," he ordered.

Kelly watched nervously as the dark haired man did as instructed. She tried not to tremble, even though she was afraid she would be used as a punch bag again, though even that seemed preferable to the other horrors she tried to hold check in her imagination.

Her jaw ached as the gag was removed from her mouth. She ran her tongue around her lips to try to correct the dryness. Even though she longed for a drink, she wasn't going to ask them for anything if she could help it.

The dark haired man pulled her up to a sitting position. She'd expected him to be rough and drag her forward, but she was surprised by his gentleness.

The one giving the orders moved towards her. Big Don stayed by the door, more solid than the concrete floor beneath her.

"Do you know my friend Finn here?" The smaller man motioned towards his dark haired companion.

Kelly shook her head. "No. I don't know any of you, and before you ask me again, I don't know where Jake is."

"That's quite all right, Kelly. Jake is going to meet us. He's going to trade himself for you." The man crouched down next to her, seeing him even close up made Kelly shiver inside. A jagged scar ran across his forehead like a neon sign. His hair combed back from his face showed it to its full advantage.

"Now, Kelly," he continued. "I expect you're hungry? Maybe thirsty as well? It's not very comfortable being tied up with your mouth bound all night long." He brushed her swollen cheek with his fingers. Kelly flinched involuntary. She tried desperately not to appear scared.

"I'm afraid Big Don can get carried away a little, but we do like to keep him in check whenever we can. He has been told not to hurt you again. Well, so long as you don't give him any trouble."

Kelly glanced at the man by the door, he grinned at her. It wasn't a friendly grin.

The soft spoken man looked at his watch. "Nearly ten. Any moment now Finn's phone should ring. It will be Jake, and he will want to speak to you."

"What if he doesn't call?" asked Kelly.

"He will. He knows what Big Don will do to you if he doesn't."

Kelly fell quiet. Her tormentor stood and motioned Finn to pull a crate over from the wall for him to sit on. As he sat down, the phone rang.

"Finn here. That you, Jake?"

Kelly almost held her breath.

"She's fine. A bit bruised but it's only cosmetic." There was a pause and Finn crouched down, holding the phone to Kelly's face.

Jake asked. "Kelly, are you all right? What have they done to you?"

Tears stung the corners of her eyes but she held them in. At first his voice comforted her, but then only served to make the situation even more real. "I'm okay, Jake. Why do they want you? What's going on?"

"You'll be fine Kell, it'll all be okay soon. Just do whatever they say. Finn's okay, he won't hurt you."

"Jake what's..."

The quietly spoken man took the phone from Finn. "Marchant here, Jake. You are going to co-operate aren't you? You do know who I'm going to have looking after your girl?"

Marchant's face betrayed no emotion as he listened to Jake. "When I get my goods back, you get your girl. There better not be anything missing," he warned.

Marchant passed the phone back to Finn. Finn listened for a few moments then said, "Now, Jake, you know I won't be able to bring her until I check out the goods." There was silence while he listened. "I promise you, Jake, as long as it's all there, she'll be okay."

He hit the end button and turned to Marchant. "I'm meeting him at three o'clock, St. John's cafe in the Precinct." Finn straightened up.

"Couldn't he think of anywhere more public?" Marchant smiled. "He must think we won't try anything in a busy shopping center. Well he'd be wrong, wouldn't he?"

"What have you got in mind?" Finn asked.

"I want him dead. Nobody gets away with stealing from me."

"What about the girl?" Finn nodded in Kelly's direction.

"I said she'd be let go and she will." Turning to Kelly he said, "When you see what I do to Jake, there'll be no way you'll go to the police, will there Kelly?"

"Can't you just let him go when you get everything back?"

Marchant laughed softly. "Oh you silly girl, Jake has to be made an example of. He knows it as well as I do, he's not expecting to get away with this. The most he can hope for is that I keep my word and let you go."

Marchant stood and turned to go. To Big Don he said. "Get her something to eat and drink, then I want you in here with her. I'll send Joe to keep you company. I don't want you getting bored, Don."

Big Don opened the door for Marchant to pass through. Finn started to follow them but Marchant paused in the doorway.

"You hang on here 'till Big Don and Joe get back, then I want to see you before you go to meet Jake."

With that parting comment, Don and Marchant left the room.

Finn leaned against the closed door. Kelly watched him nervously. Jake had told her Finn was all right, but she wasn't prepared to trust anyone.

"As soon as I have the stuff from Jake, they'll let you go," he said.

"Why? What's to stop them killing me? They won't want me to go to the police."

"Marchant likes to keep his word whenever he can. If he has Jake he'll let you go, but if you go to the police, he'll kill you."

When Marchant had first told her what Jake had done and who he really was, she'd been shocked that the gentle man she knew was some kind of gang member, dealing in drugs.

Kelly shuddered. Now all she wanted was for them both to get out alive.

28 - A CHOICE TO MAKE

Mark rubbed his eyes, it wasn't very bright in the back of the van, but despite this, it dawned on him that his employer looked different. While Mark was figuring out what had changed, The Baker was looking at something he'd taken out of the box.

Why did this guy now look familiar when he hadn't known him from Adam two days earlier?

"You see," said The Baker looking down at his prize, "I used to travel a lot in my last job."

"Oh yeah? Worked on "Wish ya were here" I suppose." Mark registered the rare smile on The Baker's face as he looked over to him. Where had he seen him before?

"Something like that. I did a cookery program at one time. I travelled the world for unusual dishes. I was a celebrated chef you know."

Marks fuddled mind cleared. His Mother used to watch that program before the cancer got her. Now he knew who he was.

"Monty cooks the World!"

"In more ways than you can imagine."

Mark sat up straight, taking in his companion's appearance. "You've shaved; you've got normal clothes on. I mean, ya still look a bit rough, but ya Neil Montgomery, aren't ya?"

"Congratulations, Mark. You have ten out of ten, now pay attention."

The smile faded and Mark looked down to the small statue in the other man's hands.

"What's that?"

"You are so full of questions, Mark, are you sure you want them answered?"

Mark was still recovering from the revelation he was sitting in the back of a van stuffed full of drugs with a famous television chef.

"Why d'ya disappear? You've gotta let people know you're alive, the world thinks ya drowned in that storm."

"Still asking questions, Mark."

Mark finally looked more closely at the small black statue in Montgomery's hands.

"What's that?" Mark asked. "It looks like some sort of weird mushroom." He looked closer. "Or is it a man?"

"Finally, you ask something that I wish to answer, but first I want to ask you a question."

"Ya?"

"Did you know that the Mayan civilization offered up human sacrifices to their gods?"

"I dunno know. Didn't pay that much attention in school."

Another slight smiled curled The Baker's lips upwards. "I suppose that is to be expected from someone like you."

"Hey, I don't have to sit here and be insulted just because I don't know history stuff."

"You're free to go at any time, Mark, but there is much I can tell you, much I can help you with."

"Such as?"

"Would you like to be powerful, Mark? Really powerful? To have the strength to walk into your house and shake your father out of alcoholism? To be able to kick your own rather distasteful habit in a second, and never crave it again because you will have all you ever need?"

"Ya talking a load of crap."

"If that's right, listen to me for ten minutes and after that, I'll give you a choice."

"What choice?"

"There you go asking questions again. Just listen, Mark."

The Baker held out the statue. Mark took it in his hands. It felt cold, as if came straight from the freezer. Mark pushed it back towards him.

"No, Mark, hold it a little longer."

"It's fucking freezing."

"Is it?"

Mark brought it towards his face to examine it more closely. The top was a blend of a mushroom cap and a man's head. There appeared to be multiple tiny faces carved into the stem, or body of the stone. As he looked closer, the cold faded and it began to warm up. As it grew hotter, the black color turned to red and Mark dropped it onto the sleeping bag.

"Shit, what *is* that?"

"That, my friend, is Grohah. Say hello."

"Hell fucking O."

"It's a good thing Grohah doesn't mind offensive language, if he did, you'd be in trouble."

"All right, ya got my attention, what's so good about a hot black statue."

"On my travels for the cookery program, I visited Mexico. It was two months after the June twenty-ten eruption of Popocatépetl. While exploring the volcano, I slipped down a crack in the earth. It wasn't too far, but as I scrambled up my hands gripped this box." The Baker indicated the gold container he'd taken the statue from.

"Well, I wasn't hurt, but naturally I was curious as to what was in the box."

"And it was that thing?"

"That *thing,* as I have already told you, is Grohah."

"Okay then, Grohah."

"There were instructions in the box as to how to contact Grohah, but unfortunately I couldn't read them. They were in hieroglyphics and pictograms, but once I had them translated, it became very clear what I had to do."

"I might not be that bright, but surely other people would be interested in something like that. What about the person who translated for you?" Mark questioned.

"He died of a heart attack; most unfortunate."

Mark wondered why The Baker was telling him all this. "Am I gonna die of a heart attack now? Is that the choice ya offering me?"

"Not at all, I am offering far more than that." He paused, stroking the statue. "Grohah is a god once worshipped by the Mayans. You won't find this information in any history books because it is not widely known. There were several gods they worshipped. Most of these are documented but Grohah is not.

"There was a secret organization of select high priests. They alone knew of Grohah and had found a way to raise him, hoping to harness his power for themselves. Historians can't decide on what happened to the Mayans but I know. The priests organized mass human sacrifices of their own people, but it wasn't enough. Ten thousand more needed to die in order to bring Grohah back. The Mayans turned on their rulers, but two escaped. One of them had the statue."

Mark interrupted him. "Hang on. How d'ya know all this? I suppose it was written in the box?"

"You are almost right. A great deal of the information was deciphered from the writings that were wrapped around the idol, but the rest Grohah himself told me."

"I thought I was the only junkie in this van, sounds like ya taking some of ya own gear."

"Once Grohah was awakened, then, through me, he learned more of the world as it is today."

"Oh, ya?"

"Remember I told you of the human sacrifice?"

Mark wriggled out of the sleeping bag, this conversation was weird, and there was no way he was becoming a sacrifice for some nut with a statue.

"Wait, Mark, I don't want to kill you. You're here to help me."

Mark picked up his bag and stuffed his jacket inside. "Fine, it's great ya don't want to kill me, because I don't fancy dying just yet."

"Don't get out of the van, Mark. I've not finished talking to you."

"Well, I've finished listening. See ya around, thanks for everything, but it really is time I was gettin' home."

"To your alcoholic father, I suppose?"

Mark's hand reached for the side door of the van.

"You do know he'll be dead within the year, and you won't be able to help him because in two days' time, you'll be dead yourself."

Mark stopped at the door. "Ya know everything, do ya?"

"More than you realize. If you leave, in two days, you will die of a heroin overdose. You will inject ninety percent pure heroin into your bloodstream and die seconds later."

"Ya don't say?" Mark pushed the handle down.

"You said you weren't ready to die yet. If that's true, then sit back down and listen."

Mark hesitated. The catch was open, all he had to do was slide the door back and he'd be out.

He let go of the handle.

"Good choice, Mark, now I can tell you more."

Mark sat on a box, but stayed near the door. There was someone on the stage outside. He heard the squawks of sound equipment and speakers being adjusted. More people were up and about now, the buzz of various radios on different stations were jumbled up together, music on one, a breakfast show host blabbering on another. The situation appeared ludicrous with all the signs of normal life outside the van.

The Baker tugged at the statue's mushroom-shaped head, it came away neatly in his hand. He held the squat stem in one hand and the head in the other. Mark waited for beams of light to shine out of it or stars to leap forward, but nothing happened.

The Baker beckoned him. "Come here Mark. Come and see what I see."

Curiosity had him. He rose from the box and moved towards the man with the icon. The easiest way to see it was to kneel down on the floor of the van.

Looking into the stem of the idol, Mark could see nothing, it appeared to be hollow.

"Put your middle finger into the space," The Baker instructed.

Forgetting the previous ice then fire experience, Mark did as he was told. He pushed his middle finger of his left hand down into the hollow space of the statue. Nervousness and fear vanished; he felt something liquid which was neither hot nor cold.

A sharp scratch made him try to draw his finger back out, but the digit swelled. The knuckle was inside the hole and it wouldn't pull back.

"Something scratched me," he murmured, just before he fell backwards onto the sleeping bag. He thought he felt the statue easing from his finger, and words reached him, but he couldn't understand the language.

Then he dreamt.

29 - BECOMING IMMORTAL

Mark climbed a mountain. He was dressed in black from his head to his ankles, but his feet were bare. They were blistered and raw, but he felt no pain. The further up the mountain he went, the hotter it became, but he had to go on.

Finally he reached the top, finding himself on the edge of a crater. The smell of sulphur assaulted his nostrils, but it was welcome. It meant he was near Grohah, and Grohah would save him.

Something on the ground caught his eye. It was a small black statue. He recognized the mushroom shaped figure. Mark picked it up and pulled the top from the statue to look inside. He could see nothing, but he knew what to do.

Putting the neck of the statue to his lips he tipped it towards him and drank the contents.

A halo of steam rose from the crater. He knew himself to be on the top of a volcano, but he had no fear. He watched the vapor take on the squat shape of the icon in his hand, and listened as the voice spoke to him.

The voice told him he had to collect ten thousand souls and then Grohah would be released from the earth that held him captive, as he should have been released hundreds of years before.

Mark took a step forward, instinct driving him.　　He walked three steps on the rubble beneath his feet; his fourth step took him over the edge.

Mark fell into the heat below, but the lava did not burn him. It immortalized him.

30 - GLASTONBURY FRATRICIDE

Lysa managed to park her car on a piece of waste ground not far from the festival site. The summer heat increased steadily, and Lysa would cook if she stayed in the car any longer.

Cars, buses, tents and campers filled the fields like hundreds of colored pins in a map. The sheer size of the site was astounding. How the hell could she hope to find Robbie in all this?

Still, she was here now so she might as well start looking. As she wandered over to the site entrance, she remembered her promise to call Finn. Not hearing from him before she left, she'd realized he must be unable to call her. She would have kept her promise to phone as soon as she found somewhere to stay, but there wasn't a single vacancy anywhere. Not having a ticket would have proved difficult, but Lysa showed identification that she was a doctor and told them she was looking for one of her patients, and they let her in on the proviso she left all her contact details.

The farther into the fields she walked, the louder the music pounding out from the speakers became. She didn't have a clue which band was playing, but Robbie would.

She glanced at her watch. Almost two o'clock. Burning on her bare arms reminded her she'd forgotten to pick up sun cream. Still, skin cancer was the least of her worries.

***   ***   ***

Mark had awoken from his dream with a new purpose. Everything was different now, and The Baker had promised him he could save his father when their work here was finished. Grohah had been wronged, and he would do all he could to release him so that he would be avenged.

He'd distributed the remainder of the biscuits for free. Most of them had been given out the day before, and those who'd eaten them yesterday encouraged their friends to take what was left. Now was the time to come into the light. For everyone.

Mark and The Baker sat on top of the van to watch the show begin. Although the sun blasted down on the metal roof, the heat did not scorch their skin.

***   ***   ***

Robbie was squashed near the stage. Sweaty bodies glued against him and each other, but it didn't matter. Chariot was his favorite band, and the music entered his ears and surged through his veins, infecting every nerve and seeping out every pore in his body. He could feel it within him, pulsing into his bones until he was just a speck in the universe of sound. He didn't notice a group to the right of the stage who had started fighting.

The crowd throbbed and moved to the music. Blood sprayed Robbie's face as he turned to see who shoved him.

Sun flashed off a blade, and Robbie fell into a girl behind him in his efforts to get out of the way. She dropped to the ground, but he trampled over her in his bid to escape. The crowd started to open up as it became apparent something was wrong. Screams alerted some of the crowd and festival goers pushed and jostled each other in their efforts to escape the mounting disturbance.

Robbie saw a gap in the crowd and headed for it, but as he scrambled quickly away from the main stage area, fights were breaking out all across the field. His feet seemed not to belong to him as he ran, but maybe it would be better not to run at all. Robbie sat down on the grass and watched. Everything was right. Everything was perfect. A feeling better than sound started in the middle of his chest and spread its warmth through him, from the inside out. Sparks fired off in his head and a total body orgasm vibrated every nerve, every pore, his lungs, stomach, kidneys, and heart. A smile split his face and he knew this was the best drug ever. Smack was history. Euphoria was now.

He looked up into the sky and watched it turn red.

*** *** ***

Lysa heard the band call for calm over their microphones. That is until the crowd stormed the stage and dragged them off. Chariot disappeared into the heaving mass of bodies. The speakers squawked and boomed before being uprooted and thrown into the crowd. They slammed over anyone in their path. Lysa ran towards the crowd, calling for Robbie, but she couldn't hear her own voice above the cries of the people all around her. She didn't notice the young boy sitting calmly on the grass until she felt the hand grab her leg and drag her to the ground.

She looked into her brother's face. "Robbie! Thank God you're okay."

He punched her hard in the stomach. As she landed on her back he jumped on top of her and began ripping at her skin with his hands.

"You're white, you have to be red. Everything has to be red," he murmured.

Lysa tried to call out, but his hands were around her neck, choking her; his nails digging deep into the flesh of her throat. Veins threaded spider webs from the corner of his eyes. The blood sped through his corneas, covering them with a deep ruby veil.

"The sky's bleeding crimson onto the grass. Can you see it?"

She couldn't answer; she would die soon if he didn't stop. She grasped at the ground for a weapon, anything to make Robbie let go, but all that came up were dry sunburnt blades of grass. In desperation, she brought up both knees, hitting Robbie on his rear with enough force to jolt him forward, making him lose his grip on her. She pushed him off and rolled away. The screaming in her ears came from the crowds around her. If she'd had the energy to yell herself she would have joined them. She gasped for air, but only breathed in the metallic smell of blood. It sickened her, making her want to retch, but she couldn't afford to. Robbie had turned and was coming for her again.

Lysa ran. There was nothing else for it. Robbie seemed intent on killing her, and there wasn't anything she could do to stop him. Her throat was bruised and ripped from his fingers, but she ignored the pain. She jumped over bodies, dodged past the dying or dead. Bluebottles already feasted on open wounds, undisturbed by the mayhem around them. Lysa's survival instincts took over and adrenaline pushed her forward.

Sirens grew louder as police and ambulances rushed to the scene. Lysa focused and aimed her feet in their direction.

Her foot slipped as her hair was tugged from behind. She fell backwards and looked up at a girl of about seventeen, with the body mass of a wrestler. She was smeared with blood. A gash ran the length of her right cheek, but it didn't seem to bother her.

This had to be someone else's nightmare. Lysa wanted out badly. The girl smiled, the blood running down her cheek into the corner of her mouth, where it hung for a fraction of a second before sliding down over her lower lip. The two seconds she had hold of Lysa seemed to last hours.

Lysa saw the hand above her captor's head. It took a moment for the closed fist to bring a metal tent peg down into the girl's skull.

Lysa blinked as the blood sprayed into her eyes, blinding her for vital seconds. Her hands were bathed red as she tried to wipe the sticky liquid from her face. The girl went into spasms before collapsing on the blood-stained grass. Lysa automatically turned and moved forward to help, but as she rose, she found herself looking into Robbie's grinning face and he already had another weapon — a heavy steel four armed wheel brace. If he hit her with that, he could kill her.

"Robbie, stop please, it's me, Lysa. Don't you know me?"

"I know you," he growled. "Bitch!"

The girl in the blood-sodden grass was dead. A clump of Lysa's matted hair still clutched in her fist. Lysa swallowed down the acid rising in her throat. The girls' head had been split open with the ease of hot water on snow, the blood still pumped in mini eruptions from her skull. At the moment Robbie moved, Lysa instinctively reached for the peg embedded in the corpse's head. She tugged it free from its haven and stumbled to her feet, brandishing it against her brother.

"That won't save you." Robbie lunged, the steel cross aimed at her head.

Lysa wanted to shut her eyes and rid herself of this terror, but instead she kept them open, plunging the metal rod forward into her brother's chest.

As she let go, he collapsed on top of the girl. He knocked into Lysa as he fell, but all she took was a step back, frozen by the horror of her actions. No, there shouldn't be this much blood. She'd only wanted to stop him. Meant to catch him on his side, but from the location of the gushing scarlet torrent, she'd punctured his heart. She fell onto the ground, grasping his arm, checking for a pulse. Nothing. Checked his blank eyes. No response. If souls existed, then hers had been slashed open. Pain in her chest, stabbing, ripping, tearing. No, no. This couldn't be real. She deserved to go to hell for this. Why wasn't she dead instead? Why had she fought him? For those still seconds in time, Lysa pulled him into her arms and soaked him with tears that ran in torrents down her face. A scream blasted through her ear, and to her right a young boy stamped on his twin brother's chest. Reality checked her back in and self-preservation took over. "Bye Robbie," she whispered. Her vision couldn't afford to be blurred by crying, so she breathed in as hard as she could, wiped her face with the back of her blood-covered hands and moved. The grass was littered with bodies. It could only have been five minutes since it started but it looked like a battlefield.

Lysa darted through the mass of fleeing and fighting people towards the first ambulance to arrive on the field. Before she could reach it, a gang surrounded it and turned it over. The crew were dragged out.

Lysa spun on her heel and ran for her car.

31 - BRUISES

Jake pretended to be interested in the discounted books. The table in the middle of the store held heaps of different volumes. He positioned himself so he could look out of the window toward the dining area in the middle of the shopping center.

It was nearly three and he wanted to make sure Finn had turned up alone. The fact that Finn sat by himself didn't mean Marchant wouldn't have others in the vicinity.

Jake watched him for a few more minutes before putting down the book and leaving the store. He made his way quickly along the railing to an opening into the dining area. Five seconds later, he was sitting opposite Finn.

"I don't want you to lie to me," said Jake. "How many has he sent with you?"

Finn looked up over the rim of the red and white paper cup. "Only two. One at the aisle by the shoe shop, and one by the aisle with the jewelers on the corner."

"That still leaves one exit unmanned. Why didn't he put anyone by the sports shops to stop me getting out that way?"

"He may have thought I'd have no trouble persuading you to come with me."

"No. Marchant wouldn't take a chance like that, he wants me dead. I know that, and he knows I know it."

"He has Kelly. He also knows you don't want anything to happen to her."

"How is she?" Jake asked.

"Big Don hit her face, she's a bit bruised but she's okay."

Anger twisted his guts. "Bastard. Is he here?" Jake asked.

Finn put the cup down as his phone bleeped. "No, he's been left with Kelly."

Jake's hands clenched into fists. "If he lays another finger on her, I'll kill him."

"Damn, my phone is almost dead," Finn said.

"Fuck your phone. I'm more concerned about my girlfriend dying. My dad is already dead."

Finn put his phone in his pocket. "Just how do you think you're going to get out of this, Jake?"

"I'm working on it." Jake looked across to the escalators. They were positioned facing the guarded aisles. No use trying to escape by using them to reach the upper floor.

"Does Marchant trust you, Finn? Does he expect you to bring me in?"

"He expects me to bring you in and the gear with you."

"He'll have someone down the bottom of the other exit. There are two ways out if you go that way. He's too good not to have it covered."

"You're probably right, but there's an elevator at the back of the bookshop. It's unlikely he'll have that manned."

Jake glanced behind Finn. He'd forgotten about that. Stuck in a little corner, sandwiched between the bookshop and a second jeweler's shop, there was indeed a small elevator. Marchant probably didn't even know it was there. Marchant didn't shop. He had everything handmade, or brought to him by one of his lackeys. His guys might know, but there was a chance they didn't.

"I have to take you in, Jake; if I don't, Big Don will kill Kelly."

Big Don being left with Kelly scared Jake. Kelly was in trouble and it was his fault. His own chances of survival were slim if he went back with Finn, but he'd risk it to save her. "You can call Marchant and tell him I'm taking you to the stuff but I don't want to be followed. Then when I've given it to you he can let Kelly go."

"He won't agree, Jake; he wants you as well."

"I know, but as soon as he lets Kelly go, I'll come with you."

"Jake, I hate to remind you but you don't exactly have any choice. He won't agree."

Finn was right, but his first objective was to keep Kelly alive. He would take his own chances with Marchant, but he wanted to be sure she was safe first. "Try him."

"I can't call him from here, there's no reception. We'll have to go to the car."

"Where is it? The car park above here?"

"Yeah."

"No way, he'll have people by the car." Jake stood. "Come on, let's take the elevator."

"Hang on, Jake, if I don't take you back with me now there's no telling what will happen to Kelly."

"If you phone him, he won't hurt her, you'll be keeping him informed; he'll wait." Jake sounded more certain than he actually was. Marchant was unpredictable.

Finn stood and turned to follow Jake towards the elevator. As Jake passed a table, a large man with a shaved head grabbed his arm.

"Hey, pal, you just knocked my drink over."

Coffee dripped down the table and splashed onto the tiled floor.

"Sorry, mate." Jake fished in his pocket for a couple of coins and tossed them onto the table. "Here, buy another one."

The skinhead stood, and although Jake was as tall as him, he wasn't expecting the punch that landed on his jaw and sent him flying into the table to his left.

The blonde woman he crashed into gave a yell, and her boyfriend shot up and dragged Jake up by his shirt.

"What are you playing at?"

"Hang on," said Finn, "that bloke hit him." Finn motioned to the skinhead.

"And you're next, mate." The skinhead lunged forward for Finn, but his fist missed its target as Finn dodged the punch.

Within seconds. the skinhead's two friends joined in. Jake's back slammed against the edge of a table; it was bolted to the floor and didn't give an inch. It felt as though he'd been hit in the back with a hammer, but Jake dragged himself back up and landed his fist into the first man who'd hit him. A second later, someone grabbed his neck from behind and as he fell backwards, he saw Finn go down as the skinhead landed a punch on his jaw. Out of the corner of his eye he spotted one of Marchant's men watching the disturbance. It was at that moment the uniforms arrived.

Finn and Jake were carted away to the City Center Police Station. Each of them slung in separate cells.

*** *** ***

Needham entered the tiny room. "How do you like being on the other side of the door, Finn?" he smiled.

"I suppose it's worth it not to blow my cover. How's Jake?"

"He'll live. You can leave him to us. Marchant has no reason to keep his girl now we've got him. There's a brief outside arranging your release as we speak. Marchant's money buys the top men."

"Marchant's filthy money can buy most things, but he'll want Jake out as well."

"We've said we need to keep him for questioning, but we've kindly agreed to let you go."

"Very nice of you, Boss."

"You just make sure nothing happens to that girl."

Finn stood up and rubbed his jaw. "Do us a favor, Boss, when you see Bill, tell him he didn't have to hit me quite so realistically."

The D.C.I. moved aside for Finn to exit the door. "It'll look good if you have a few war wounds." A grin spread across his face. "A couple of scars will improve your looks. A good plastic surgeon would charge a fortune for those."

Finn turned as he passed through the door. "Why don't you hire Bill out then? If the department made a few bob we might even get decent coffee in the canteen."

The uniformed officer outside the door led Finn down the corridor, at the end of which stood a tall well-dressed man in a grey suit, Armani, Finn noted. Marchant's man.

After a few brief words, Finn accompanied the solicitor to his car and was driven back to the gym. He said a quick goodbye to the Armani suit and went inside.

Finn pushed open the heavy green door. Now to see if Kelly was okay and to try and persuade Marchant to let her go. Lysa hadn't called him, and he pulled his phone out of his pocket to see if there were any missed calls. It was dead.

He was probably worrying about nothing; it was just the stress of the job getting to him. Lysa would be fine. She'd only gone to a festival to look for her brother.

He needed sleep, but there was no time for that luxury. Finn climbed the spiral staircase to Marchant's office, but before going inside he rubbed his jaw. He'd apply for that desk job when this was all over.

.

32 - AFTER THE MASSACRE

The cold water was welcome on Lysa's face. The white coat over the hospital blues was too big for her small frame, but at least the clothes were clean and free from blood. Lysa walked slowly back down the pale green corridor into the casualty department. A phantom wound gaped open in her chest, and guilt screamed inside her head for Robbie's death, but she couldn't allow her own pain yet.

Helping out at the local hospital with the chaos of emergencies and injuries allowed her to erect a temporary barrier to her grief. Other people's distress and despair deflected her own.

Another victim to cover up — a young girl of about eighteen. She reminded Lysa of Tina, the girl who'd died in Liverpool. As far as Lysa knew, Tina had not been violent, but there were certain similarities in the cases. Both girls had hallucinated. Tina's boyfriend had told her Tina was shouting about worms coming for her before she collapsed, and by his own admission she had taken a new drug. Lysa had told a doctor of her suspicions and they were testing everything they could to find some trace of whatever was causing this mass violence among the music fans.

"Doctor Warner," the nurse broke into her thoughts. "Doctor Cryton wants to see you."

"Thanks, I'm on my way." Lysa left the room and hurried down the corridor to Doctor Cryton's office. The door was slightly open so she knocked lightly.

"Doctor Cryton?"

"Come in."

Lysa entered the room. It was much like any other hospital doctor's office — painted white with uniform beige roller blinds at the windows. They were pulled up and allowed the sun to bounce its light off the walls. Doctor Cryton sat at his desk, pouring over test results.

"I believe you've seen cases like this in Liverpool?" He said, looking up.

"Not quite the same. In the few cases I saw, we found no history of violence before death. Maybe they hadn't taken as much of the drug as these new cases have."

"A possibility, but did you manage to pinpoint a cause? A specific drug in the system?"

"Only a small trace of cocaine, but that doesn't cause the reactions we've been seeing. It must be mixed with some other, more potent substance."

"You'd be right about that, Doctor Warner." He motioned her to sit in the chair on the other side of his desk and passed a small piece of paper over to her.

Lysa read the words on the paper but it made no sense. "What on earth is Morning Glory?"

"A plant. A blue flowering plant that originates in Mexico."

"Is this what they've been taking? How did you find out?"

"It took some time, but eventually the lab found it. The thing is, there only seems to be a fine trace of it in the bodies of the victims, not really enough to produce the types of reaction we've been seeing."

"So we're no closer to knowing what's causing this?"

"In a word, no, but at least we have something to go on. Morning Glory is a hallucinogenic, and you can find a more common version of it in most garden centers, but that's not the type that produces these symptoms."

"So where did it come from?"

"Someone must have brought it in from Mexico. This species is quite rare, and for anyone in this country to know about it seems unusual."

"And there's only a trace of it in the bodies?"

"There's slightly more in the victims who are still alive, but it seems to melt away on death. The longer the victim has been dead, the smaller the amount detected."

"So even if we checked the bodies in Liverpool, there would probably be nothing left to find."

Lysa was scared to ask the next question on her lips, but she had to. "Can we help the victims who haven't yet died?"

"We're doing our best, but it's not looking hopeful."

Lysa remembered Robbie's face as he'd tried to kill her. A physical pain gnawed at her chest, but she was afraid to allow herself to grieve, because if she did she was scared she would never stop.

"I have to tell you, my brother was among the victims. I don't know where his body is, but he tried to kill me before he died."

Doctor Cryton's face registered his surprise. He made no comment, but allowed Lysa to continue.

"My brother was a heroin addict, Doctor Cryton, but he could easily be persuaded to take whatever was available. He would have taken this new drug if it was offered to him. My main regret is that I didn't warn him about it."

"Did you have the opportunity?"

"I bailed him out of jail, and was helping him through his withdrawal. I didn't tell him about the new drug the kids were taking in case it tempted him." Lysa shook her head. "I should have told him. At least he would have known the dangers."

"Doctor Warner, your brother must have known the dangers of taking heroin, but the drug meant more to him. Even if you had warned him about this, do you think he would have refused it?"

"No," Lysa sighed. "He'd have still taken it."

"Then, hard as it may seem, our job is to try and help those who remain, and we have many in our wards and in our corridors that need us." Doctor Cryton paused, allowing Lysa a moment to compose herself.

"I'll quite understand if you have to find your brother and make arrangements for him to be transferred back home. If you wish to go back to Liverpool, you are under no obligation to stay here."

Lysa swallowed hard, trying to get rid of the rock that seemed to be permanently wedged in her throat. "No, Doctor Cryton. I'll help out here for as long as I can, but if it's possible, could I have one of the doctor's rooms? I was unable to find accommodation, and it would be easier if I could stay at the hospital for as long as I'm here."

"Of course, there should be no problem with that. I hope we won't need you for too long." Doctor Cryton let a wry smile escape his lips. "I don't mean that I want you to leave of course, I just hope the emergency doesn't go on for too long."

Lysa remembered the long forgotten phone call to Finn. If he'd heard about the chaos, he would be worried about her. "If I could make a phone call, Doctor Cryton, there's someone who will be concerned about me."

Doctor Cryton stood up and moved from the desk. "Of course, I'm sure there is. Use mine. Make your call in private. I'll find someone to organize a room for you."

With a smile, he left the room, closing the door quietly behind him. Lysa reached for the phone.

Tapping out Finn's number, she hoped it was a good time to call.

33 - NO TIME TO REST

"Just how did you manage to get involved in a fight in the shopping center?"

Marchant's tone was steady, but Finn detected an undercurrent of rage in his voice.

"Jake knocked some bugger's coffee over. He turned out to be a psycho, next thing we knew there were security men and cops all over the place."

"You do understand, Finn, it's not the money he's cost me, but the fact he thinks he can get away with stealing from me."

Marchant looked out of the window of his office, though the vertical blinds to the gym below. He had his back to Finn. It was as if he didn't want the men in the room to see how angry he was. Big Don stood silently next to the door and two other heavies leaned on the wall to the right of the window.

"Look, Boss, I'm sorry. What more can I say? I couldn't predict what happened."

Marchant turned slowly. "Couldn't you?"

Not for the first time on this assignment Finn felt Marchant was on to him.

"Can't your brief get him out?" Finn asked.

"If that were possible, he'd be standing next to you now wouldn't he?" Marchant's tone was slightly raised. It was the first time Finn had ever sensed real anger from him.

"What are we gonna do with his girl then? Let her go?"

Marchant's eyes flashed ice. "We? What am *I* going to do with her, Finn?" Marchant moved from the window to approach Finn. "Let her go? I think not."

Finn chanced pushing him further. "But if we can't get to Jake, what use is she?"

"You don't really think I'll let her go? Even if I scared her enough not to go running to the police, which I very easily could, what makes you think she's no use to me?"

Finn stood his ground as the thinner man stopped two footsteps away from him. To move back could prove foolish. "I just thought we could do without the hassle of having her here, if we can't use her to get Jake."

"Did you now? And did you ever think that Jake might talk, that he may be offered a deal, and that's why I can't get him out?" Marchant's voice was back on its even keel, he had regained control.

He reached into his pocket and brought out a small keychain. Finn's stomach churned, the keys were never a good sign. Marchant moved away from him and walked to the display case on the wall. Finn hoped this didn't mean Kelly was going to be tortured because Jake was in police custody.

He swallowed his fear and said, "So if we keep her here, he won't talk?"

"Precisely, Finn."

Marchant had two keys. The first he used on the upper lock on the cabinet, the other on the lower lock. The glass doors of the case swung silently open.

"But what if they find something to keep him banged up for? How long can we keep her?"

Marchant carefully selected a dagger from the case and then locked up the cabinet while he continued to speak. "We keep her for as long as I say. Or until Jake's been taken care of."

Finn heard the implication, but Jake would be kept in solitary for his own safety.

Marchant turned to walk slowly back to his desk. He sat on the edge and placed the dagger next to him. "I have friends in the police force. We won't need to keep her long." Indicating the antique knife he said, "But, there's always a little insurance I can take out. His girlfriend is quite pretty."

Jake was in real danger. He had to let his superiors know Marchant was planning to have Jake killed by an inside contact. If by any chance Jake was protected in time, then the threat would fall to Kelly. As he was absorbing this information, Marchant pointed the remote and the television sprang into life. The news report came live from Glastonbury Tor.

At the sight of the blood-stained grass and devastation, everyone in the room fell silent. As the reporter gave the latest information, the emergency number to call flashed on the screen. Finn glanced at the dead phone on his hip while fear crept into his heart. Panic rapped in his bones as he thought about Lysa. He only had her home number, but not her mobile. He would have to drive down there and look for her.

He scanned the faces of the men in the room. They were all mesmerized by the screen, but there was no chance he could slip away. Marchant turned his head and caught his eye.

"What's wrong, Finn? Do you have people down there?"

His expression had given him away. Shit! There was no point trying to deny it, it would make Marchant suspicious.

"Err yeah, close friends of mine moved down there a couple of years back. I'm godfather to their kid."

Marchant laughed. "Godfather. I don't think you're Corleone material yet, Finn."

Big Don laughed at Marchant's joke and the others joined in.

"What do you think Don?" Marchant chortled. "Finn Brando?"

Big Don grinned. "Not yet, Boss; let's give him a few more years, and a few more pounds on the belly!"

Finn was the only one not laughing, so he turned up his mouth in a slight smile. "The phone lines will be crazy. I'd like to go down there, check they're okay."

"Go on, Finn take a day, hell no, take two. That's the best laugh I've had in ages." Marchant waved his hand at him.

Finn moved to go. "Thanks. Boss; I'll be back..."

Marchant cut in. "Now he thinks he's The Terminator." He laughed louder.

Finn didn't tell him that line was from a different movie, why ruin his mood? He waved as he left the room and spun down the spiral staircase as fast as he could without breaking into a run. For once, he didn't smile at the girl on the desk. He had to find Lysa, make sure she was all right. He also had to talk to Needham in order to keep Jake safe.

Gleaming sunlight blasted his eyes as he stepped outside. He reached into his top pocket for his sunglasses and put them on before jumping into his car and plugging his phone into the charger. It fired into life. Finn was about to tap out the emergency number from the television when he realized he couldn't remember it.

He called the station.

All the lines were busy.

Finn started up the engine. He had to drive to Glastonbury. It was only now, with the dread in his stomach making him feel sick, he realized how much he had come to feel for Lysa.

Maybe he was in love with her. After only a few days? If it wasn't love, it was *something*, and it was real enough to have him in a near panic.

The heat in the car was stifling, so he flicked on the air conditioning and dropped his charging phone onto the passenger seat for easier access. As it hit the upholstery it rang out.

Finn turned the key to turn the engine back off and picked up the phone.

"Finn here," he said.

"Finn, it's Lysa."

A wave of relief started at his head and made its way down his body to his toes as he heard her voice.

"Lysa, thank God. I've only just found out what's happened."

"You weren't worried about me, were you?"

"Oh no, my girlfriend gets involved in deadly riots every day. You could have been killed."

"What's that?"

Finn tried to recall what he'd said. "That you get involved in deadly riots every day?"

"You called me your girlfriend."

Finn smiled. "Oh, I did. Do you mind?"

"Well, you might not want me to be after you hear what I've done."

"You can't have done anything that bad."

"Oh I have…" He caught the pain and sadness in her voice, but was still relieved to be talking to her, to know she was okay. "No matter what you've done, would you like us to keep seeing each other? Take it as it comes?"

"Yes, and I'll understand if you change your mind later," she replied.

For those few precious seconds they were like any other couple starting out in a new relationship even if she did think she'd done something terrible. Their life was more complex though, and they had to deal with it. Reality rushed back.

"I'm so glad you're okay," Finn hesitated before asking. "Did you find Robbie?"

The silence on the end of the line told him it was bad news before she spoke.

"He was killed in the rioting. I've not found his body yet. I'm helping out at the nearest hospital, but casualties have been ferried out to surrounding hospitals, there are so many dead."

"If you've not found his body, how do you know he was killed?" Finn asked.

The line was silent for a second or two. She replied slowly, "I, I stabbed him in the chest with a tent peg. I killed him."

Finn swallowed hard. In his job he'd seen some pretty bad things, but the mental image of a young lad with a metal stake sticking out of his body shook even him. The fact Lysa killed the brother she loved so dearly stunned him.

"Will you have to arrest me?" Lysa asked.

"Surely it was an accident?"

"No. He was trying to kill me but I grabbed the peg and stabbed him."

"Then say nothing to anyone just yet. It was self-defense."

"But you're a policeman, and I've confessed."

"You're in shock. I'm coming down, Lysa, I have to see you. Can you stay in the hospital until I get there?"

"Yes, but keep your phone turned on. I've been trying to call you."

"Sorry, my phone died and it's been hectic."

"Ask for me at reception when you get here and they'll page me."

Finn heard a beep at the other end of the line.

"Got to go, Finn, I'm needed back in casualty."

"Look after yourself. I'll be there soon."

Finn stared at the phone. He had two days away from Marchant, he couldn't get through to the station anyway, and so what was the point in letting his superiors know where he was? Policeman or not, he wasn't going to report Lysa. Maybe the criminal life was rubbing off on him. They'd talk about how to handle it later.

He dropped the phone back onto the passenger seat.

Torn between feelings for Lysa and fear for Jake and Kelly, Finn turned the ignition. He couldn't go to the station, if it got back to Marchant, the game was up. Finn put his foot on the pedal. He had to be with Lysa.

.

34 - DRIFTING AWAY

Jake lay on the mattress counting the specks of peeling paint on the ceiling. The small airless cell was stifling in the summer heat, but that was the least of his worries.

His thoughts tumbled over each other. Marchant had Kelly. Big Don had access to Kelly. Big Don was an animal. Marchant's brand of evil was as cold as the Antarctic and just as unforgiving. There was no deal the police could offer him that would make him put her life at risk.

One thing he couldn't figure out was why he was still here. He'd have expected Marchant to have him out almost before his arse had touched his cell. The last thing he needed was for Marchant to think he'd done a deal in order to save his own neck.

A key turned in the lock.

"Hello, Jake, we've got a message for you."

Two men entered the cell. Jake recognized the big one with the twisted nose. The story was it had been broken with an iron bar when he'd been on a job for Marchant. Marchant had offered to pay to have it fixed, but Phil had decided he liked it the way it was, despite the way it made him snort when he spoke.

They closed the door behind them and Jake heard the click of the key turning as someone outside re-locked it. A smell of garlic filled the entire cell, betraying their recent meal.

"How did you two get in here? Why hasn't Marchant got me out?"

Phil sniffed noisily before answering, "For some reason, the police think they have grounds to keep you here."

"Who let you in?" Jake asked again.

"You should know by now, Jake, Mr. Marchant has contacts."

"Is Kelly all right?"

"That depends on you."

"I haven't told them anything, do you think I'm stupid?" Jake stood up as the men approached.

Phil blew air down his nose without the benefit of a handkerchief. Jake took a step back, expecting to be covered in something disgusting, but to his surprise nothing happened. Phil seemed to have mastered the art of clearing his nasal passages quite invisibly. "Are you sure?" said Phil. "Mr. Marchant wouldn't like it if you've been talking. He may feel it necessary to dispose of your pretty girlfriend."

Jake's voice hardened. "He'd better not hurt her. I'll finish him if he does."

The men advanced and gripped Jake by both arms. The thinner man stayed silent while Phil spoke again. "You wouldn't be threatening Mr. Marchant would you, Jake?"

This was trouble. Jake tried to struggle free, but they gripped his arms at either side and pushed him down, pinning him to the mattress. He felt the scratch in his arm as the quiet man injected something into him.

The smell of Phil's pungent breath mingling with the sweat from the big man's body made Jake want to puke. The room circled around him. All strength left his body; there was nothing he could do to save himself. "Pleasant dreams, Jake. Pity you won't wake up again."

"At least I don't fucking stink, you bastard," Jake whispered, his speech sounded slurred.

Heat and intense pain seared his throat. It would be blood, they'd gashed open his neck.

He heard a distant tap on the door and the squeak of the hinges as it opened to let his assassins back out. Their conversation came as if from down a long corridor.

"Mr. Marchant will have a bonus for you shortly, sergeant. He likes to reward those who help rid him of little irritations."

"As long as no one finds out I let you in. It's my job on the line if they do."

Jake heard no more as the door slid shut. As the blackness swallowed him, the last face he saw was Kelly's.

.

LORRAINE MCLEOD

35 - TRINITY

Mark was destined for higher things. He and The Baker had
surveyed the damage from the top of the van. None of the
rioters who surrounded them had come near. It was as if they
couldn't see Mark and his companion perched on the roof.

Police and ambulance crews had asked if they were hurt.
When they'd replied they were fine, the rescuers advised them to
be checked out at hospital anyway. Mark and The Baker smiled
and nodded to imply they would, although of course they had no
intention of going anywhere near a hospital.

The police were clearing the fields of tents, campers, and
vehicles, so they were now parked on a narrow road. It served to
separate farmer's fields from a wooded area.

The Baker seemed agitated.

"Not enough died; Grohah has not been released." He turned
to Mark. "Why hasn't it worked? Surely enough took the drug,
added to those who died in the nightclubs it should have been
enough."

"I thought you had all the answers," Mark said calmly.

"Don't try and be smart with me," the older man snapped.

"They might not all be dead yet, the hospitals might be
keeping some alive."

"No! They should die. There should be no cure, I followed the instructions meticulously."

Mark sat staring ahead, his hands lay loosely on his lap. "Yes, you may have, but those instructions were, how old? Medicine has advanced a hell of a lot since your recipe was written."

"There were the extra ingredients Grohah added, they should have died!"

Mark looked out into the darkness, it seemed simple to him why Grohah had not been released. He did not understand why The Baker had become so distressed. They only had to wait for the rest to die, and maybe kill a couple of hundred more, and it would be complete.

He turned to impart his thoughts to his companion. "They'll die soon, and even if they don't, we'd only have to kill a few more and we'll have done it."

"And just how do you know? You were only initiated this morning, what makes you the expert?"

If Mark could have looked in a mirror he would have seen blank eyes in his reflection. He answered, "It's the visions. Don't you see them?"

"Of course I do, I found Grohah before you. He talks to me constantly."

The Baker lied. Grohah had said he would. Grohah had finished with The Baker. He had stopped talking to him when the killing started. He spoke only to Mark now and he would only send the visions to him. Mark looked coldly at the older man before speaking.

"Liar."

The Baker glared. "How dare you call me that? You were nothing but a pathetic addict when I picked you up."

"Is that right?"

"You know it is."

"Don't you wonder why Grohah sent you to find me? Do you really think it was purely to help you connect with all these people?"

Mark watched the lines on the older man's face relax as the realization that he was no longer in control crept into his expression. "It was pure coincidence that I picked on you," The Baker replied. "There were hundreds I could have chosen from."

"Do you not notice the changes in me, Monty? Do you mind if I call you that?" Mark smiled slowly. "No, of course you don't. It is your name, after all."

"Your voice has changed a bit, and you talk a bit smarter," Monty replied. "But why don't you just get to the point? You obviously have something to tell me."

"All right. Grohah is finished with you. He needed you to start things, and it was useful you could make Euphoria, but now he has almost enough deaths, he no longer needs an old man like you."

"You're the one who's lying. Grohah promised me immortality."

"And you'll have it."

Steel flashed for a second before Mark brought it swiftly across The Baker's throat. The blood sprang out in a fountain, showering Mark's face and chest.

"You will have your immortality, Monty, but you'll have it within me." Mark threw himself on top of his victim, bathing in the warm liquid which continued to pour from the man's neck.

He sucked The Baker's essence into himself. The final stage was near. Mark had a strong young body, just what Grohah needed, but he had kept his promise. The Baker had his immortality within Mark.

Now, they would be three together.

36 - A BODY OF BLUEBOTTLES

Finn arrived at the hospital a little after nine o'clock. Lysa was busy on the wards and it was another half hour until she could meet him.

Hunger scraped at his stomach. The bright lights of the hospital canteen revealed the tiredness in Lysa's pale face as she walked down the corridor towards him. Things always seemed worse when you were hungry Finn's mother had always said, and food seemed a good idea to Finn right now. They filled their plates from the self-service bar and paid the cashier. Blue Formica tables and grey plastic chairs filled the room. They found a clean one and sat down. Lasagna waited in front of Finn. Lysa settled for a chicken salad.

"Whoever said hospital food was awful hadn't stayed in this place." Finn commented.

"This is only for paying customers. You don't want to be up on the wards. They only get cardboard tasting pizza or processed fish."

"So it's true then?"

"What is?"

"The rumor that more people die from hospital food than the illnesses they came in with."

Lysa failed to see Finn's attempt at humor. "I haven't heard that."

"It was a joke," Finn explained, putting a forkful of lasagna into his mouth. He watched her pick at the chicken salad. "Sorry."

"Robbie's here."

Finn hadn't even asked her whether she'd found her brother, he'd been so relieved to find her safe.

"I'm sorry, Lysa, I should have asked about him."

Her lower lids filled with water, and she tilted her head slightly to stare at her plate. She wouldn't look up. "I murdered him, Finn."

Finn reached across the table to her. He placed his right hand over her left while her free hand twisted a piece of iceberg lettuce around the end of her fork.

"He was trying to kill me. He was one of the crazies on the fields."

"He was probably so drugged up he didn't know who you were."

The fork scraped the plate as she twisted it, the lettuce forming a tutu around the ballerina's cold steel.

"He knew me, but it wasn't him behind those eyes; it couldn't have been."

Her fingers didn't move underneath his hand. He squeezed them. "Come on, Lysa, let's go for a walk, get out of this place."

She looked up with wet cheeks. Pulling a ragged paper handkerchief from the pocket of her doctor's coat she said, "I can't; I might be needed."

"There are plenty of other doctors around. If you don't get a break for a while, you'll end up in a ward yourself."

Lysa blinked, as if trying to hold back more tears, and wiped at her face with the remains of her paper tissue. Finn moved around the table to her. "I thought you were starving?" she asked. "You're not eating your meal."

"Now why would I want to finish a plate of hospital food, even if it is lasagna?" Sometimes, other things were more important than filling a hungry belly.

Finn guided her through the chairs and tables to the exit. They travelled down a maze of pale blue and grey corridors, passing countless people with red eyes and swollen faces before finally emerging into the fading sunlight.

They hardly spoke as Finn led her to his car, his arm around her waist.

There was plenty of countryside to choose from for a quiet drive, and eventually they came to a small car park adjoining the woods.

"I'm here for you, Lysa. Even doctors are allowed to cry, you know." Finn sat back in his seat. He wanted to reach out to her, tell her everything would be all right. Her grief re-opened wounds of his own he'd been trying to heal for the past year. It would never be *all right* again, but it would eventually become easier.

"We're estimating seven and a half thousand people have died," said Lysa quietly. "Could reach near nine thousand if all the casualties don't make it."

"And it's just over two hundred who've died in the nightclubs. Have the police any idea where this drug came from?" Lysa asked. "As doctors, we can do little but try and treat the victims. Those who didn't take the drug and aren't too badly injured have been sent home. We need the beds for the worst casualties."

"I do know the people I've been involved with sold some of this stuff on, but I don't know where it came from. I was investigating a heroin and cocaine racket, and it turns into this." He was the policeman. He should have been able to do something to stop this carnage, but he couldn't even phone through to his station.

"A week ago, I'd only seen three of these new drug cases, but now the hospitals are overflowing with dying and injured people." She was looking to him for answers that he didn't have.

"Come on, let's go for a walk." Without waiting for her to reply, Finn opened his door and climbed out of the car and she did the same.

The evening air was still warm and felt comforting on his skin. They took a dusty well-trodden dirt-path that wove its way through the woods with the curves of an earthworm. The air was slightly cooler under the trees.

"Not cold are you?" asked Finn.

"No, I just felt nervous; it's probably the stress of the last few days."

Finn pulled her closer to him. "I'm really sorry about what's happened to Robbie, and I don't know what's behind this drug, but I can promise you that I'm going to do my best to find out."

"That means you'll have to go back up to Liverpool. It's the only place you have any leads."

"So come back with me. We can stay here the night, get some rest and head back up in the morning."

"I can't, Finn. They need all the doctors they can get in the hospital."

Finn spotted a sawn off tree stump that was big enough for the two of them to sit on, so he moved away from the path. The undergrowth felt like an old woven mattress beneath their feet. As they neared the stump, Finn was aware of another smell intruding on the aroma of leaves and the cool forest, but couldn't quite place what it was. He sat down and Lysa squeezed next to him, picking a blade of deep green grass from the base of the tree.

He brushed a blonde strand from her cheek. "From what I heard on the news before I left Liverpool, they're moving the causalities all over the country, there'll be plenty for you to do back home."

The softness of her skin on his hand stirred those feelings up again—feelings he thought he'd never experience again after losing Amy. He breathed deep, hoping what he was about to say wouldn't be too much for her to hear. "I think I'm falling in love with you, Lysa."

She said nothing, just twisted the grass in her fingers.

"Oh shit, I've gone and opened my big mouth when I shouldn't have," Finn said standing up. "I'm sorry, I shouldn't have said anything. I know it's too soon, I must sound crazy, especially with what's happened to Robbie."

Finn was aware that his rambling would make her think he was even more of an insensitive idiot than he already felt. He wished she'd speak so he would have to shut up.

"Lysa, just forget I opened my mouth, would you?" he said.

She smiled as she looked up at him. "I don't think you're stupid, sit back down." She patted the stump.

Finn did as she asked, but he still wished he'd kept his mouth shut. Why did he act like this when it came to emotions? He could go undercover and be as cool as a snowman, but give him a girl he liked, and he carried on like a schoolboy. He wiped his hands on his trousers. His palms were moist, despite the coolness of the shade. She kissed him.

Finn stopped worrying about offending her and kissed her right back. Unfortunately, he pulled her toward him a little too far and they both tumbled into the undergrowth behind them. They landed with Finn on his back and Lysa on top of him.

Lysa bent down to kiss him and he gently rolled her over so he was now looking down at her.

She reached up to stroke his cheek and smiled. And screamed.

Finn turned his head to follow her eyes as she scrambled out from beneath him.

A moving body of bluebottles covered the head of an upside down corpse hanging from a branch above them. The neck gaped open in a red-mouthed voiceless howl, but no blood dripped from the wound.

Lysa shook. From where she now stood, their discovery was hidden by the thick leaves and branches. It was only from directly below the body, it could be seen.

"We were..." she started, but Finn had disappeared under an overhanging branch to get a better look.

"Finn, come back. Whoever did it could still be around. It's probably one of the crazies from the festival."

Finn studied the corpse. From the size and build of the body, it was probably male, though without being able to see the face and examine it properly, he couldn't be absolutely sure, but he was ninety per cent certain it was a man. There was no way to establish an accurate age until he was cut down.

"I'm okay, Lysa, we'll go in a minute," he called back. He tapped out the emergency number on the phone. It took three attempts before the operator answered. He passed his message quickly and accurately to the police, telling them he was an officer and he would meet them on the road to show them the way to the body. Then he tried calling his own station.

Finally, he got through. He was talking to Needham as he ducked under the branches to go back to Lysa.

There was no sign of her.

37 - INFATUATED BY POWER

Mark grinned as he drove along the road towards the motorway. The Baker was dead, he had taken his place, and when the last casualties died in the hospitals, Grohah would be released into him, enabling the final revenge to be completed. It didn't matter that The Baker's body had been discovered, he'd known it would happen sooner or later.

It was pure luck on his part to find the woman. He'd trekked through the trees and bushes so he could hide the body on the other side of the woods from where he'd parked the van. That way, even when the body was discovered, no one would report his van being seen at that section of the road. Mark had stayed in the woods for a while simply to soak up the nature, the feeling of freedom the animals and the birds enjoyed. He'd been sitting up in a nearby tree when he'd seen the couple in the grass.

Her capture was purely to test his new powers.

It wouldn't be long now. The visions were more frequent and the feeling of Grohah being with him was stronger. The excitement built in him like a child waiting for Christmas. He didn't exactly know what was coming, but he believed it was going to exceed his expectations.

Mark grew stronger each passing minute. Taking the woman so easily was proof of that. He'd become the cat stalking a bird. She hadn't heard a thing. The first she knew was when he grabbed her, but she'd been unable to struggle against him. His presence had overpowered her as much as his strength. He was able to try out the mental hypnosis Grohah had told him about. It was amazing to reach into her mind and see her thoughts and feelings. The fact he could subdue her with his mind alone delighted him. He'd been surprised to discover it was the lady doctor from Liverpool. The strange thing was, she seemed not to recognize him.

It was near midnight before he stopped.

Lysa sat quietly in the back of the van. Hypnotic suggestion made her sit patiently. How far could he go? What could he do with her? He was a kid with a powerful new toy.

Sitting down to face her, he reached into her mind. Her thoughts were blank, but Mark wanted her to remember things. He sent messages to recall the events of the previous day, wanting to know who she was, what she felt.

Glastonbury—the music, the massacre; he saw it all through her eyes. Felt her terror as she ran for her life, her grief for her brother. Saw the man she was with, discovered he was an undercover policeman.

Now that was interesting.

Feeling her tiredness was strange. Tramping the hospital wards, helping the injured, trying to comfort the relatives. Foolish woman. Why didn't she realize those who had taken Euphoria could not be helped?

Mark learned the death count was almost ten thousand when you added in the deaths in the nightclubs. The time was getting nearer.

She felt passion for Finn, and experiencing her desire made him realize he hadn't thought about sex since he'd joined up with Monty. He didn't worry about his lack of libido. There was a gorgeous woman in the back of his van who'd do exactly what he wanted and he was more interested in her mind.

Pride filled him, excited him, but the voice came and told him to rest. He had used enough of his new mental powers for now, and he needed to let the woman sleep.

Mark understood. He lay Lysa down on the makeshift bed and told her to sleep. She did.

When he had finished with her, he would kill her. That gave him more of a rush than sex would have. He went to sleep dreaming of the best way to do it.

38 - LEAVE WITH YOUR LIFE

Kelly spent another restless night in the basement of the gym. She didn't like the way the big guy, Don, looked at her. She prayed someone would find her soon and that Jake was okay.

The handle of the door turned and one of the goons came in. They'd untied her yesterday, and she was able to move around, but all they'd given her to use as a toilet was a mop bucket. She tried to eat as little as possible to avoid having to utilize it.

A short man with dirty blonde hair put a tray down on the floor. It contained a couple of slices of toast and a plastic cup of tea from a machine.

"How long are you going to keep me here?" It was a question she never tired of asking, but as yet she hadn't had a constructive reply.

"Mr. Marchant will let you know when he's ready."

She sighed at the expected answer. "And just when will that be?

He ignored her question. "Look, it could be worse. You could have Big Don looking after you. Only he'd be more inclined to look after himself, if you know what I mean."

Kelly shuddered.

He stood in the doorway ready to leave the room. How could she make him stay longer, maybe leave the door unlocked?

"Can you stay and talk to me for a while?" she asked. "I'm going mad locked up in here not knowing what's going to happen."

He closed the door, but to her disappointment, he sat down on the floor with his back to it.

"Okay, I've got ten minutes, but then I have work to do."

Kelly sat on the gym mattress and sipped the tea. It was tasteless and hot, but it felt good to her dry throat.

"I know you're not supposed to tell me anything, but can't you at least give me some hope of getting out of here?"

"As you said, I'm not supposed to say anything."

"If I ask just one question, will you answer it truthfully for me?" Kelly tried what she hoped was her best sad dog look.

"All depends on the question."

"Are they going to kill me?"

He looked at her without expression. "I don't think so, but I don't know for sure."

"Has Jake been in touch?" she asked.

"I can't answer that, Mr. Marchant wouldn't like it." He stood up to leave.

As he turned the handle and opened the door, Kelly leapt up and threw the remainder of the hot liquid into his face. He instinctively put up his hands, and in that vital second she rushed through the door.

The corridor split in two directions, and Kelly took the one to the left, but her gaoler was only seconds behind her in the hallway.

A door to her right was slightly open, so she darted through, shutting it behind her. It seemed to be a storage room, with plastic chairs stacked against one wall and folded down trestle tables against another. She spotted a small window above the chairs.

Kelly leapt up onto the chairs as her pursuer opened the door. She pushed hard on the window latch, but it had been painted shut. In desperation she put her fist through the glass, cutting her hand, but in her need to escape, she didn't feel any pain.

A hand gripped her leg before she could push the rest of the glass out of the window.

"Come on, you can't get away," the short man said.

She slipped as he pulled her down and the stack of chairs toppled over, crashing noisily to the concrete floor.

"Do you want to get yourself in even more trouble than you already are?" He gripped her arm and dragged her out of the room, closing the door behind them.

"How much more trouble can I get in," Kelly snapped. "Do you think I'm stupid? I know they're going to kill me."

He didn't speak as he hauled her back down the corridor and pushed her back into the room. He followed her in, shutting the door quietly behind him.

"Look, the only chance you have is if you co-operate and don't try any more tricks like that."

"Why should I? The way I see it, I've got nothing to lose. If Jake was coming back he'd have been in contact by now."

He slapped her hard across the face. Kelly fell back with the impact, her cheek burning.

"That was for the tea in my face," he said. "Now, I'm gonna do you a favor. I'm not going to tell Marchant you tried to escape, just that you got a little frustrated and threw your drink at me."

"Why? What difference does it make?" Kelly didn't rub her cheek, although it hurt like hell.

"Because it don't look good that you got past me okay?"

"What if I tell him I did?"

"You're not that dumb," he answered. "If he thinks you tried to get out, you'll be dead by the end of the day. Your only chance is to make him believe that you won't go to the police. If he thinks you tried to escape, then he'll never believe you won't go straight to them."

What he said made sense. "All right, I won't try anything again."

He turned and left the room. Kelly heard the click of the key in the lock. She was alone again with her thoughts.

It must have been about three hours later the door opened for the second time that day. Now the big guy, Don, and Marchant accompanied the short man.

They stood back as Marchant approached her. Kelly didn't bother to stand. She stayed on the gym mattress, arms tucked around her drawn up knees.

"Have you come to kill me now?" she asked.

Marchant's mouth turned up slightly at the corners. "What makes you think that, my dear? I have something to show you."

Kelly still didn't move. "I've heard that one before," she muttered under her breath.

"What was that, Kelly? Didn't your mother ever tell you it's rude to whisper?"

"No. She told me not to talk to strangers."

"I can see what Jake saw in you." Marchant's smile was that of a snake before it struck.

There was something odd in what Marchant had said, but she couldn't figure out what.

He reached out a hand to her. "Stand up. I said I have something for you."

Kelly stood without taking the offered hand and leaned against the bare brick wall.

"Why so distrusting, Kelly? I won't bite."

The idea of touching even his hand repulsed her.

"What makes you think I'd be interested in anything you have?" she asked.

Marchant reached into his pocket. Kelly thought he would probably pull out a gun and finish her off, so the brown paper envelope he offered surprised her.

"What's that?" she asked suspiciously.

"Open it and see for yourself. It's your passport out of here if you want it."

"What's the catch?"

Marchant shook his head. "Really, Kelly, all you have to do is open the envelope, and then, if you agree not to go to the police about anything that's happened here, you will be free to leave."

Kelly took the envelope. Her fingers hesitated before opening it, afraid of what they would find.

Slowly she reached inside and brought out three photographs. They were white side up, she was afraid to look.

"A little keepsake for you, Kelly," Marchant said quietly.

Kelly turned the photographs over. Even though his hair was short and dyed black, she recognized Jake immediately. He lay on a single bed, a hypodermic needle by his side.

His throat cut.

"No!" Kelly screamed. "These are fake. I don't believe you!" But, the self-satisfied look on Marchant's face told her it was true. Jake was dead.

"They were taken in his police cell. The heroin overdose stopped him screaming before his throat was slashed." Marchant held out a piece of paper. It was a photocopy of the death certificate.

Kelly understood. Marchant was telling her if he could get to Jake in a police cell, he could easily arrange for a convenient death for her.

"I get it," she said. The shock and helplessness of finding out about Jake defeated her.

"I'm glad that you do, Kelly, I don't like unnecessary killing. There should always be a reason." He reached out a hand to stroke her bruised cheek. A shiver of fear sprinkled through her pores. For the first time since she'd been kidnapped, Kelly understood real, unmistakable fear.

She couldn't speak. Everything was out of control, unreal. She was in serious trouble and her responses were shutting down. His touch on her skin seemed to be the trigger. She'd been scared of Don, but the hope of Jake coming for her had got her through.

Now he was gone, the terror she'd been holding in check was escaping.

Panic banged against the inside of her skull with iron fists. She froze as Marchant ran his hand over her cheek and down to her neck. There were three men in the room and no one would hear her scream—that was if she was able to make a sound at all. She dropped the photographs and death certificate to the floor.

He took his hand away and her body sagged against the wall.

"Joe here will take you home," Marchant said stepping back. "I suggest that you move out of Liverpool. Transfer to another college, somewhere you won't have any painful memories."

Kelly nodded, and walked forward on trembling legs to the door as Marchant stood aside for her. The short man, Joe, took her arm and led her out. She didn't notice how they left the gym, in fact she didn't even realize what color car Joe drove her back to her flat in. He led her up the steps to the door, opened it with her keys, and guided her inside.

Kelly sat down on the red canvas futon. The flat smelled musty from the windows being closed in the stifling heat. Everything felt strange. Numbness enveloped her.

"I'm going to leave now," Joe said. "You remember, no going to the police or make no mistake; Marchant will have you taken care of."

She nodded in reply. No police.

He hesitated before leaving. "Look, if it's any consolation, I liked Jake. I wish things hadn't turned out like this."

She made no response.

"Do as he says, get out of the city. Get a transfer or whatever it is you students can do. I'm sorry for hitting you earlier, but I knew Jake was dead, and because he was a mate, I didn't want to see you end up the same way."

Kelly turned her head to look at him. "I suppose I should thank you then."

"Just doing a last favor for a mate. You pack up and go back home or whatever. Make it soon."

Kelly noticed the look of concern in Joe's face. He seemed genuine. She nodded, and he appeared to have a sad smile on his face as he left the flat.

The click of the door behind him left her alone, but to feel safe, she'd have to pack up her belongings and leave.

39 - STAYING ON THE JOB

Finn hadn't slept all night. He was tired and needed a shave and he wanted to punch the walls of the local police station. Needham had ordered him to stay there until further notice, and the local cops had enough to do with the events of the previous couple of days. Lysa was just another missing person among many on their list.

Finn had managed to get through to Needham, but now his boss wanted to see him in person. They were running an internal investigation. He'd wanted Finn to get straight back up to Liverpool, but, with the discovery of the body in the woods, he had to stay.

Finn turned as the door to the interview room opened.

"They say you can go see the body now if you want." The uniformed officer held the door open as Finn moved swiftly for the exit.

Finn found his car and drove back to the hospital. There were so many bodies needing the cause of death identified, the police labs alone couldn't cope. The one from the woods had been transferred to the hospital Lysa had been working in.

Finn flashed his card to the white-coated coroner. The man looked only slightly older than Finn, but already there were a few flecks of grey in his dark brown hair.

"I'll need to ask you to wear gloves, just in case you want to handle anything."

"Sure," replied Finn, putting them on and moving over to take a closer look at the body on the slab. It was unrecognizable.

"We've identified him as the television cook, Neil Montgomery," the coroner informed him.

"He disappeared a while ago," mused Finn. "I remember reading about him in the papers. Last heard of near Mexico, wasn't he? On a ship that went down in a storm?"

The coroner said sharply, "Mexico? Are you sure?"

"Yeah. His son said he went on holiday to Mexico and he never came back. There was an investigation into his disappearance. Police in Mexico discovered he'd been booked on a ship that went down in a freak storm, but his body was never found."

"And there was no record of him coming back to England?"

"There's a record of someone using his passport coming back into the country, but nobody actually remembered seeing him. Neither did anyone recognize him from the photographs."

"Are you aware we think the source of this new drug is from a rare Mexican flower?"

Finn looked up from the body. "You think he brought the stuff back into the country?" He shook his head. "From the amount of deaths we've had he'd have had to smuggle a truckload back in. One bloke on a plane just couldn't have done it."

The coroner pushed his glasses further up the bridge of his nose. "It's only guesswork at the moment, but we found a trace of this flower, Morning Glory in a couple of the casualties. It seems it has been mixed with other substances, as we've also found small quantities of cocaine. It leaves little or no trace in the body after death. It almost evaporates."

"If this could be true, and a television cook brought this stuff in, how did he get it to the kids in such quantities? He wouldn't have known the right people..." Finn noticed the distinctive black ring on the man's thumb. "Can I see that ring?"

"We also found these in his pockets, and also on some of the victims." The coroner turned and picked up a clear plastic bag which appeared to contain crumbs. He passed the bag to Finn and moved back to the body to remove the ring. He prized it from the digit, and handed it to Finn.

"Enlighten me," said Finn, inspecting both the ring and bag. He'd seen this ring before.

"Now, I'm not a policeman, but to me it would seem that he used his own cooking knowledge to bake the drugs into biscuits of some sort. We haven't had the results of the tests yet. but we're expecting to find traces of Morning Glory in these, as well as cocaine."

It seemed incredible, but he was making a connection between the TV cook and the black clothed Baker. "How the heck would he get these plants into the country? We have restrictions at all entry points."

The coroner pushed his glasses back up the bridge of his nose. "He could have brought the seeds in. Then he may not have been noticed."

"You mean to say he grew them, and then mixed up this new drug?" Finn was having difficulty processing this, even though the ring was evidence that The Baker and Neil Montgomery were one and the same person. "Why not just get into smack or cocaine dealing? Why go to all the bother of making this stuff that kills everyone who takes it? I mean he's not going to have any repeat customers."

"Maybe he didn't want any."

The coroner's remark made some sort of sense. But why would a famous cook, with enough money to disappear, want to kill around nine thousand people?

Finn took a copy of the coroner's report and said his goodbyes. He still had to phone Needham. The lines were still busy, but he'd promised to fax him a copy of the report, so he made his way back to the local station.

The first thing he asked when he got back was if there was any news of Lysa. There wasn't.

Finn faxed the coroner's report up to Liverpool, but he had to figure out the latest piece of the puzzle before contacting Needham personally.

The black-clothed Baker in Liverpool was, without doubt, the chef Montgomery, though from the way he'd looked the last time he'd seen him he'd never have guessed. His thoughts were interrupted by a woman police constable from across the room.

"Hey, Finn, there's a fax for you here. Came in while you were out."

Finn crossed the tiled floor and picked up the paper. A quick scan confirmed Kelly Winter had been seen back at her flat, one of Marchant's men had dropped her off.

Finn wondered how she would be feeling. She probably knew about Jake's death. It wouldn't be long before the police questioned her. She wouldn't tell them anything, which explained why he was wanted back home. They probably thought he'd be able to talk her into giving them the information they needed. He felt sorry for Kelly. She was a nice kid; she didn't need to be mixed up in all this shit.

Finn screwed up the paper and tossed it into the nearest bin.

Marchant's connection to Montgomery was his only lead. If Marchant had Montgomery killed, then maybe whoever committed the murder now had Lysa. If Marchant knew Lysa was with Finn, and he suspected something, then he might have taken Lysa for insurance the same way he took Kelly. It wasn't a great theory, but it was the only one he had. As Marchant was maybe his only link to what had happened to her, there was no other way forward.

"Tell them I'm on my way back, but not to contact me. I'm going back in," Finn told the young policewoman who'd given him the fax.

"But Inspector Needham said he had to speak to you."

"You tried to get me to call, but the lines were busy," Finn answered. "And if you hear anything about Lysa Warner, anything at all, make sure someone contacts me on the number I've left."

"But weren't you supposed to fax him?"

"I've sent him the coroner's report, if he wants to know any more, tell him you couldn't find me."

"All right," she answered, "I'll try."

Finn hated going back to Liverpool without Lysa, but as the police here had turned up no leads at all, his gut told him Marchant was his only clue, even if it didn't really seem to make any sense. Hopefully his cover wasn't blown yet.

He prayed Lysa hadn't suffered the same fate as Neil Montgomery.

40 - TOO LATE

Lysa sat in the back of the van while Mark drove down the motorway. He'd given her a sandwich in the morning, which she'd eaten without comment. He found it strange, but thrilling, that he could control her so easily.

Dreams kept him company all night. Messages fed into his mind constantly, telling him to keep Lysa's mind in his, showing him how to envision tendrils from himself to her to keep her captive. It was second nature now.

There were only a couple more hundred people left to die and then Grohah would take control. Then Grohah, himself, and Monty, would be one complete and all powerful entity.

It was easy to conjure up images from Monty if he wanted to. He could recall things from his victim's memory as easily as if it were his own. He found he was able to do this with Lysa also. It was more enjoyable to rape her mind than her body.

What would it be like when the last few died? How would he feel? He couldn't be driving the car in case he crashed. That could ruin everything. A signpost for a service station came into view, and he pulled off the motorway for a while. By now, Lysa would be feeling the call of nature, and it would be a good exercise to see if he could control her from a distance.

As he pulled the van into an empty space, he mentally let go some of the tendrils that tied her to him. He watched her carefully; he had to let her free a little, so he could see how much control it took to bring her back.

Giving her a comb he said, "You could do with tidying yourself up a bit before you go in there."

Her eyes flickered a moment as he severed another tendril, but still she showed no fear of him. Mark tried something new.

He stole images of Robbie from her mind, and focused, making her think he himself was her brother.

After only a few seconds she threw her arms around him. "Robbie. Thank god you're all right, but how?" She shook her head. "I thought I'd killed you."

This was so easy.

She pulled back to examine him. "How did the wound heal up? You should have been dead."

"Nothing happened, Sis. Someone at the festival slipped you a tab. You were hallucinating, screaming I was trying to kill you."

"No," said Lysa. "It happened, it was real."

Mark smelled her scent, being so close to her excited him. How far could he take this? "Honest Sis, you had a bad trip. You were screaming I was dead."

"Then why aren't I in hospital? Why didn't you take me there?"

"And ruin your career?" said Mark. "How could I take a doctor to hospital with drugs in her? I just put you in the van and drove you away. I know how to look after someone in this state better than a doctor." Mark shrugged his shoulders. "No offence, y'know?"

Lysa sat back on the mattress. She looked around the metallic inside of the van. "Where did this come from? You didn't steal it, did you?"

"Nah, it belongs to a mate. He went off with a girl so he said I could take you back home in it."

It was easy to make her believe him. Mark became stronger each minute, but there was less of the real Mark with each victim who died in their hospital bed.

Lysa looked down at herself, realizing how scruffy she was. "I have to go and clean up Robbie. Use the toilet. Where are we?"

"At a service station. You can go and sort yourself out while I get us something to eat."

"Where's my bag? My clothes?"

"I had to get you out of the site so quickly there wasn't time to pick them up." Mark gave her two twenty-pound notes. "Go get what you need at the shop."

Lysa took the money, not even questioning where it came from. This was fantastic. Later, he'd see if he could make her believe he was Finn. That would be really interesting.

They walked together across the car park. Mark went to the fast food kiosk and Lysa went to pick up what she needed. Mark kept up the image of her being connected to him; he could see where she was through her eyes.

He ordered two lots of fish and chips and a few cans of coke and headed back to the van. It was only a couple of minutes until Lysa joined him.

She'd washed and put on some make-up, and her hair was swept back into a low ponytail with a lilac hair-tie. There wasn't much she could do about the crumpled clothes. She'd taken off the hospital trousers , and had left on the doctor's white coat. It was long enough to cover her decently. She climbed into the passenger seat. "How long have I been out of it, Robbie?"

"Two days," Mark lied.

The shock in her face pleased him. He passed her the food.

"I can't believe it. I don't understand how it happened." She tucked into her fish and chips. Mark watched her, impressed with his new abilities.

She looked up suddenly from her meal. "I have to ring someone. There's someone who will be worried about me."

"It's okay," he answered. The can of coke hissed as he pulled the metal ring. "I know about Finn. He turned up at the festival. He already knows what happened. He's going to meet us back in Liverpool. He said to tell you he doesn't want you caught up in his investigation."

"But surely he'd have wanted to come with me? He wouldn't have left me in this state."

"Come on, Lysa, this is the real world." He put a chip into his mouth. The vinegar stung an ulcer on his tongue but he relished the pain. "An undercover cop being caught with a drugged up doctor?"

"How do you know about Finn's job? He wouldn't have told you anything about it."

"He had to tell me when you flipped out."

Lysa didn't seem convinced. "He wouldn't have told you. He tried to lie to me about it. Knowing your connections, he would never have told you. You could blow his cover too easily."

"He was so worried about you he had to. What other choice did he have?" Maybe he'd gone too far with his Robbie guise. Perhaps it was time to switch to Finn.

"Where is he now?" Lysa asked.

"On his way back to Liverpool, I told you already."

Lysa screwed up her paper and drank her cola. "Is he going to see us back at the flat?"

"Yeah."

The information he'd taken from her wasn't enough. He needed to know more to sound convincing, but her mind was sharpening. He was only receiving glimpses, and it was harder to keep control while he was making her think he was Robbie. His head was starting to hurt.

"Come on then, let's get going," she said, snapping her seatbelt shut.

Mark put his hands to his head. His temples throbbed. The time must be near now. He felt more of the victims dying; heard the voices in his head.

Monty talked to him, telling him it was too late now. He would be swallowed up with him soon. It wouldn't be long. He couldn't see Grohah or Monty, but he heard a low grumbling sound. It was like a voice, but was neither male nor female. He could put no face to it, but as it chanted, he understood he'd made a mistake.

Lysa spoke from down a long tunnel. "Are you all right Robbie, what's the matter?" He vaguely heard the seatbelt unlock as she leaned across to him. He let loose the vision of Robbie dead on the field of blood.

He heard the scream, but he couldn't silence her. The last tendril snapped, recoiled, and whacked him in the center of his brain.

The scream he heard now was his own. He was going somewhere unimaginable, but something inside was still Mark, and didn't want to take her with him.

"Get out!" he screeched, looking up at her. His hands were pressed to his head so hard he it wouldn't be long before he crushed his own skull.

He barely comprehended the stunned look on her face. Shock waves started from the base of his neck and shot through his body like a flash-fire. The chanting inside his ears rose to a crescendo.

Although he couldn't see his face convulse, he could feel the spasms rage in his body. She tried to help him but he kicked out at her uncontrollably, catching her across the face, sending her head smashing against the metal frame of the window. Somehow he prized one hand from his head and pushed open the passenger door, but the pain hurt so bad he pressed both his hands back quickly, and with his feet, he shoved her unconscious body out of the door to the ground. She fell with a thud to the tarmac, but some part of him was pleased she was out.

As Mark was absorbed deep into what remained of his soul, he was aware he was trapped in a body that no longer belonged to him. A body he could no longer control, but one he would now watch from within, witness to whatever this entity decided to do with it. The incessant noise started to die down. He wished he could feel nothing, but Grohah had not allowed him that privilege.

No power remained that he could control. No ability to reach into another's mind and make them feel what he wanted them to. Too late; he understood he had been tricked, and new eyes now looked out of his sockets. He saw what they wanted, when they wanted him to. There was silence finally in his mind.

The new owner of Mark's body stepped out of the van into the bright sunshine, drank in the warmth, and walked out into the service station.

41 - NARROW MISS

Finn pulled into the service station as the clock turned three p.m. He didn't notice the young lad in the white hire van. Why should he? He decided to check in with Somerset station to see if there was any word of Lysa. There was none.

Even undercover cops had to eat and go to the toilet, so Finn locked up the car and walked toward the building that promised both services. On his way across, he noticed a crowd of people gathered around an ambulance and crew. They seemed to be picking someone up from the ground.

Probably collapsed due to this heat, Finn thought.

Ten minutes later, Finn was sitting down eating a plate of chicken from the restaurant. It was air conditioned inside, and a welcome relief from the sticky afternoon.

Looking out of the window, he saw the ambulance drive off and the crowd disperse. Couples talked and nodded to each other as they watched the white and green vehicle re-join the motorway. For a fleeting moment, Finn wondered who it was, then he returned his concentration to eating his meal.

He'd finally checked in with Needham, only to hear what he'd expected. They wanted him to talk to Kelly Winter. Finn was saddened that Jake had been killed. At least the overdose would have dulled the pain of his throat being slashed, which of course was theatrical and unnecessary. The drugs would have killed him. Marchant plainly wanted people to know it was a hit, not an accident. Finn still had to find out how Marchant got his supplies into the country. Most likely it was by sea, but he had to get a time and date. No word about Lysa's disappearance from Needham either. Even though he wanted to start a one man search of England for her, it would achieve nothing. It was time to give his other boss a call.

He finished his meal and stocked up on snacks and canned drinks for the car, then made his way back to his vehicle and called Marchant.

"Hello, Finn. I didn't expect to hear from you so soon. Missing us, are you?"

"Everything's crazy, I'm coming back."

"So it's true then? The rumors?"

Finn would have frozen if it hadn't been eighty-five in the shade. "What's that, Boss?"

"Don's been pining away for you up here. Is there anything I should know about?"

The rare hint of amusement in Marchant's voice told Finn he'd had a brief panic attack about nothing at all. "Hey I've seen some dogs in my time, Boss, but none as ugly as Don. Give me credit for having some taste."

Marchant's tone became serious. "I don't want you back up here yet. There's something I need you to look after down there."

The pit of Finn's stomach felt like a boulder had dropped in it. He wanted to get back to Liverpool as soon as possible. "Yeah what's that then?" he asked.

"A little bit of business. I want you to oversee a delivery and make sure everything goes smoothly for me."

Finn had no choice.

"Okay. Where do you want me to go?"

Finn listened as Marchant gave him instructions to go further south. Cornwall. It was the last place Finn wanted to be, but at least he was going to find out where Marchant's shipments came in.

Finn should have contacted his station. He should have organized men to be at, or around, the pickup place to make the bust. It would be his reward for months of living with the dregs of the earth. But he didn't.

It would take too much manpower. Manpower the force couldn't provide at the moment. It would take too long to organize. Needham would never be able to arrange it in time. The shipment was coming in tomorrow night.

But he was trying to fool himself.

He started back up the motorway to Liverpool. He was putting his job on the line with Needham, and his life on the line with Marchant, but he had to find Lysa first. If he could find her before the shipment was due, then he might just make it back to Cornwall in time.

Might.

42 - KIDNAP

Kelly piled the last bag into her car and took a final look at the flat she'd shared with Jake. She missed him, wanted him back with her, but she was never going to see him again, never going to look into his eyes or make love to him. Tears should be rolling down her face, but fear and a need to get away wouldn't allow them to come.

She slammed the boot down on the car and walked around the front to open the driver's door. She was sliding into her seat when a car pulled in front diagonally, blocking her exit.

Kelly panicked. Her stomach felt as though it was about to fall out of her body. It was all she could do not to lose control of her bladder.

Finn came out of the car running. He yanked her door open. "Get out!" he ordered.

"I, I told Mr. Marchant I wouldn't go to the police, I'm leaving like he told me, really I am."

Finn's answer was to take hold of her arm and pull her out of the car. Kelly managed to grab her bag. She looked around the street to see if she could call anyone for help, but there was nobody around. She wanted to scream, but it stuck in her throat.

Finn guided her quickly around the front of her car and opened the passenger door of his own, pushing her inside. "Don't think about getting out," he barked.

Everything had been a lie. How could she have been so stupid as to believe them when they said they'd let her go? God she must be really naive.

*** *** ***

Lights hurt Lysa's eyes so she squeezed them shut again. She instinctively put her hand up to her head and felt the dressing over her left temple. It hurt like hell.

The bright bulbs overhead and the box of curtains surrounding her told Lysa she was on the wrong side of a hospital bed. She couldn't recall how she'd come to be here.

A boy in a van. She didn't know why, but she'd thought he was Robbie. He'd had some kind of seizure and she'd tried to help him, but that was all she could remember.

It felt as though her skull was split in two, but it wasn't, otherwise she'd be wired up to monitors and drips. Surely Finn had come with her? But she couldn't remember him being in the van with her and the boy.

The usual hospital sounds filtered through to her brain. A television in the background. Some silly afternoon chat show where the general public made a spectacle of themselves. Cheap programming.

Lysa shoved her elbows into the mattress and tried to sit up. Big mistake. The pain in her head ricocheted from one side of her skull to the other. She sank back down into the crisp pillows.

Why wasn't Finn here? She tried to remember the last time she'd seen him, but her tired memory couldn't cope with the strain, and sleep claimed her.

43 - WHO TO TRUST?

Kelly sat quietly in the passenger seat. The last thing Jake had said to her was that Finn was all right. She had to believe his last words to her, but she didn't feel inclined to trust anyone after the events of the past few days. He didn't speak, other than to tell her to be quiet and he wouldn't hurt her. Huh, as if she could believe that.

Finn drove through town, into a run-down area that Kelly didn't recognize. Was he bringing her here to kill her? He stopped the car outside a three-story dilapidated Victorian detached house.

"Come on," he said, his tone softer now.

Kelly sat still in her seat. No matter what Jake had told her, she didn't want to get out of the car.

He turned to face her. "It's okay. I'm not going to hurt you."

"Well why have you brought me to a dingy place like this? Are you going to kill me and leave me in a cellar to rot?"

Finn laughed. "Well we're going into a cellar but I'm not going to kill you, or leave you anywhere to rot."

Kelly wasn't convinced. "Well if you're not going to kill me, why do we have to go in there?"

"Because, it's the only lead I have at the moment."

"What do you mean?"

"I'm looking for my girlfriend. She went missing a couple of days ago. The guy who lived here is dead, but there may be some clue in there as to where she is."

"Why'd she run away from you? Hit her did you?"

"Of course not. She was involved in all that trouble down at Glastonbury. I found her and then managed to lose her again."

"I'd say that was pretty careless of you."

"Yes it was."

Kelly was feeling a little more at ease, but she still didn't want to go inside the house. It looked far too creepy.

"Why can't I stay out here and you go in?"

"Because, although the guy who lived here is now dead, I think he may be connected to my girlfriend's disappearance. Marchant also wanted this guy dead and he might send someone to check the place out, and I wouldn't want them to find you sitting outside. You can trust me, Kelly. I promise I won't hurt you."

"Then why the strong-arm tactics before? You could have just asked me to come with you. You didn't have to drag me into your car."

"I had to get you away fast before the police came for you. Marchant would never believe you hadn't grassed him up."

"I wouldn't say anything, I promised him I wouldn't."

Kelly felt tears well in her lower eyelids. She had relaxed a little but her body was shaking and she couldn't control it. Finn leaned over the handbrake to take her arm. She tensed at his touch, sending tremors through her body.

"Do you want to tell me what happened?"

She looked up at him. "You were there, surely you know. You are part of it all."

"I had to go away but I came back as soon as I could. Jake would have wanted me to."

"So you know he's dead?"

"Yes. There was nothing I could do about it."

She saw him look at the bruise on her cheek, and he reached up to touch the purple mark, but she flinched away from him.

175

"Look, Kelly I told you I didn't bring you here to hurt you and I meant it." He nodded towards her cheek. "Who did that? Don?"

"No, the smaller one. Joe."

"Did Don touch you at all?"

Kelly shook her head. "No."

He looked relieved at her answer. "I'm surprised it was Joe who did this."

"I'd tried to escape. He caught me."

"You've no reason to trust me, Kelly, but I hope you will. If I'd tried to persuade you to come with me you'd have said no. That would have delayed things, by which time someone may have seen us and been able to describe me as the person you left with."

"Why would that matter? If you were ever arrested for anything Marchant would have you out in no time."

"It's Marchant that I can't afford to have find out it was me who took you away."

Ah, this was too confusing, but she wanted to trust him.

"You don't want Marchant to find out I'm with you?"

"Or the police."

"Are you running away from both of them?"

Finn laughed. "I wish I could."

"Why would the police be looking for me?"

"They'll want to question you about Jake, and they know Marchant had you in the gym."

"How do you know the police knew?"

"Word gets out."

Anger overtook Kelly's fear. "You mean the police knew that bastard had me locked up and they never bothered to get me out!"

"They want Marchant, and they thought they could use Jake to get to him. The fact that Marchant had you would make Jake do what they wanted."

"Except Marchant knew that so he had Jake killed?"

"That's about the size of it."

The tremors that had shaken Kelly's body disappeared as anger took over. There was something odd about Finn. He seemed to be against both the police and Marchant.

"Who *are* you?" she asked.

"You know who I am, Finn. My last name is Hastings."

"That's who you say you are, but you don't want Marchant or the police to find you, and you don't want either of them to know I'm with you, so are you going to tell me what's going on?"

"I'm just someone who owes a mate a favor."

"Why would you put your neck on the line for a mate's girlfriend? It seems to me that you're in some kind of trouble of your own. What am I? Some kind of bargaining chip?"

"Look, if the police take you in for questioning it will get back to Marchant. If you tell them anything he'll have you killed."

"I know that. I promised I'd get out of town, and say nothing to anyone."

"You've already broken that promise."

Kelly looked up. "No I haven't."

"You've spoken to me."

Kelly shrugged her shoulders. "What does that matter? You're one of them anyway."

"One of whom?"

"One of Marchant's men, of course." Kelly grew impatient. "You still haven't told me why I'm here. Never mind all that rubbish about hiding me from the police. I was leaving anyway."

"If I tell you anything at all, you have to promise not to tell a soul."

"If you're trying to double-cross Marchant he'll feed you to the fish. If I learnt nothing else I learnt that much."

"I'm supposed to be down south on a job for Marchant. If he finds out I'm here, there'll be hell to pay."

"So you really came back for your girlfriend, and you thought you'd take me for some insurance?"

"Look. Jake phoned me last week, just after he'd done a runner. He said if anything happened to him I was to look after you. He made me promise."

It sounded feasible... "So you're really supposed to be down south?"

"Yes."

"Doing what?"

"I told you, a deal for Marchant."

"Then why don't I believe you?"

Finn shook his head. "All I can say is that I'm telling you the truth. If the police pick you up, which they will, then eventually you're bound to tell them something. Then you'll wind up as fish food yourself."

"What if the police picked me up and I told them nothing at all? Then Marchant would have no reason to kill me."

"But you would tell them. They'd convince you to."

"How do you know? Had much to do with them in your time?"

Finn put his hands to his head and pushed back his hair. He breathed in deep and asked, "Have I done anything to hurt you so far?"

"Yes you have, you pinched my arm when you dragged me out of my car."

Finn sighed. "That was necessary. I mean have I tried to deliberately hurt you?"

"I suppose not."

"And do you think I will?"

"I don't know. I'd hardly spoken to you until today."

"If I wanted to hurt you, I'd have done it by now. I just want you to come inside with me and then I'll take you to a safe place until I've sorted something out for you. Is that too much to ask?"

"Are you going to lock me up in there?"

Finn leaned back in his chair. "Look. If you want to leave, then leave. I give up trying to help you." He fished inside his pocket, took out a ten-pound note and dropped it on her lap.

"There. I'll even provide the taxi fare. Seeing as how I kidnapped you and brought you out here, but if you leave, you stand a very good chance of the police picking you up. Then it won't be long until you give them the information on Marchant they want. After that, you'll most likely be history."

Kelly looked at the money, picked it up and handed it back. "Okay, I'll come with you, but you'd better not lock me up in there."

"At last. We're starting to get somewhere." Finn smiled at her. It was a nice smile, not like the one Don had.

Finn opened his door. "Ready then?"

Kelly nodded. "Ready."

They both hit the button on the doors. This was the type of area you needed to lock up.

*** *** ***

The body that still looked like Mark walked into the Saturday evening service. Still and silent, each member of the congregation offered up prayers to their God. Mark was so small in his own body. He could sometimes see what was happening, but the rest of the time it felt as if he was floating in a colorless void.

At the moment he could see, and from somewhere in his soul, he wanted to know what a demon like Grohah was doing in a Christian church.

The entity waited at the back of the church. It took from the minds of the congregation, learning about their God, their beliefs. It watched the procession enter and walk slowly toward the altar.

Mark gazed from inside himself, powerless to do anything. Sometimes he could hear Monty's voice chipping away at him. Everything seemed crazy. Maybe he was going insane? He'd taken so many drugs over the last year he might have lost his mind. He'd heard it could happen.

He remembered killing Monty. That was probably why he kept hearing the cook's voice. He was haunting him, revenge for the brutal way in which Mark had killed him and left him to rot in the tree.

After the priest climbed the low steps to the altar, Mark's body walked down the central aisle. The evening sun shone on the stained glass window ahead of him, lighting up the picture of the Virgin Mary and her baby. Mark no longer had the capacity to panic. If he had, it was exactly what he would be doing right now.

The priest looked up as Mark's body walked towards him, expecting him to step sideways into one of the wooden pews.

He didn't.

As the controller of the body, Grohah walked straight up to him, climbing the three wide steps to the pulpit. A barely audible murmur went through the congregation, but the priest did not step back.

"I think you may be more comfortable in the benches."

Grohah fixed him in his stare. The priest stepped back and motioned him to take the microphone.

"You are all here for one purpose — to worship your God." It was not Mark's voice, but one much deeper, almost a growl, that seemed wrong for his body.

Nobody spoke. They watched and listened in silence.

"I am your God. I am the one you should worship. I will take you to everlasting life."

If the priest wanted to protest, he didn't.

"You must believe in me. I have come to release all of you. You must go out and bring others to me. It is the only way they will be saved on the day of reckoning."

A man in the congregation stood up. "Who are you? What gives you the right to come in here and disrupt our service? You look like some scrapheap junkie."

Grohah smiled with Mark's lips.

"You are right, that is exactly what I was. This body has been fed with all the poison on the earth, but just before I destroyed it completely, I was saved."

"Saved by who? By God? God would not want you to come in here and bear false witness on his altar."

"I bear no false witness. Look at me, look at my clothes, my appearance." The entity paused, moving from the pulpit to the front of the altar before continuing. "Was Jesus a rich man? Did he wear the clothes of kings? Did he not go into the temple and speak of his father?"

A murmur rippled through the congregation. Heads nodded.

"Come out here to me, look into my eyes and see the wisdom within. Do not look at my torn clothes and dirty hair. See what is inside."

Knees moved sideways to let the man pass through the bench. He walked up the altar to the body that once belonged to a young addict called Mark.

"Look deep into my eyes. What do you see?"

The man looked in. Mark could see the images Grohah fed to the man. Images of children left on mountaintops to die. Young women and men flayed on a bloodied altar. Men in fine feathered robes, drinking blood.

He showed the man his own death, and the terror it held stopped his heart.

The congregation watched as he slumped to the floor. Nobody moved to pick him up. Their eyes went from the fallen man to the young scruffy boy who held their minds.

"He has come to me. He will be the first of many. Do not worry about him; he will be revived with me."

Grohah walked over to the celebrant who stood at the side of his altar. The old priest was mesmerized by the tatty youngster who had captivated his congregation.

Grohah embraced him, and the priest kissed him on the cheek. One by one the people came forward out of the aisles and walked up to the altar. The occupant of Mark's body placed a kiss on each of their foreheads and they went and resumed their place in the benches.

When they were all seated he spoke again.

"I have chosen you especially to lead my followers. Your mission will be to bring others to me, to bring them into our new life."

He picked up the man from the floor. His lifeless body held no weight for him and he carried him as easily as he would a tiny baby.

"This man is the first of many to come into our new world. I have chosen this church as my temple, and you must remember who you have become. You are my followers. You have my kiss on your foreheads and you are forever mine." He brought the body in his arms down so it now rested at the height of his waist. If anyone thought the language seemed strange coming from a teenage youth, they didn't voice an opinion.

Grohah motioned the priest to him. "I will stay here in my temple. You will show me where I can sleep. Turning back to the congregation he said, "You will all arrive back here at sunrise. I will speak to you again."

Still carrying the body, he followed the priest out of the side door into the sacristy. Mark felt himself being pushed lower and experienced Grohah's energy entwined in his own. Grohah would show these people what power was. Tomorrow one of them would give themselves as his sacrifice, and he would become more powerful each day.

44 - CLUES IN THE BASEMENT

The flick of the light switch illuminated the damp basement. The floor shone and moved as a carpet of cockroaches melted into the walls. Despite the insects and general state of repair of the house, Finn was surprised at the cleanliness of the small room. Even the tattered curtains that hung on the solitary window appeared washed, and the linen was neatly folded on the end of the bed, indicating the occupant had vacated the premises.

Kelly walked down the steps and entered the room behind him. "You mean someone actually lives in this place?"

"Some people don't have a choice, but then again, the man who lived in this place certainly didn't need to."

"Why's that?" Kelly asked, moving further into the room, wrinkling her nose up at the musty smell that permeated the whole place.

"Because he was a very well paid chef, and pretty famous at that. What I have to figure out, is why on earth would he want to live here? He has a house in London, and one in the country."

Kelly screamed and jumped back as a cockroach scuttled past her foot. Turning, she leapt onto the mattress. "You couldn't pay me to live here."

"Good, because I wouldn't have enough money." Finn spoke quietly as he carefully examined each section of the room. Nothing but a few cockroaches peered out from under the bed. He wasn't impressed, even though they waved their antennae in some strange kind of insect greeting that he had no desire to respond to.

Finn glanced at Kelly standing on the bed, her face revealed a fear of all things crawling. Her eyes flitted from one part of the room to another, no doubt seeking out more of the shiny insects. Every time the electric light glinted on something she appeared to jerk. Finn went back to checking out the room.

He worked quietly, examining each part of the small space in detail, but still managing to move swiftly from one section to another.

"When can we get out of here?" Kelly asked.

Finn investigated the cooker, having finished with the sink unit. His voice carried a strange echo from inside the oven. "Soon. There must be a clue in here somewhere." He pulled his head out and looked across the room to where she still stood shivering on the bed.

"They're only insects you know, they can't eat you."

"Well thanks for the information, but I'd still rather not hang out with them."

"I see your point, but they know more than I do about this guy. They must have seen him at work. The oven's spotless, not a crumb anywhere."

"Ugh, how could anybody eat in here, with all these crawling things?"

Finn laughed. "Maybe he cooked a few up in the biscuits he's been baking. It would probably add to the crunchiness."

Kelly trembled. "That's disgusting. When can we get out? This place gives me the creeps."

Finn started to pull the cooker away from the wall. "If you get down off the bed and look under the mattress while I do this, we can get out as soon as we're finished."

Kelly glared at him.

"I'll take that as a no," he said, scraping the oven on the floor.

Kelly watched him, as if waiting for something sickening to run out from underneath.   Nothing happened.

Finn rested a moment, leaning on the hob to catch his breath.

Kelly suddenly slapped her arm, but there was nothing there. "I've got to get out of here," she said. "I'm imagining all kinds of stuff now."

Finn moved around to the back of the cooker. There was nothing to be found.   "Come on, you'll have to get down off that bed. I need to look under the mattress."

Kelly shook her head. "No way, I'm not getting down from here until we're ready to leave the room."

"The sooner I check the bed out, the sooner we can leave."

Kelly didn't sound convinced. "If I get down something might crawl on me."

"If you stay on there much longer, something will definitely crawl on you."

Kelly looked in the direction of Finn's gaze. Right next to her foot was a very large, very shiny cockroach.

Her scream bounced off the walls as she jumped off the bed, kicking the neatly folded blankets to the floor. She couldn't form words, but ran out of the door, up the stairs, and out of the house. It looked like she'd prefer to take her chances with the police or Marchant rather than face the thing on the bed.

"Good thing she didn't walk in here before me," murmured Finn as he picked the blankets up from the floor. Two sheets of folded paper fell out of them.

Finn picked them up and glanced quickly over them. The paper contained scribbled notes. The handwriting was smudged and stained with what appeared to be grease and food. Time was an issue, so reading it properly would have to wait. He had to press on, so he folded them back up and put them in his pocket.

He swiftly checked the rest of the blankets and under the mattress. Finding nothing else of interest, he followed Kelly back up the steps to the waning sunlight outside. She was leaning against the car waiting for him.

"You could have told me before it nearly crept on my foot." She blinked her eyes and held her chest tightly with her arms, but couldn't prevent her body from shaking.

"Sorry, I didn't see it until I told you," replied Finn. "Anyway, you wanted to get out of the place."

He unlocked the car and let her in. She slid into the seat, smoothing down her clothes.

"Did you find anything?" she asked.

Finn took the papers out of his pocket. "Only these, but I'm not sure what they are yet."

She held out her hand and he passed them over to her. He'd not tell her, but he was glad to be out of the damp basement as well. A bath in his own home would feel fantastic right now; the dirtiness of the cellar seemed to cling to his skin. Six months since he'd been in his own house, the house he and Amy should have been sharing. Sighing, he put the key in the ignition and turned the car over. As he pulled away from the curb, Kelly spoke.

"There's a kind of recipe on one page, but I can't figure out what's on the other. It looks like some sort of story."

"I'll look it over when we get home. Right now I reckon we need some food inside us before we do any more."

She folded the papers back up again. "And where's home?"

There was no option. Finn would have to take her back to his own house. The flat where Marchant thought he lived wouldn't be safe.

45 - MUCH TO DO

Finn owned a small semi-detached house he had inherited from his mother who'd died two years previous. On the way, they stopped to pick up some food as there wouldn't be anything in the house. After showing Kelly to the spare room, he quickly searched around for any evidence relating to who he really was, and hid it away in his floor safe. No missed calls on his phone, so no reports of anyone finding Lysa. Even though he was avoiding calling Needham, he knew if they had any news, someone would call him. Exhausted from the events of the last few days, he took a shower to clean up and relax before falling into the bed he hadn't used for over half a year and went straight to sleep.

By the morning, he felt refreshed and was busy cooking breakfast when Kelly came into the kitchen.

"Were those papers we found any use?" she asked.

She'd washed and dressed in a white dress with tiny red flowers belonging to Amy. Although he'd moved Amy's clothes to the spare room, he'd not yet been able to give them to a charity shop or throw them away. Seeing Kelly in them stung.

She noticed his gaze on the dress. "Sorry, I should have asked first," she explained. "I have nothing else to wear and I found this in the wardrobe. If I can wash my things through I'll change as soon as I can." She paused, giving him an opportunity to speak. When he made no reply she asked, "Will your girlfriend be upset I borrowed her clothes?"

Finn understood why Jake had been so protective of her. She was a delicate china doll with flame-red hair. Seeing her as Jake had seen her brought him back to the present.

Amy was past, but would always have a place in his heart. Lysa was now. It was time to let go of the clothes. "It's fine, they don't belong to my girlfriend. They belonged to someone else. She'd be happy someone could use them."

She wasn't showing any grief over Jake. Finn wondered if she was trying to block it out. Better to let her bring up Jake herself if she wanted to. Changing the subject he said, "You were asking about those papers?"

"Oh yes. Did you find out anything more?"

"They only tell me what I already knew he was doing," he answered, passing her a plate of toast.

"And what's that?" she asked.

"The guy was baking drugs up in biscuits. Marchant has been buying from him but we thought it was just some twist on a regular drug, but this stuff seems to send people crazy. The recipe seems to relate to the drug, but the other page I don't have a clue about."

"And that is?"

"Some kind of story. It's a bit difficult to make out, but it seems to be some sort of tale about sacrifices and souls. Like a horror fairy tale."

Kelly sat at on a pine chair that matched the table. The dining furniture wasn't really what Finn would have chosen for himself, but he hadn't been able to bring himself to change it as Amy's mother had bought it as an engagement present.

"Does it have anything to do with the recipe?"

"Yeah, sort of. If the guy believed in the story, then he wanted to kill people to release some kind of demon."

"Has it worked, do you think?"

Finn raised his shoulders and shook his head. "It seems to have worked in so much as people are being killed, but as for releasing a demon? Who believes in stuff like that?"

Kelly nodded. "I suppose you're right."

"To be honest, I didn't pay too much attention to the story; I concentrated more on the recipe. I figure if we know what's in the biscuits, then maybe the doctors can work out a way to help the victims."

"That makes sense." She looked around the kitchen. "This is a nice house, but not really what I'd expect of some big time gangster."

"I'm not a big time gangster."

"Oh no that's right, you're just one of the gofers, aren't you?"

Ignoring her jibe, Finn dished the eggs onto the plate with the bacon and tomato. He passed her plate to her, then brought his own over and put it on the table next to her.

"Hope you're not a vegetarian," he said, turning back to the worktop and pouring hot water in the coffee mugs. He brought them over to the table and sat down. "There's sugar in the bowl, if you want it."

"You're very organized. I'd never have thought you were so domesticated."

Finn put his bacon on his toast and dipped it in his fried egg.

"All men aren't incapable of looking after themselves, you know."

"Sorry, but the house is so tidy, it looks like no one even lives here. Does your girlfriend live with you? Doesn't she mind you having another woman's clothes in your spare room?"

"Those clothes belonged to my fiancée. She left them behind."

"Why don't you get rid of them?"

"Because, I've not been able to."

Kelly looked puzzled. "I'm sorry. I must be missing something here. You're looking for your girlfriend, but you keep your ex-fiancée's clothes in your spare room?"

He was reluctant to go into the explanation, but if he didn't, she'd probably not stop asking questions.

"The clothes belonged to my fiancée who lived with me last year."

"You seem to make a habit of losing your girlfriends."

"I didn't lose my fiancée. She died."

Embarrassment turned her cheeks the color of her hair. "Oh. Oh I'm so sorry, I didn't mean, um, I don't know what to say...."

Finn picked up his mug, "That's ok, you weren't to know."

"But still, it was so tactless of me," she replied.

"It was a comment made without malice," he smiled. "When I find Lysa, I'm going to ask her to move in with me. I might stand less chance of losing her again then."

"When you find her."

"It's not been that easy."

"Sorry, I didn't mean to upset you." Kelly sounded flustered. "All I seem to be doing is putting both of my feet in my mouth at the same time. Look. Why don't I get out of your way and go to my parent's place? That's where I was going anyway."

"That's the first place the police will look once they find out you've left your flat. I've told you, you won't be safe if the police get you."

"You're going to a lot of trouble on my behalf. Surely, as long as I don't say anything, Marchant will leave me alone?"

"Do you really want to take the chance? You've been held by them once already. Do you want to end up in a worse place than the basement of the gym?"

Kelly shook her head and silently started to eat her breakfast.

Finn saw her eyes fill up and remembered she'd been through a lot, and she was still young. The ringing of his mobile phone cut into his thoughts.

"Excuse me," said Finn, making his way into the living room.

"Hello, Finn here," it was safer not to give a surname.

"Mr. Finn Caffrey?"

Of the people who had the mobile number only the police force and Lysa knew his real surname. Marchant thought his last name was Hastings.

"Who is it?" Finn asked.

"This is Doctor Channing of the Royal Infirmary in Birmingham. We have a Doctor Lysa Warner here. She's been involved in an accident and gave you as the only person she wanted us to contact."

A rainstorm of relief washed the tension from his body. "I'll be right down for her. Tell her not to leave until I get there."

"Mr. Caffrey, Doctor Warner is in no state to leave here under her own steam. I can assure you, she will be going nowhere until we are confident she has someone to look after her."

Finn sank down on the couch. Thankful that Marchant didn't have her, he'd not considered she might be seriously hurt. Nausea swirled in his stomach.

"What do you mean? Is she injured?"

"I did say she had been involved in an accident," the doctor repeated. "Miss Warner has suffered a serious concussion. Although she has made good progress and is able to look after herself, we would be much happier releasing her, considering her injury, if she had someone with her for a few days."

"What type of injury?"

"A concussion is a head injury," Dr. Channing replied.

"Yes, sorry, Doctor; of course. I'm not thinking straight, I've been very worried about her." Finn tried to calm himself, "Dr. Channing. Tell Lysa not to worry. I'm on my way as soon as I hang up the phone."

"I will, Mr. Caffrey. I'll look forward to your arrival."

Finn hung up the phone and raced back into the kitchen to Kelly.

Grinning, he said, "I've found Lysa, or rather she's found me. She's in hospital in Birmingham."

"That's great, Finn. I'm happy for you."

Finn picked up his car keys from a hook on the wall. "I want you to stay here till I come back. There should be enough food for today."

Kelly stood up and moved to the bin, scraping the remains of her breakfast into it. "Don't you think you're leaving me here on my own. Anyone could turn up for me."

"You'll be quite safe here. No one knows about this place."

"You mean to tell me Marchant doesn't know where you live? How did you think you could hide me here anyway?"

Damn! What a stupid mistake. Kelly still thought Marchant was his employer, and so of course he'd know where he lived. He couldn't tell her this was his real home and Marchant thought he lived in a flat at the other end of the city.

"I told you, Marchant thinks I'm down south on a job. He'll never think to look here for you."

"Surely the police know where you live? You must have a conviction for something? I'm sure they must know who you are."

She couldn't be more right.

"You'll be okay, just so long as you don't put a foot out of the door. I'll be back as soon as I have Lysa."

"What about the job you're supposed to be on? Won't Marchant find out you didn't do it? Then what?"

Why did she keep asking awkward questions? Agitation picked at the back of his neck, now he had another problem. He was supposed to be in Cornwall to oversee Marchant's job this evening, it would take seven to eight hours to reach Cornwall even without stopping at Birmingham to pick up Lysa.

Unless he was a magician, he couldn't be in two places at one time, and he didn't want to waste seven months undercover and miss the bust that could finish Marchant for good.

Kelly interrupted his thoughts. "If you don't do the job for Marchant he'll send someone looking for you, and the first place he'll look will be here."

She wasn't right, but he couldn't tell her that.

"Okay, you can come with me. Maybe you can look after Lysa while I go and do the business for Marchant. At least I'll know she's with someone."

Kelly picked up his left-overs and threw them in the bin. She put the plates and cups in the sink.

"I think we'll have to leave the washing up till later. Are you ready to go?"

Finn nodded in the direction of the door. "Let's make a move then."

All Finn took with him were the two sheets of paper he'd found in Monty's flat, his credit cards, his wallet, and his mobile phone. A thought niggled at the back of his mind. He would have to notify Needham of the shipment, but if he did, then

Needham would want him in on the bust. That would mean wasting too much time on the phone to Needham, when he could be on his way down to Birmingham.

They set off down the motorway. How the heck could he wrap up the case on Marchant, keep his job, and pick up Lysa all in a few hours?

Not to mention track down Neil Montgomery's killer.

It was going to be a busy day.

46 - RIDING THE WAVE

Craig Jones rode the wave like a pro. The sun in his face and the surf beneath his feet gave him a reason to live. Unfortunately it didn't pay his bills.

He jumped off his board and paddled back out into the sea, waiting for the next wave. The summer had been too hot and the sea too calm for many decent waves this season. Even the surf championships had been postponed, maybe cancelled altogether. It was disappointing. He'd hoped this would be his year.

Craig had been surfing all his nineteen years. His parents had sat him on a board when he was only a baby and pushed him in on the waves. It was the only thing he knew how to do well.

If he had to work, he helped his father on his boat, taking tourists out to the Scilly Isles. Unfortunately, that job only earned him pocket money. The positive thing was though, as his father trusted him to sail the boat, he would let him take it out on his own. He would be taking it out tonight.

The money would enable him to take out the pretty little blonde who was waiting on the beach for him. It was a different girl every two weeks in the summer. There were a lot of benefits to living by the sea.

Craig paddled back in and carried the board up the sand, digging it in upright next to Sarah.

"You weren't out long," she said.

"Decided to come back and spend time with you."

"I'd love to be able to surf. You don't see many waves in Glasgow."

Craig lay down on the sand next to her. "I don't suppose you do. It rains all the time up there don't it?"

Sarah laughed. Craig liked her laugh and her accent, even though he sometimes had to ask her to repeat what she'd said.

"Not all the time silly, we do see the sun now and again."

"Really?"

"Yes really. No waves though," she said shaking her head. "No ocean inland."

He pulled her down on the sand next to him. She looked good enough to eat in her yellow bikini. Desire grew, and he rolled her onto her back, kissing her. When he ran his hand down her shoulder to her breast, she pushed him away.

"Not here, Craig! People are looking."

Craig rested his brown elbow in the hot sand, looking down at her. "All right then, I'll take you out on the boat tonight. I've got a job on, but I'll pick you up when the club lets out."

"I don't know Craig. Mum and Dad will want to know where I am."

"Tell them you're with your mate. The dark-haired one."

"Janice?"

"Yeah that's it, Janice. Get her to cover for you."

"I can't. Janice and her mum are sharing our caravan. They'll soon notice if she's in and I'm not."   Craig lay down on the sand, staring into to the cloudless sky. "Forget it then, but you'll be going home soon, and I wanted something to remember you by, to keep me going till you come back again." Craig had used the line so many times before he'd lost count. It always worked, especially when he used his sad voice.

Sarah sat up and looked down at him. He kept his gaze on the sky.

"I could bring her with me? If you had a mate she could get off with?"

Craig thought about Janice, with her short dark spiky hair and her cute bottom. Maybe he could fix her up with his mate Den? If not, two girls could prove better than one.

"Okay, I'll give Den a ring. See if he can make it. Bring her with you."

Once he'd picked up the delivery tonight, he was on a promise. Maybe he wouldn't even phone Den.

47 - TWO WOMEN

Lysa had never wanted out of a hospital so badly in her whole life. It felt ironic, considering all the exams she'd taken to be allowed to practice in one.

When the staff had been busy giving out medication, she'd slipped into the nurse's station pretending to look for her chart. They knew she was a doctor, so they wouldn't pay so much attention. She pocketed a scalpel, sterile swabs, a roll of gauze and a few bandages. With everything that had happened in the last few days, she wanted emergency supplies.

Knots in the brown woolen skirt she'd been given irritated her. Pulling off the tiny tangles, she wondered where the skirt had come from, hoping nobody had died in it. Creases added a pattern to the garish red blouse that accompanied it, and no matter how much she tried to smooth them out, they glared stubbornly back at her. She hoped Finn to pick her up soon. If she could borrow some money from him, she could at least buy herself a shirt and a pair of shorts. Even her blood stained hospital white coat seemed preferable to this outfit.

Since this morning when she'd finally been able to stay awake long enough to ask the doctor to phone Finn, she'd been impatient to get out. She'd been able to recall everything that had happened to her, and the logical part of her mind told her she'd had no choice but to kill Robbie. If she hadn't, she wouldn't be sitting here now. It didn't help with the grief, but she hoped eventually it would make the guilt easier to bear.

Her mother probably wouldn't know he was dead yet, and Lysa couldn't decide if or how she could tell her she'd killed him. The fact her son was dead would be hard enough for her to cope with. The knowledge that her daughter, who was committed to preserving life, had killed him, would hurt her too much.

The television set at the end of the ward ran a continuous news program. The repercussions of Glastonbury were still being discussed on most TV stations, especially as kids were still out there murdering each other. Thankfully though, the numbers appeared to be slowing down.

Lysa moved across to the window, her back to the ward entrance. A magpie sat on a corrugated metal roof opposite her. One for sorrow, Lysa thought. She heard him call her name before she saw him, but as she turned from the window, her attention was caught by the pretty redhead at his side.

He walked so fast, he almost ran down the ward. The girl followed behind at a slower pace.

"Thank God you're all right. I've been going crazy."

Lysa wanted to know who the girl was, and why she was with him, but she didn't ask.

"I'm okay," she replied. "This morning was the first chance I had to contact you."

Finn wrapped his arms around her and held her as though he didn't want to let go. The warmth of his body felt comforting.

"You had me so worried; what happened to you? One minute you were in the woods with me, the next you were gone."

Lysa looked over his shoulder at Kelly who now joined them. She pulled back slightly, alerting him to her curiosity. He drew back a little and half turned to the younger woman.

"Lysa, remember the girlfriend of my friend I told you about?"

"The one you had to go back to Liverpool for? I thought that was all made up?"

"The excuse I gave you was made up, but part of the circumstances were real." He looked from Lysa to Kelly. "This is Kelly Winter. I've brought her along with me because I don't believe she's safe back home by herself."

"Can't the police look after her?" Her voice was shaper than she intended it to be, and he reacted to her tone with an uneasy look in his eyes. "Just for now, I don't want the police to speak to her. I don't think it would be in her best interest."

Lysa didn't trust Kelly's smile. She was far too pretty, and if she'd travelled down here with Finn, she must have noticed how attractive he was. Her sudden jealousy of the young girl surprised her.

"I have to keep Kelly out of the way," he explained. "Marchant had Jake killed, and if he thinks Kelly will talk to the police, he won't waste time in having her taken care of as well."

Oh, the poor girl, her boyfriend was dead and she'd been suspicious of her motives. She must be devastated, grieving, as she was herself for Robbie.

"I'm sorry, Kelly. I do know how terrible you must feel, I've recently lost my brother."

The genuine concern in Lysa's voice released an ocean of tears from Kelly, who slumped down on the bed, her body shuddering.

Lysa instinctively sat next to her, putting her arms around the shaking girl. Her weeping was the trigger for Lysa's own grief over Robbie. As Kelly's tears soaked the cheap red blouse, Lysa's sobs splashed down and mixed in with them. They both held each other tightly, sharing their grief, although they were strangers. Finn pulled the curtain around the bed. Lysa was grateful for the small amount of privacy, though she had seen and heard much crying recently.

"Shall I go find us some coffee?" he asked

Lysa nodded, and he smiled and slipped behind the curtain.

*** *** ***

Finn's training and common sense told him to leave them alone for a while. He was an intruder on their sorrow, so he left the ward and walked down the corridor until he found a hot drinks machine. So many people with red eyes had swollen faces, sore and tired from crying. It was actually a very inhospitable place. There was nowhere private for anyone to grieve.

A row of grey plastic chairs with fold-down seats were fastened to a wall. Finn flipped one down and sat to drink his coffee. It burnt his tongue, but he wanted to wait a while before going back to the ward. He didn't know how to help either of them. Even though he'd been trained how to break the news of a death — he'd done it several times in his career — those occasions hadn't been like this. He hadn't known the people involved. He'd been removed from it. Even his own experience of grief over Amy didn't seem to help him know what to do. Although he'd only known them both a short time, their pain touched him.

He sat there a while, trying to make sense of the past week. So much had happened so fast. The recipe in his pocket was probably proof enough Montgomery had cooked up the drug that had been the cause of so many deaths. Maybe the doctors could figure out some kind of antidote if he gave them the recipe? It was evidence though, so he couldn't just hand it over. He had to contact Needham to get his permission to give the doctors the information.

He instinctively pulled out his mobile phone. He was about to punch in the number when a passing nurse startled him with a curt command.

"Get outside with that. You can't use it in here."

Finn looked up. She appeared as stern as her voice. "Sorry, I forgot. I'll call later."

She gave him the type of look that said he was lower than a worm. "I don't know what can be so important you have to try and use that in here. It'll only take a minute to walk outside."

If only she knew. He watched her waddle down the corridor away from him. She reminded him of a matron from an old comedy movie. He hoped she wasn't looking after Lysa. He could make the call when they were all out of the hospital.

Finn dropped his paper cup in the metal bin by the drinks machine. Feeding the machine more money, he collected two coffees to take back to the ward.

The women's voices could be heard behind the screen as he approached. He couldn't hear any crying, so he opened the curtain and stepped inside.

Lysa looked up, her eyes bloodshot from tears, like so many others he had seen in the previous few days. Finn passed her a paper cup, and offered the other to Kelly.

She disentangled herself from Kelly and took the cup from him. "Thanks, I could do with this."

Finn needed to be on their way, but didn't want to rush them. Kelly came to his rescue.

Wiping her face with a tissue from the locker next to the bed she said, "As soon as we drink this, we'll be ready to go. I've told Lysa we have to be in Cornwall soon."

"Oh, right. As soon as you're ready then."

When would he have a chance to talk to Lysa alone so he could make sure she didn't tell Kelly who he really was? It would have to wait until the opportunity arose, but he hoped it would be soon. He already had enough to worry about without Kelly finding out his real identity. They talked about the deaths, and the fact that the world seemed to have gone crazy. From the way Lysa avoided saying anything about his connections with the drugs and the police, he assumed she hadn't revealed anything about him to Kelly.

By the time the three of them were back in the car, Finn was at least an hour behind schedule. Lysa was now dressed in a blue shirt with black shorts, having persuaded him to stop at an open air market they'd passed on their journey to the motorway. Kelly had also bought a white shirt and a short denim skirt. While the girls bought clothes, a hold-all, and some toiletries, he'd taken the opportunity to call Needham, but had been told he was not available. Damn. The recipe might be able to save lives and he couldn't get it through to anyone.

Lysa still hadn't told him what had happened to her. Maybe she wanted to tell him in private? Maybe she didn't want to tell him at all?

By six o'clock, they were all hungry, but Finn had to meet the shipment at ten, and he still hadn't organized the police to be there for the bust. He pulled the car into a service station to take a break so he could try Needham again, asking Lysa if she and Kelly would go and pick them up something to eat. He nodded toward his phone when Kelly wasn't looking, and Lysa took the hint, leading the younger girl off towards the Little Chef.

Finally, he was able to get through to Needham. His boss wasn't very amused he was giving him so little time to notify the Cornwall police and the coast guard, even though they were experts at intercepting smugglers. Finn gave him the location and Needham said he would organize back-up. Instructions were to check back in with him at nine-thirty. He would keep the line clear. Needham wouldn't let Finn disclose the recipe to anyone until he'd seen it himself.

That done, they had enough time to eat their meal and push on, maybe finding a bed and breakfast to stay the night.

He wouldn't be getting much sleep.

48 - WATCHING FROM THE INSIDE

At times, Mark was aware he had done something really bad, but most of the time he was merely an observer, privy only to the life beyond his body he was allowed by his captor. It all seemed so strange. Now that he was incapable of doing anything for himself, he was conscious of what life was all about, and how much of it he had wasted.

He'd caught a glimpse of what Grohah had done to the man in the church, but he felt no sorrow for him. Death meant nothing to him. After all, he was as good as dead himself. He could see and hear, but couldn't feel physically. He knew people would follow the entity that possessed his body. He knew how good it could make people feel. It would make them think they were powerful, but really they were weaker than they could ever know. In the last twenty-four hours, Grohah had taken possession of five churches with his own priests already appointed to worship him. It would take an immensely strong person to defeat the demon, and Mark didn't think there was anyone who was tough enough. He was captive inside himself, and he didn't know if there was a weakness in Grohah. There probably wasn't.

Mark started to slip away. That meant something bad was going to happen. He hoped he didn't have to see it.

*** *** ***

Catherine stood at the steps of the altar. What she was about to do would be a joyful release. Her previous painful life slipped away as the as the boy with the knife approached. He took her hand and led her up the steps. She had done well. She had brought more followers into the temple, and now she would receive her reward. She had waited all her life for this moment.

She lay on the slab, smiling up at the boy. As the knife plunged into her heart, she expected release into a new and wonderful existence. Too late, she found herself in the blackness.

Lost. With no hope of finding her way home.

She felt her energy go to Grohah and briefly grasped his need to sustain himself with more lives, or he would slide away and be imprisoned again. He would not let that happen. He would regain his followers. His rage was more immense than they could imagine, and it gripped her heart, wringing out the last droplets of her life.

*** *** ***

Natalia wanted to cry, but then they would find her, and she would be in trouble for sneaking into the church. She watched as the man on the altar lifted her mother's body up high above his head. She shouldn't have climbed the stairs to where the choir usually sat next to the organ, but her mother had said something wonderful was going to happen, and she'd wanted to make sure she could see.

She hid her face in her hands and curled up as tightly as she could under the bench, holding her breath in case the man could hear her breathe. Her mother had left her with her auntie Karen, but one of Auntie Karen's boyfriends had come to the flat, and she didn't like the noises they made in the bedroom. She put on her best sandals, the ones Mum had bought in the school jumble sale, and made her way to the church.

Now she was scared because Mum was gone, and Auntie Karen would be mad at her when she knew she'd sneaked out.

Natalia waited until all the sounds from below had gone away and all the lights were turned out. She crept down the stairs to go out of the doors, but they were locked. She wasn't afraid of the dark, but she was afraid of the man who'd had the knife, and now she had to go toward the altar to find another way out.

All the doors lining the left side of the church led into small rooms like boxes. It was strange to have such a tiny room with only a pad on the floor and a black mesh screen in the wall. Maybe the man with the knife put the dead people in there.

As she neared the altar, she wouldn't look towards the center. She wanted her mother to come and give her a hug and tell her everything would be alright, but she hadn't done that very much before. Maybe now she was a ghost, she would.

She turned the handle of the heavy wooden door that was next to a statue of a nice lady who was holding a baby. The door was almost too heavy for Natalia to push, and it squeaked as it opened. Natalia stopped pushing it and slipped through the small opening she had already made.

White robes like ghosts hung on pegs right in front of her. She was scared, but she had to find a way out. She would have to tell Auntie Karen what had happened, even if she did get into trouble. Natalia suddenly felt cold and one of the white garments moved. Natalia screamed. It had come to life and was going to get her. Then, she saw the open window ahead.

She scrambled up on top of a wooden table. The window was small, but so was she, and she squeezed her tiny frame through it. She landed with a thud on the pavement outside. She'd scraped her knees but she didn't care.

She screamed again as a hand grabbed her from behind.

49 - THE PAYOFF

Marchant checked the time. It wouldn't be long now until the shipment came in. In two hours, his largest amount of drugs so far would be smuggled into the country. He would make a packet.

The money he earned from this little venture couldn't improve on his house though. It was perfect as it was, and this was his favorite room. He relaxed into the plush leather chair and aimed the remote control at the CD player and closed his eyes as the sounds of the London Philharmonic Orchestra filled the room and his head. The day's anxieties melted away as he prepared himself for the evening to come. Not that he ever let anyone know if he was anxious about anything. His outward appearance of total calm unnerved most people. Especially those who worked for him. With the exception of Finn.

Finn puzzled him, although the man hadn't put a foot wrong or given him any reason to doubt him. Hadn't Finn done everything he'd told him to do? He recalled watching Finn in action with Don when they'd gone to sort out one of the dealers. Finn had shown no hesitation in breaking the man's knees. He'd displayed no remorse when the wimp had screamed out for him to stop.

Violins played as Marchant mentally filed Finn away in his 'not sure' box. The only person he could trust with certainty was Don. Even though the man was an animal, he knew Marchant was top of the food chain. He'd learned early on in their business arrangements. Controlled breathing sent him into a relaxing sleep. His internal body clock would wake him an hour later, and refreshed, he would set off for the gym to await news of the shipment.

*** *** ***

Finn screwed up his eyes and wished he could find his sunglasses. Finally they were booked into a bed and breakfast with vacant rooms. With a smile on her round face, the landlady explained they wouldn't have had the rooms except the people who had booked them had left to go to their sons who were in hospital. Finn thought it odd she seemed so pleased to relay the tale to them.

While Kelly settled into her room, Finn quickly told Lysa about Neil Montgomery and the latest developments. He gave her the recipe and notes to look at, despite Needham's instructions.

"If I get this to the hospital labs, they may be able to do something," Lysa looked up from the page with the recipe.

"Needham won't authorize it until he's seen it."

"But we might be able to save people with this. We have to give it to the doctors."

Finn shook his head. "The best I can do is find the local nick and send it to his private fax number. He can then pass it on to the police labs and let them work it out."

"That's ridiculous, why can't we just copy it and give it to the doctors?"

"Procedure. If something went wrong, say the docs created some sort of medication from our copy and it went bad, we'd be in the shit."

"Procedure sucks."

"I know, but that's the way it works."

Lysa lay back on the bed and stretched out. "God, I'm aching all over, and it just stinks that our hands are tied this way."

"That's how it has to be."

Finn flopped down on the flowered quilt next to her. He'd much rather stay here with Lysa than go out to the cove, but this might be the bust they'd been waiting for. Needham's voice rattled around in his brain telling him not to blow it. Remember the password to identify himself to the customs men. The drugs guys don't care who they hit on the head. If you're a smuggler, you're fair game.

He pulled his thoughts away from Needham and the bust tonight. He didn't want to ask Lysa the question rattling around in his head, but he had to; it was eating away at him.

"Do you want to tell me what happened when you disappeared?" Immediately, he was sorry he'd asked. He shouldn't be prying if she didn't want to tell him.

Her eyes misted as if she were far away. Maybe she didn't want to remember.

"I'm sorry, Lysa. You don't have to tell me anything. It's none of my business."

She pushed herself up the bed, arranging the pillows behind her back against the headboard.

"No, it's all right. I can remember most of it, but it doesn't make much sense."

"Go on."

"Well, I don't know what happened in the forest, but I woke up in the back of a van with someone I thought was Robbie."

"But Robbie's…"

"I know. I said I *thought* it was Robbie." Lysa paused. "This is the bit I can't figure out. There was a teenage boy who I thought was Robbie. He looked like Robbie, spoke like Robbie. He told me I'd been slipped drugs at the festival and he'd taken me away in his mate's van."

"But surely you knew that didn't happen."

"Somewhere in the back of my mind I thought it was wrong, but I thought I'd killed him, and there he was talking to me. It was easier to believe what he said."

Finn reached out for her hand as she talked, and she gripped his fingers.

"He said you'd told him to look after me, and that you'd had to leave. He knew you were an undercover cop and I remember thinking you wouldn't have told him that."

"Too right, I wouldn't."

"Well, I said that to him, but he convinced me that you had. I thought if I could have been wrong about killing him, then maybe I was so mixed up, you probably had told him. How else could he have known?"

Finn wanted to know who was clever enough to convince Lysa he was her dead brother. Lysa continued. "Anyway, he said we had to get going, and I belted up ready to drive off," she paused a moment, thinking. "This is the bit that confuses me," she said. "He put his hands to his head, and then all I could see was…" Lysa stopped, and swallowed hard, as if fighting back tears at the memory. Finn squeezed her hand. "I saw the field. All of the bodies, and the metallic smell of the blood, so much blood." She stopped again, pain crossing her face. "Then I saw Robbie lying dead with the tent peg sticking out of him. When I looked at the boy in the van again, he was no longer Robbie. He was different. Just a bit older than Robbie, and now I know I'd seen him before, back home in the hospital. He screamed as though he was in terrible pain and I wanted to help, but he screamed at me to get out. Then, everything went black. It must have been then I was knocked out."

Lysa took a breath as she finished her story. It sounded incredible she could have been so easily fooled into thinking someone else was her dead brother.

Finn said quietly. "He must have hypnotized you somehow. You know how easily those TV hypnotists do it."

"But this was just a boy who brought his girlfriend in to the hospital last week. He's an addict himself. I don't see how he could have hypnotized anyone."

Finn wanted to hit himself on the head. The answer had to be staring him in the face, but he just couldn't figure it out. His concern for Lysa seemed to have impacted his usual line of rational thinking. Maybe now she was safe, he could get his mind back on track.

But first, he had the bust to sort out. He forced himself to sit up, to get ready to leave. "You know I'd like nothing better than to stay here with you tonight, but I have to go now. I want you and Kelly to stay together all night until I get back, even if you have to sleep in the same room."

Lysa gave an uneasy laugh. "What can happen to us here? We should be perfectly safe."

"*Should* being the operative word. I don't want to take any chances."

"All right. As soon as you leave, I'll go in and see Kelly. We'll go down and get something to eat."

"It's only a bed and breakfast. They won't do an evening meal."

"There's a takeaway on the corner. We'll go there and get something."

He didn't want them going out without him. Probably nothing would go wrong, but so much was happening lately he didn't want to take any chances.

"All right, but come straight back, and stay together."

Lysa grinned. "Last time I heard that, I was twelve years old taking Robbie to the park. That was my mother's catch phrase."

"Sorry, but I've already lost you once. I don't want it to happen again."

Lysa squeezed his hand again. "It won't."

Finn wanted to stay with her and make sure nothing would go wrong, but he had a job to do. He'd spent months waiting for this night — lived with people he hated with a vengeance, done things he hated himself for, but were necessary to win Marchant's trust.

This was payoff night.

50 - TREADING WATER

Craig met the man at the usual bar in town. He knew him as Pete, but he guessed it wasn't his real name. The name didn't suit the owner. Anyone called Pete should be scrawny and wimpish, like his own Uncle Pete. This Pete was the total opposite. He looked more like a mountain gorilla.

The guy's quietness disturbed Craig.   He only seemed to speak when it was absolutely necessary, almost as if he didn't want to wear his voice out.

He steered the boat out into the black night water. It appeared more logical to bring the stuff in during the daytime. There were so many boats about then it would seem to make more sense, but maybe these guys knew more than he did. It didn't matter; he was still being paid well.   Thinking about seeing Sarah when he got back brought a smile to his windswept face. The evening ahead should be a good one.   Den had been up for a blind date with Janice so they'd all be having some fun when the job was finished.

The other boat would be waiting at the designated location. They changed the rendezvous each time, just to be on the safe side. He'd been blessed with 20-20 vision and had no problem guiding the boat to the dark shape up ahead. It was a good thing he knew the area so well. Anyone who didn't might easily run straight into the other boat, but Craig prided himself on knowing exactly where it would be.

The boat hardly made a sound as they pulled up alongside the other craft. Craig loved the sea at night when it was this quiet. When he was out alone on a night like this, he would imagine he was the only person in the world. There was no need to drop the anchor. He wouldn't be there long enough.

Pete's large frame appeared beside him. He signaled to a figure on the other boat and a plank scraped the rail on Craig's deck as it was laid across to form a bridge between the two. Craig knew the drill and passed the wheel to Pete. He didn't care about his wetsuit being cold and damp from the afternoon's surfing. The adrenaline was running now, as it did every time. Craig liked the feeling almost as much as the money. He pushed the facemask to the top of his head, and checked his flashlight was secure around his wrist.

He quickly sprang over the plank to the other boat. It amused him that Pete appeared to be afraid of crossing it.

Craig dropped down into the cruiser. He admired the sleek lines of the boat. One day, he would have one of these.

"Hope you've got enough room on your tub for this lot kid. There's more than usual."

Craig recognized the owner of the vessel. He'd dealt with him often enough over the past eighteen months. He wondered how much he was paid for running this gear. It was probably a heck of a lot more than they paid Craig.

"How much more?" he asked.

"Take a dive and see."

Craig pulled his face mask down and dropped over the side of the boat. He expected the momentary shock of the cold water, knowing he would soon warm up. He flicked on his light and swam underneath the boat.

What the beam revealed was crate upon crate of oranges, sealed in transparent waterproof wrapping. They trailed beneath the boat, tethered to the underside by thick rope. At least triple the usual number.

Craig swam to the surface and pulled himself up and over the rail of the cruiser. He pushed his mask up again.

"Are you getting paid more for bringing this amount in?" he asked the older man.

"Sure am, aren't you?"

"I fucking well will be. I'm not shifting that lot till I've had a word with King Kong over there."

The older man grinned as Craig leap back up the rail and over the plank to his own boat.

"What d'you think you're playing at? You never told me I was bringing that amount in."

Pete turned from the wheel to face him. "Is there a problem? Can't you handle it?"

"It'll take longer than usual, but if there's a chance I'm going to get caught for that amount, I want more fucking money than I usually get."

"You get paid for the hire of yourself and the boat to bring it in, not by the amount."

"If I was caught for the normal amount, I'd do about ten years, if I'm caught for that lot I'll be drawing a pension before I get out."

Pete sighed, as if the conversation was a strain to him.

"All right. I'll try and get you more money when we get back on land."

Craig shook his head, "No way. You sort it out now or you can dive in yourself and bring the stuff up. Then you can steer the boat back yourself as well. But you'll have to mind out for the rocks, or you'll put a hole in her and we'll go down."

"You wouldn't do that. It's your father's boat you'd be wrecking."

"I can swim. As far as I'm concerned, it was stolen. I know where the nearest land is, I'll be fine mate."

Pete looked uneasy. Craig guessed that Pete couldn't swim. He watched as the man took out his phone.

Craig sat on the rail as Pete negotiated a higher rate of pay for him. When he was satisfied the risk was worth the money he put on his oxygen tank, nodded and jumped back in the water to start moving the gear.

Craig's arms ached. He'd not need to work out for a few days. Still, it was worth the extra effort for the extra money. The floatation aids he untied from the boat and secured on the bases of the crates helped, but Craig was relieved when he hauled the last one up. Climbing back on deck he watched Pete stack the last crate and wondered if he'd ever regain the feeling in his fingers.

He should have worn his neoprene gloves, but they made it more difficult to untie the knots.

Taking the wheel, he negotiated the rocks that could so easily scupper a boat if you didn't know the area. But the ocean was Craig's home.

*** *** ***

The damp rocks dug in hard against Finn's back, and the smell of washed up seaweed reminded him of his grandfather who used to make soup from the stuff. He shuddered at the thought. Even a Brussels sprout looked appetizing compared to that bulbous mass. He glanced up to the cliff top. Marchant's contact sat comfortably above in a brightly painted fruit and veg van, waiting for his signal. Finn looked back out to sea. It was a fairly inventive idea really, smuggling the cargo in oranges. Once loaded in the van, it would look genuine, especially mixed in with the real fruit and vegetables. When the driver up top had explained it, Finn had to admire the ingenuity of the operation.

Finally, he heard it. The engine was quiet but unmistakable in the silence of the night. Finn glanced at his watch. Nearly an hour late. He'd been beginning to think the deal had been called off.

The engines quit, and Finn hoped the police and the coast guard were in place. He glanced around the deserted beach, imagining them hidden in the shadows of the surrounding rocks. If they were, they didn't make a sound. Would they wait until the boat was unloaded, or strike when the crates were in the van?

He heard a splash and returned his gaze to the sea. He could barely see the shape wading through the water towards him even though it was a clear night, with the moon offering a pale illumination. Finn's feet made a sucking sound as he pulled them free of the damp sand to move forward to approach the figure.

The man was twice as wide as Finn and about a foot taller. He carried a crate of oranges in his arms. His shoes hung over his left shoulder, tied together by their laces.

"They for Nell Gwynne?" Finn asked, looking at the crate.

"No, they're for the grocery store," the man replied flatly.

"Then meet the grocer. I'm Finn."

The man put down the crate. "Pete," he said, introducing himself. "And I hate getting wet," he added, shaking his trouser leg. Droplets of salt water flew off and melted into the damp sand.

Another figure appeared out of the darkness. It was a young man in a wetsuit. He appeared to be a bit young to be the owner of the boat. Pete looked like he hated even the thought of being near the water.

The lad put another crate down on the sand.

"You're new. Where's the other guy?" the younger man asked.

"I'm Finn. The other guy, as you call him, is on the top of the cliff waiting for me to send this lot up."

This seemed to satisfy the lad and he turned and waded back into the ocean. "I'm Craig. This'll take a while," he called over his shoulder. "Pete there won't give me hand, doesn't like the water."

Pete made no comment, but picked up a crate and walked towards the cliff wall. Finding the rope dangling down, he tied it to the crate and tugged it twice. The man above started hoisting up the cargo.

"Aren't you going to help him?" Finn asked Pete. "He'll be all night doing it on his own."

"If you want to get wet, you can. I can wait until the sun comes up if it means I don't have to go back in the water."

Finn didn't fancy going in the water either, but he wanted this over with as soon as possible so he could get back to the girls.

Off came his shoes, socks, and trousers, and then, with a little apprehension, he waded in.

His feet numbed as soon as the water lapped around him. He shivered and stood still for a minute as the froth ran around his ankles. Craig laughed as he passed him with another crate.

"Cold isn't it? Well now you've taken the plunge you might as well go right on in. We'll be faster if at least one of you helps out."

Finn breathed in and forced himself forward. Now he knew why Pete wouldn't help, but moving the crates from the boat to the shore would be done quicker. How could this water be so damn cold when the days were so hot?

***   ***   ***

"Do you think Finn will be all right?" Kelly asked, sipping coke from a can.

"I hope so," replied Lysa. Then, seeing the younger girl was worried she added. "I'm sure he will be. He knows what he's doing." She paid no attention to the radio, even though one of her favorite songs was playing. Her focus was on an emotional Kelly, and after hearing what had happened to her in Marchant's gym, Lysa could see the events of the past week were starting to take its toll on her.

"I can't believe Finn's one of them. They're so horrible, and he seems so nice."

"Jake was involved with them too, and you loved him, so he couldn't have been horrible."

The girl was fighting tears, determined not to cry.

"I didn't know anything about what he did until that man Marchant had me kidnapped. I couldn't believe some of the things he told me Jake had done."

"Try not to dwell on that side of his life too much. From what Finn tells me, he only stole those drugs so he could get enough money to disappear with you to make a new life."

"It was still wrong though, the things he did. How could I have not seen it? Am I really that stupid?"

Not stupid, just young.., "You just have to believe he regretted his choices and was trying to change his life for you."

Kelly shook her head. "Then if it hadn't been for me, he'd never have stolen those drugs and he'd be alive now, and so would his father."

Lysa moved out of her chair and crossed to the bed, putting her arms around Kelly. "He made his own choices. Even if he'd never met you, he could have ended up dead from some gang war. You can't blame yourself."

The song on the radio faded out and the newscaster related the latest summary of national events.

"It'll be hours until Finn's back," said Lysa. I think we should try and get some sleep."

If either of them had been listening to the radio, they'd have heard about six year old Natalia Freedman.

51 - INNOCENT

Woman Police Constable Margaret Holmes covered up the tiny girl. It would do her good to sleep. No child should see the things Natalia had seen.

Margaret wanted them to catch the ringleader of the sect, the one who'd murdered the child's mother. If it wasn't for the fact she'd witnessed so many strange things in this job, she'd never have believed two of the three members they'd rounded up could be priests from the church, and the other their housekeeper. From what Ken Hopper had told her, they all seemed to have been hypnotized by the person who'd invaded their church.

Natalia coughed as she turned over. Her small eyelids flickered, but stayed shut. Suddenly, Margaret filled with intense anger toward the person who had caused such a young child so much pain. Ken had sworn he would find the bastard who'd done it.

But even he hadn't been able to get much information out of the three they had down in the cells, and if Ken couldn't make them talk Margaret couldn't think of anyone who could.

Officially of course, he couldn't tell her what the suspects said. She knew so much because he trusted her. After all, she'd kept their affair secret for almost two years. She was his confidant in everything. Even though all the trio had said was something about a meeting, she had faith in Ken. He would find this cult leader, she was sure he would. He'd dealt with all sorts, even religious nuts like this lot, preaching on about how only they would be saved. Why people were taken in by this rubbish was beyond her. They were all crazy.

Margaret picked up the phone to dial Natalia's aunt again. The ring tone grated on her nerves. Where could the woman be? Well, by morning she would know what had happened and most likely be banging on the door. Margaret silently cursed whoever had leaked it to the press, as if the child hadn't gone through enough already.

She put the receiver back down and her gaze lingered on Natalia. At least she had peace for the night. God knows what the morning would bring for her.

52 - EXECUTING

The last crate bounced of the jagged rocks and scraped over the cliff edge to the top. A smattering of soil fell to the sand. Finn rubbed his arms and glanced at his watch. Hope the back-up arrives soon.

He turned his attention back to Pete as he heard the rustle of paper. Craig's teeth shone in the moonlight as he grinned and counted his money.

"Now I can go pick my girl up."

"At quarter past one in the morning?" asked Finn.

"Yeah, she's with a mate of mine down the club. I've only got to take the boat back, get changed, and I'll be there by the time they're coming out."

Finn shook his head. "She must think a lot of you to put up with that."

"They all do, mate." Craig smirked.

Finn didn't remember being so confident at that age. Then again, Finn had never been that confident with women at any age.

"Come on," grumbled Pete. "I want to get out of here and into some dry clothes."

Craig disappeared into the water. What the hell had happened to the coast guard? Surely they couldn't have got the destination wrong.

Pete had already started to make his way around the cliff, to where the rocks made an uncertain stony staircase to the top. They would have to climb up to meet the van. Finn looked around for any sign of life other than him and Pete, but so far there wasn't any.

Anxious to get back to Kelly and Lysa, Finn followed Pete towards the rocks.

***   ***   ***

Don poured himself a drink from Marchant's private bar. Only the quiet rippling of the brandy in the glass broke the silence in the office of the gym. He sat on a barstool that might easily topple over. His size made him appear as though he was sitting on a tripod.

Joe never drank alcohol, and he hardly ever sat down. Marchant glanced at him now, standing by the door, unmoving. A blue-suited statue.

Marchant willed the phone to ring. He wanted to hear everything had gone to plan. He appeared as calm as ever to Don and Joe, but the millions of pounds resting on this deal threatened to pierce his cool exterior. Damn that silent phone. He couldn't afford for anything to go wrong.

His calm shattered as the door flew in.

***   ***   ***

Shadows sprung out of the cliffs with the agility of panthers. Finn and Pete didn't stand a chance as they were thrown to the ground. Sand filled Finn's nose and mouth, choking him, stinging his eyes.

Over the voice reading him his rights, Finn heard Craig start his boat. Someone on a loudspeaker ordered him to stop, but the engine burst into life as the handcuffs snapped around Finn's wrists, scraping his skin. The sound of a louder engine assaulted his ears, and the area around him dazzled and hummed with the helicopter searchlight and blades

Pete spewed forth a stream of obscenities Finn didn't even know existed, and the roar of more engines on the water filled his ears. As he was flipped over on his back, he tried to spit the sand out of his mouth. Unfortunately, his captor thought he was spitting at him, and struck him a blow across the face with something much harder than a hand.

The coast guard surrounded Craig's boat. Finn struggled to sit up so he could look out across the water and he caught sight of Craig firing his flare gun. Oh no. Stupid kid...

The blast of gunfire thundered, and, in the helicopter's beam of light, Finn thought Craig disappeared over the side of the boat, but couldn't tell if he'd jumped or been shot.

Hands on his shoulders dragged him roughly to his feet. Pete glared at him as they were hauled towards the steep rocky steps. Climbing with hands cuffed behind your back was no easy task. Finn slipped a couple of times, but took some gratification when Pete lost his footing also. The big man swore more intensely with each scrape on the sharp rocks. Finn stayed quiet as much as he could. There would be time at the station to tell them who he was.

*** *** ***

Marchant instinctively reached for the gun under the desk, shooting the first man entering the room clean through the head. The bullet exited his skull, narrowly missing a second man and only stopping when it embedded itself in the wall. The blood from the fatal wound drenched the second guy, but it didn't deter either him or the others behind him. They ran over the body and into the room.

Marchant couldn't hope to win and flicked a switch underneath the desk. A panel slid open in the floor and he dropped into it. There wasn't much time. Don and Joe might hold them off long enough for him to escape.

***   ***   ***

Don didn't see Marchant drop through the escape hatch. He was too busy dodging bullets. The bar didn't give him much cover, but it was better than nothing. They were outnumbered. His only chance was to stick up his hands and hope they wouldn't shoot him.

He felt the pain rip through his right palm as the bullet tore away his last two fingers. He opened his mouth to say he was giving himself up, but he didn't get the chance to form the words. He was blasted back into the bottles of spirits without even knowing who had come for them.

***   ***   ***

The hatch in the floor had only gained him a couple of seconds, the heels of his shoes hammered on the concrete staircase as he headed toward the basement. His pursuers' footsteps echoed his own, but at least he had the advantage of knowing where he was, and he didn't need the lights.

He passed the room where he had kept Kelly, and on to where the corridor split into two. Taking the right, he ran for the fire exit, then stopped dead. It would probably be covered. He heard his hunter take the other corridor, giving him a precious extra few seconds. His hands pushed up the bar on the fire exit, forcing the door outward, but instead of going outside he ducked into the room at the end of the corridor.

Even in the dark he could make out the large old fireplace in the corner. Crossing the room as quietly and quickly as possible, and without a thought for his expensive suit, he pushed himself inside, edging up the chimney as though he was a spider going home.

He couldn't avoid knocking soot down on his upward journey while trying not to inhale. The police would be too stupid to notice it. Someone in the room below flicked on the light switch. Marchant slowed his breathing so he wouldn't take so much dust into his lungs and cause a coughing fit. Muffled voices reached his ears.

"Not in here. Even the window's bricked up. He must have gone out the exit."

"No way," came back another voice. "We'd have seen him. He couldn't have slipped past us."

"Yeah? Well maybe you're not so shit hot as you think you are."

The argument faded away as the men left the room.

He couldn't go back to his house. It would be being watched for sure. Fucking shit police. Now he would have to wait in this sooty prison until it was safe to leave.

He would find out who was responsible for this. Whoever had crossed him would wish to die quickly.

53 - BEING SWALLOWED

Mark grew smaller as the entity became more powerful. Its intention was to kill, and there was nothing Mark could do about it.

Although the sun was up and it would be warm, he neither saw, nor felt it. All he was aware of was almost constant blackness, with only a rare few glimpses of life. Would this go on forever, or would his periods of consciousness become fewer and fewer?

When Grohah was in need of a new sacrifice, and as the time for the kill came closer, the anticipation seemed to give the demon strength and Mark was often pushed down again. After some of the things that had happened, he welcomed oblivion. His current state of awareness wouldn't last long. The entity would make a new kill and he would melt back into the blackness. Regret filled all that was left of him. There was always a price to pay for power, even if it was fleeting.

Sun flashed briefly through overhead leaves. The entity was building up for something. It passed its thoughts on to him, let him know its time was nearing, but laughed at his weaknesses.

Mark wanted to be angry, but the emotion wouldn't stir.

54 - ON THE MOVE

Someone pounding on the door roused Lysa from sleep. Her limbs were stiff from sleeping all night in the chair, but she forced them to work. It had to be Finn, thank God he was back.

When she opened the door, the bruises and cuts on Finn's face were enough to shake the last remnants of sleep from her eyes.

"What happened?" she asked, reaching for his face. Finn waved a finger at her. "Never mind that. You opened this door without even asking who it was." He walked into the room. Kelly still slept, despite the noise he'd made.

Lysa followed him across the room. "I knew it would be you." She sat on the edge of the bed as he sank down in the chair she had just vacated.

"And just how did you know that?"

"Because," said Lysa, whispering so as not to wake Kelly. "You had to come in the front door to even get up to this room, and then you had to know exactly which room I was in."

"Ah, but anyone could have just asked the landlady."

Lysa took his hand. "Ok, sorry, I should have been more careful. It's just that my first thought was that it would be you and I needed to see you were ok. We were so worried. She squeezed his fingers. "You haven't answered my question yet."

"And what was that?"

"Call yourself a policeman?"

Finn shot a glance over to the bed at her remark.

"She's fast asleep. We were awake till gone two this morning. If you didn't wake her banging on the door, my whispering certainly won't."

Finn nodded. "All right. I took a hit so as not to blow my cover."

She grimaced and shuddered slightly. "Did it go well? Will Kelly be able to go back home?"

He shook his head. "Not that well. We got the contacts down here, seized about three million pounds worth of drugs, but Marchant seems to have vanished into thin air."

"But I thought the police back home were ready to nab him at the same time."

"They went in all right, and he was there. Don was killed, and Joe's in intensive care with a head wound. Two officers were killed as well, but Marchant seems to have got clean away."

Finn could be in real trouble, Marchant was probably looking for him by now. No wonder he'd been annoyed with her for not checking before opening the door. "Does he know it was you who set him up?"

Finn shrugged his shoulders. "He's not stupid. Once he finds out I'm not banged up with Pete, it won't take him long. I don't think he ever really trusted me anyway, but if he's out to find me, there's a good chance he will." He drew in a breath before continuing. "That's why I want you to take Kelly away somewhere until we know where he is. If he comes after me and you're in the way, it won't worry him one bit. He'd kill you just to make me suffer."

"No," Lysa answered without hesitation. "I'm staying with you. Don't forget the other crazy who kidnapped me is still out there somewhere."

"Yes, well, that's another thing."

"What do you mean?"

"I want you to look at this." Finn reached into his pocket and took out a photo-fit and a police artist's drawing. He handed them to Lysa.

"That's him. That's the lad who brought his girlfriend into the hospital. He's the one who kidnapped me."

"I thought as much, though I wished I was wrong."

"Why?"

He looked as though he didn't want to tell her. Her hand was still on his, but now he switched and took both of her hands in his and paused, then said, "This person is believed to have committed a ritual murder in south London."

Lysa shivered. "What do you mean? Ritual murder?"

"It appears he killed a woman in a church as some kind of sacrifice. We only have a couple of witnesses, and all we can get out of them is a description. For some reason they thought we should know what he looked like so we would be saved."

"What?"

"They see him as some kind of savior. He appears to have brainwashed a whole congregation in one go. They call him Grohah, and say he has come back to claim his people."

"And they told you what he'd done?"

Finn shook his head. "No, we only found out when a beat bobby picked up a victims terrified six-year old daughter from the street after she fell out of a church window."

This couldn't be real. That kid from the hospital could never have convinced a church full of people he was some kind of messiah. "How did you find this out?" Lysa asked.

"Apart from our drugs bust, it was the main topic of conversation at the station. The pictures have been circulated all over the country. They'll even be in the papers today. Someone leaked it to the press last night."

"Can you tell me anything about this kid? Anything that could give a clue as to where he'll go next? What he might do?"

Lysa tried to recall the time she'd spent with Mark. She wished she could remember more, but all that came back to her was the moment when she'd known he wasn't her brother, seconds before she'd blacked out.

She dug deep into her memory. "He screamed at me to get out," she replied. "He said, 'I was wrong, he's taking me'." Lysa tried again, "Other than that, I only recall what he said when I thought he was Robbie."

"Is there anything else? Anything that would point us to him?"

"No. He just told me you would meet us. That he was taking care of me, and to go and tidy myself up."

"What am I missing?" Finn pulled his hands away from her and rubbed the back of his neck.

"I don't know, but maybe you should rest for a few minutes. I'll go and see if the landlady has any breakfast ready."

***   ***   ***

Finn leaned back in the chair. The long night was catching up with him. There was something he wasn't seeing. If he just rested his eyes for a minute it he'd be able to think straight again. As soon as they were closed, sleep claimed him.

Finn wanted an ice cream. He was so hot and the vendor wouldn't serve him, he kept telling him to go away. Finn was angry when the guy jumped out of the van and started shaking him.

"Look I just want an ice cream," he said.

The vendor became a woman. "Come on, you can finish your sleep in the car." The woman turned into Lysa. Finn blinked a few times then cursed himself for falling asleep.

"Why didn't you wake me up? I have to find this Mark character before he kills anyone else."

Who's Mark?" asked Kelly.

It was becoming too complicated to try and continue to lie to Kelly.

"There's something I have to tell you," he said turning to Kelly. "I'm sorry I didn't tell you earlier, but I hope you'll understand my reasons."

Kelly raised her eyebrows. "You're not a mad axe murderer are you?"

"Not quite," he said, pulling himself forward on the chair. Lysa took Kelly's arm and they both sat on the bed facing him.

"So what is it then," Kelly asked.

Finn looked at Lysa before continuing. "I have had to do some pretty bad things in my job,"

"Yeah well gangsters do, don't they?"

"So do policemen. Especially, undercover policemen."

Kelly didn't speak. Her wide eyed expression showed her surprise.

"I've been working undercover for the last seven months, getting Marchant and his men to trust me. It hasn't been easy, and I wish I could have prevented Jake's death, but there was nothing I could do."

"So that's why you didn't want the police to pick me up? In case Marchant got to me the way he got to Jake?"

"Partly. I knew my superiors wanted me to talk to you. They think I can get you to give evidence, but I didn't want to put you through that until we had Marchant. He's far too dangerous."

"And what about when you do have him? Will you try and convince me to give evidence then?"

Finn knew what he should say. What Needham would want him to say. Maybe if he hadn't got to know Kelly so well he would have said it, but not now.

"No. I won't ask you to give evidence, and I will advise you, off the record, not to give evidence against him. If you do, he'll find a way to get to you. We don't have the resources to protect you for more than a couple of months, and he'll have someone find you. Even if he's locked up, it won't stop him getting what he wants."

Kelly pushed herself further back onto the bed and sighed. "He convinced me well enough not to open my mouth. I've never met anyone so poisonous in my whole life. I have no doubt he would kill me, there's no way I'll be giving evidence against him."

"Good."

"So what do I do? Won't they grill me for hours until I say I'll do it? They'll need someone to say what he is."

Lysa gripped her hand. "No they won't. Finn won't let them." She turned to Finn. "Will you?"

Finn shook his head. "No. You say you'll only talk to me. They'll have someone else in the room as well, but whatever I ask you, refuse to answer, or you say you don't know. You'll feel safe with me because you'll know I'm on your side. Eventually I'll tell my boss you're too frightened to talk, and they'll leave you alone."

Kelly nodded. "Okay, but you know something?"

"What?"

"I always thought you were too nice to be one of those goons. That day in the basement, you didn't drag me around like the others did."

"I hope Marchant didn't notice," smiled Finn.

"Is there anything else I should know?" Kelly asked.

It was Lysa's turn to answer. "There's more. I was snatched by a young guy who now seems to be causing trouble all over London. His name is Mark."

"He kidnapped you? What happened?"

"I don't remember much. All I know is that I woke up in this van, and...well, this is going to sound crazy but he convinced me he was my dead brother."

"What!" Kelly shook her head, looked at Lysa, then Finn. "How?" She turned back to Lysa, "How could he convince you of that? You're right, it does sound crazy..."

Lysa sighed. "I have no answer to that, but then suddenly he started screaming, and I saw Glastonbury, saw my brother when he died, and then I saw Mark's real face. I passed out and the next thing I knew was when I woke up in hospital. "

"This whole thing is insane." Kelly moved to the edge of the bed, gripping the mattress tight. "I'm kidnapped by a monster who kills my boyfriend. You get kidnapped by some sort of psycho kid who's now running riot in London, and you," she said, turning to Finn. "You turn out to be a good guy instead of a bad guy."

"Would you rather I was still a bad guy?" Finn asked.

"Holy shit no! I'm just trying to get my head around all this."

"I know it's a lot to take in," said Finn, "but I really have to get going."

"Get going where?" Kelly asked.

"South London," replied Lysa. "Mark has to have some connection to Neil Montgomery; he took me right from where the body was."

"A body? What body?" said Kelly.

Lysa looked at Finn, asking him with her eyes if they should tell Kelly any more, but Kelly saved him from answering.

"Never mind, don't tell me. There's enough death in my life, I really don't need to hear of one more."

"Okay, I have to leave," said Finn. "I'll drive first, and then Kelly can take over while you sleep," Lysa said turning to Finn.

Both women stood and moved to leave the room. Finn jumped up behind them.

"Oh no, I don't want you two involved in this. He's dangerous and you've already been kidnapped by him once. I don't want anything else happening to you. And as for you, Kelly, you're only nineteen. I'm supposed to be looking out for you."

"You forget though, Finn," Kelly called over her shoulder as they descended the staircase. "Lysa and I have two things in common. We've both been kidnapped and lived to tell the tale, and we've both lost someone we love. We're tougher than you give us credit for."

Finn followed them out to the car. Maybe Kelly was right. Maybe they were a lot tougher than he realized. As it was two against one, he thought it better to let them drive, and besides it would give him time to think.

Kelly took the rear seat while Finn slid into the passenger seat next to Lysa. At least if he kept moving, it would make him harder for Marchant to find. He was sure to be looking for him by now. He worried about Mark. It seemed the kid was dangerous, and apparently had the knack of hypnosis. How else did a junkie convince a whole congregation to follow him?

What if he tried to find Lysa? If he took her once, he might be able to take her again.

55 - COP HUNTING

Marchant unlocked the garage door. It tried to resist being opened, but a heavy shove from Marchant made it give way. With the fluidness of a snake, he moved to the BMW and slid inside. It was good of Jake to have left a change of clothes in his old locker. Soot and dust had gone right through his suit and shirt and caked his skin while he'd waited hours in the chimney for the police to leave the gym. The pain in his joints from being immobile for so long was finally easing and the few cuts and scrapes could be ignored. Even though the Reebok shirt and trainers together with the Calvin Klein jeans were oversized on him, they were better than grimy clothing. Once he was in London, he would buy himself shirts, ties, and suits, and a suitcase to put them in.

He dropped several newspapers on the passenger seat. The headlines were split between two stories. One, a ritual murder in London, and the other a drugs bust in Cornwall.

His drugs.

Rummaging around in the glove compartment of the car, he found the fake passport and identification he kept there for such an emergency as this. The car was registered to the fake identity. He believed in being prepared for any eventuality. He even had fake credentials for Don.

Tucking the passport into his pocket, he turned his attention back to the newspapers. Reading from cover to cover, scanning each page for information about the drugs bust. He smiled at the photograph of himself. It was an old one and the likeness was poor. A smile curled one corner of his lips as he read he was now a 'wanted' man.

Calmly scanning the text, reports revealed Don was dead and Joe was in intensive care, but there was no news of Finn. More information about the seizure of his goods in Cornwall the previous evening revealed that Craig had been shot dead after firing at the police. He hadn't known the kid had a gun.

He read with interest the piece about the policeman he'd shot through the head, paying little attention to the photographs of his wife and children. But still, through five different newspapers, he could find nothing about Finn. Frustration nudged his composure, but he refused to let it control him. Before he left the country, he would track Finn down. When he found him, he'd make him tell the truth. Then, he would cut off his balls and stuff them up his arse.

56 - YOU CAN'T REASON WITH A DEMON

Mark found it strange, communicating with the entity. It was the first time he'd been able to convey any message. Up until now, he'd been forced to listen and not been able to reply. He still had no control over his body.

He now knew Grohah had stolen his body in order to be part of the world again and regain his followers. A demon, who wanted to be worshipped as he was all those long years ago.

Through thought, Mark tried to tell him he was wrong, tried to convey he would eventually run out of people to kill. But the spirit told him there would always be people willing to die, and as long as there were, he would go on. He needed death to survive, so maybe that meant that without the continued killing he couldn't survive. Grohah laughed from inside and shook the whole body. It rumbled all around the darkness that encased Mark, and the laughter told him if Grohah didn't survive, then neither would Mark.

57 - THE RECIPE

Surrendering to the tiredness of rushing around from city to city, the hum and vibration of the car had lulled Finn to sleep. He woke to find that Lysa had explained the information about Neil Montgomery to Kelly, even though the girl had said she didn't want to know. They had to work together with all their information out in the open. Needham had ordered Finn to go back to Liverpool, but Finn had no intention of leaving London until they'd been able to follow up the lead on Mark. Determination drove him to figure out the puzzle and track the kid down.

It was just after noon when they arrived in London. Lysa had called ahead to her friend, Gail, and briefly told her she was in trouble and she and two friends needed a place to stay for a few days. Finn was impressed at how fast Lysa found them accommodation. On arrival at the flat, he scanned the external entrances and made a mental note of how many other residences there were on the way up the stairs. Gail opened the door and Lysa made fast introductions. Gail could stay only long enough to welcome them before rushing off to the hospital, which suited Finn. Doctors here were as busy as everywhere else.

After a quick lunch, the three of them sat on the carpet in the small living room. Finn laid the photo-fit and the recipe on the floor in front of them.

"All right then, what do we know for sure?" asked Lysa.

"We know Marchant had Jake killed. He as good as told me," replied Kelly.

"We can say that is a certainty," confirmed Finn.

"We also know Neil Montgomery baked up those biscuits and turned people into killers," offered Kelly.

"And Montgomery was then killed himself," replied Finn.

Lysa said nothing but studied the recipe, then turned to the second page. "I think," she said, after a few moments, "that this is more than just a recipe."

"Why?" asked Finn.

Lysa moved closer to the other two and spread both pieces of paper on the floor between them. She pointed to the page with the story. "We've been concentrating on the ingredients list because we've been trying to figure out what was in the drugs, but if we'd paid more attention to what's written on the this page, I think we'd have got further, faster." She turned to Finn. "There's a reference to the Mayan 2012 calendar, but nothing about the end of the world like the fear-mongers spout. It's more like a new phase of life. It also says, for the new world, ten thousand souls must be delivered to release Grohah." She picked up the photo-fit and papers that Finn had brought from the station. "In this report it says Mark claims to be Grohah."

Finn remembered the fairy tale horror story he'd not paid much attention to. With everything else he'd had to think about–Marchant, the drugs bust, and finding Lysa again, he'd forgotten the name of the demon in the story.

"Damn! I'm slipping," he shook his head. "I should have made that connection."

"I read the page too, and missed it until now."

"I'm the cop. I should've paid more attention. I should have realized."

"You're also human," cut in Lysa. "The main thing is that we found it now. It fits with what the reports were saying about Grohah and the priests.

"What the hell *is* Grohah?" asked Kelly.

"Well I don't know that, but whatever it is, it needs ten thousand people to die before it can get out." Lysa turned to Finn. "Remember when we were talking, adding up how many people had died, we reckoned it was nearly ten thousand."

Dwelling on the past wouldn't help them no matter how annoyed he was with himself. Analyze the evidence, piece it together. Concentrate. "So, Montgomery baked up those biscuits to drive the kids into killing each other, but he needed such high numbers it would have taken him too long to carry on using the nightclubs. He needed a high concentration of people who would take drugs without much persuading…"

"So he hit Glastonbury," Lysa finished for him.

Finn continued, "And somehow, Mark became tied up in this. They had to know each other in Liverpool. Montgomery baked up the drugs in order to release this Grohah, but it's Mark who claims to be this so-called savior."

Kelly leaned back against the base of the couch. "If that's right, and then this Mark snatched Lysa right at the place you found Montgomery's body, then maybe they travelled to Glastonbury together. Maybe Mark killed Montgomery."

"That's a possibility. Maybe he was after drugs and he killed him to get them," suggested Lysa.

"I could go with that theory, that Mark killed Montgomery for drugs, apart from one thing. Mark took you. I don't see why he would do that." Finn said to Lysa. There was something else he was sure, but he just couldn't work out what. "You said you thought he was Robbie for nearly all the time you were with him?"

"Yes."

"Why did you think that?"

"Because at first, he looked like Robbie. He knew all about me, he knew about you."

"Did you tell him about me?"

"Of course not."

"So he hypnotized you?"

"I suppose he must have. I remember being convinced he was Robbie, but I knew you wouldn't have told Robbie who you really were."

"So he had to have hypnotized you somehow," Finn reiterated.

"But he was a junkie wasn't he?" cut in Kelly.

"A junkie who could have killed Montgomery, as we have no other suspect. I had thought it might have been Marchant, he did want him dead, but he would have bragged about it when I talked to him if he had." Finn paused; the whole conversation sounded insane. He picked up the story page again, "But Montgomery was trying to raise some sort of spirit. What if…"

"You don't mean to say he managed it?" said Lysa.

Finn leaned forward. "When Mark brought his girlfriend into the casualty, did he appear to be the sort of kid who'd slit a man's throat? Or slaughter a woman on a church altar?"

Lysa didn't hesitate. "No. He just seemed like any other young kid strung out on drugs." She frowned, "Except for one thing."

"What was that," asked Finn.

"He seemed to care what happened to her, he said he didn't know her that well, but he came into the hospital with her. Most of them wouldn't risk getting themselves into trouble for someone they didn't know that well." Lysa paused. "Most of them wouldn't even risk it if it was their own mother."

"So, what does that mean?" asked Kelly.

"That he cares about people?" ventured Lysa. "And if he cares about people, then he's hardly a killer. He didn't hurt me. In fact, the one thing I remember is the way he screamed at me to get out, like it was so important."

Finn studied the paper again, re-reading the text Lysa had pointed out to them. Lysa was right. Judging from Mark's past, he didn't seem like a killer, but the circumstantial evidence pointed to the fact that he was.

"All right then," he said. "This means that although we would never have him marked down for a murderer, he is a junkie. Also two policemen who were at Glastonbury identified this photo-fit as the lad who was sitting on top of a white van with another guy. I'm now thinking the other man could have been Neil Montgomery." He turned to Lysa. "You were found unconscious on the ground outside a white van, and you've identified Mark as the person who most likely responsible."

Lysa interrupted him. "This is crazy. Are you trying to say some spirit that Neil Montgomery raised has possession of Mark, and that's why he's become a murderer?"

"Can you think of a better explanation?" Finn asked.

No one spoke. It was as if no one wanted to. The situation didn't seem real, but what else could it be? Finn needed to leave, but he didn't want the women with him.

Kelly broke the silence. "Well, I can't believe this for one minute. I reckon this Neil Montgomery was a bit nuts. He found this recipe and reckoned he'd give it a try. Who knows, with all that junk in someone's system, maybe it could turn you into a murderer. But I reckon that Mark just wanted more drugs from him. He wouldn't give him them, and so he killed him."

"But why kidnap Lysa?"

"Because she was there? Maybe he thought she could get him more drugs? He knew she was a doctor."

Kelly's reasoning seemed feasible, but Finn wasn't convinced. "That would make sense except for one other thing."

"What's that?" asked Kelly.

"The fact that Mark walked into a church, and convinced a whole congregation of seemingly normal people that it was perfectly fine to murder a woman on their altar. Even, I might add, convinced the priests as well."

"There is that, I suppose," conceded Kelly.

"Okay. Let's assume you're right Finn, and Neil Montgomery raised a spirit, and now somehow that spirit has control of Mark. What can we do about it?" Lysa shook her head. "You'll be laughed out of the police force if you go to them with that."

Lysa was right. Needham would think he'd cracked from the strain of going undercover. It sounded incredible.

"If I am right," he replied. "We have to figure out how to track him down, and how to stop him." Finn was silent, trying to think of a way to not only find Mark, but to keep everyone else safe also.

Kelly broke into his thoughts. "If you're right," she said, "and I'm not saying you are, then, it seems to me he wants people to follow him, believe in whatever rubbish he's saying. Otherwise, how could he have convinced all those people to let him murder the woman?"

"Sounds possible, considering the insanity of everything," said Finn.

"Well then, if that's the case, won't he be trying other churches? Or other places where people gather? Religious festivals or stuff like that? Can't you find out from the police where there might be anything going on over the next few days."

"That's brilliant! Of course you're right. If this spirit wants followers, churches would be the best place to find them."

"Just one problem with that, Finn," interrupted Lysa. "There're a lot of churches in London."

"Well. we'd better get moving then."

"Where to?" asked Lysa.

"Local nick, of course. Come on. You two are coming with me."

58 - GETTING CLOSER

Marchant drove around the area where Finn had his flat twice to
check for police. Satisfied there were none, he slipped through
the unlocked main entrance and up the windowless staircase to
number two. A shove on the door broke the flimsy frame and he
was inside in seconds. By the phone, he picked up a pad with a
Dr. Lysa Warner's address and phone number on it. Finn hadn't
mentioned any medical issues and he'd never heard him talk
about a doctor. It would be interesting to find out who she was.
He slid the pad into his pocket. Clothes hangers squeaked as he
pushed them along the rail in the wardrobe. There were few
clothes, and there was nothing to give away the fact that Finn was
an undercover policeman, but Marchant could smell it in the air.

Moving from the wardrobe to the few drawers in the room, he
found nothing else of interest. Time to move to the next
destination—the address he'd found on the pad.

Arriving at Lysa's apartment block, he locked up the car and
easily found her name on the intercom. He pressed heavily on
the button for L. Warner. No reply. Irritated, he rang the bell for
the downstairs flat.

A voice crackled over the speaker. "Who is it?"

"I need to check on Lysa Warner in flat three, I can't get a
reply."

"Who are you?"

"I'm her uncle. I have to speak to her. Her father's ill," Marchant lied.

There was a short silence before the voice spoke again. "How do I know you're her uncle?"

"Well you don't, but this is urgent. Her father is ill, he has severe food poisoning. We think she may be ill as well; they attended the same party." He softened his already quiet voice a little more. "Please let me check on her. She hasn't turned up for work."

The voice appeared to consider this, and in a few seconds, and without another word, the door buzzed, and Marchant was in. Making his way quickly up to the first floor, he found flat three and gave the door a sharp kick, aiming squarely at the lock. The door didn't budge. Annoyed, he kicked it harder, and this time it flew in. From the mess that greeted him, it looked like someone had been there already. To avoid being caught out by the owner of the intercom voice, Marchant closed the door before moving from room to room, examining each as quietly as he could. Another address book. This time he found Finn's mobile phone number inside. So, they were connected, and in more than a professional manner. Had she been his doctor, she'd hardly have his number in her personal phone book. Flicking through, he found the number for the Queens hospital. That must be where she worked. Lysa Warner joined his mental list. If he could find her, there was a good chance he would find Finn.

As he left the flat, he was almost knocked sideways by a grey haired woman whose size filled half of the small landing. She was whistling.

"You the bloke..." she paused, "looking for Lysa then?" she said trying to grasp her breath. Ah, she was wheezing, not whistling.

He recognized her voice from the intercom. "She's not in, but I reckon you should call the police, it seems she's been burgled." Without a backward glance at the red faced woman, he ran lightly down the stairs.

A few streets further on, he stopped and called the hospital number from her book. Being transferred around several departments displeased him, but finally he was put through to casualty. Lysa Warner was on leave.

Might as well use the same lie again. "Look it's really urgent, her father's ill and I need to get in touch with her. I'm her uncle."

There was a short silence on the other end of the line before the nurse replied. "All I know is she called this morning and said she was staying away longer than first planned, and would be with a friend in London." She sounded almost apologetic as she continued, "I don't know where the friend lives though, and even if I did, I couldn't give you the address."

Marchant thanked her and hung up. He started checking her book to find out how many friends she had in London.

Focusing on Lysa Warner would lead him to Finn, he was sure. His instinct was never wrong, and once he had dealt with him, he would be away overseas.

It cheered him to make such good progress.

59 - PLAYING THE BAD GUY

Finn answered the phone without paying attention to the call display, expecting to hear Needham ordering him back home.

"Finn, how are you?"

He hoped surprise wouldn't register in his voice as he recognized Marchant's soft tone. "Boss. Are you all right?"

"Fine, Finn. Just fine."

He motioned the girls not to speak as he leaned forward on the settee. "Thank Christ for that. I read about Don and Joe. It was too bad."

"Lucky I was able to get away," replied Marchant. "How did you manage it, Finn? The drugs squad are usually pretty good. You must be exceptional to get away from them."

Marchant sounded the same as ever to Finn, but that meant nothing. Marchant would now consider him extremely suspect. "I was lucky too. I was in the sea, just around some rocks taking a piss when it went down. I crouched down with just my head above the water. They couldn't see me with the rocks in the way."

"Not even with the helicopter searchlight?"

"It missed me. They must have thought they got everyone."

Marchant wouldn't believe his story, but it was worth a try to keep up the pretense; there might still be a slim chance to bring him in.

"Okay then, Finn. I need you to meet me. I can have us both out of the country in twenty four hours."

"Say where, and I'll meet you as soon as I can."

"Will you really, Finn? That's very good of you. I'll call you back later."

The phone flat lined.

Finn looked over to the girls, but Lysa spoke before he could tell her who'd called.

"That was Marchant, wasn't it?"

"The one and only."

"And he wants you?"

Finn nodded. "He wants me to leave the country with him."

Kelly shook her head. "As if you would. He must have an idea who you are. You're the only one not shot or stuck away in a police cell."

He sighed. If only it were that simple. "He knows I have to meet him, he's banking on it."

"But you can inform the police, have them ready to pounce on him," replied Kelly.

Lysa cut in. "He's too clever for that, he'll have you meet him somewhere it'll be easy for him to escape."

"Or somewhere it will be easy to kill me."

Kelly turned sharply. "Then you can't go."

This was getting more complex every minute. Mark had to be found so they could try and stop whatever Neil Montgomery had started, but it was also Finn's job to catch Marchant. Then there was the safety of Lysa and Kelly.

"Well, I reckon we should start moving around the local churches, trying to find out if Mark has been there. Then we might at least get an idea what he's up to. If Marchant calls me back, then I'll deal with it when it happens."

Having made a decision, he felt better. It wasn't ideal that Lysa and Kelly were involved, but if he suggested they stay in the flat, they would shout him down and he didn't have the time to argue.

"I've been studying cult religions in college," said Kelly. "I think I should go out looking for these people. They usually target young, single men and women—those who feel alone. I could fit the picture quite easily."

"No, it's too risky," replied Lysa. "What if you're sucked in? They brainwash people."

"You managed to get away from Mark when he had you in the van." Kelly pulled a ring of yellow elasticized material from her wrist and gathered her hair up in it.

"I'd have to agree with Lysa. You could end up being the next one on the altar." Kelly going in on her own wasn't an option. She was just a kid.

As though she read his thoughts, Kelly pointed at the papers on the floor. "I'm the right age, I know about this type of thing, and I don't for one minute believe in anything supernatural. It's just another psycho riling people up." She turned to Finn. "Anyway, you'll be there to bail me out if I need you."

"No. I don't like the idea at all. I don't have the authority to allow it."

"You don't need the authority. I'm going to do it anyway, so you might as well be there to back me up."

Kelly seemed far removed from the frightened girl Finn had first encountered in the basement of the gym.

She stood up. "Well, are you two coming with me or do I go on my own?"

Finn stood, and held a hand out to help Lysa up. "The thing is, the police will already have checked out all the local churches. I don't think we'll find much there."

"We're not going to the churches. We're going to where the students hang out."

Of course. Why hadn't he thought of it?

Half an hour later, Finn and Lysa sat in the Students Union Bar. Finn was conspicuous by his age, and was glad Lysa was sitting with him. Maybe the students would think they were a couple of new teachers.

They chatted about nothing in particular, as between them they kept an eye on Kelly. She sat on her own, sipping on a drink. He didn't like it. It made him uncomfortable. If anything happened to her, he would be responsible.

After about half an hour, two young guys sat down to chat with her. It was hardly surprising. She was an attractive girl. Finn watched her talking to them. After about five minutes, he saw her lean across the table and say something. Abruptly, they rose and left the table, one of them shrugging his shoulders as they went.

"I wonder what she said to those two." Finn asked

Lysa smiled. "I don't think you need to worry too much, I reckon Kelly can pretty much look after herself."

"Well, I don't think we're going to get very far with this. What are the chances of someone approaching her?"

"Well, as you said, the police will have the churches covered, so he'll have to recruit somewhere else. Where better than a university bar?"

Finn thought. Where? Where better than a student bar? If the churches were out of the question where could he go next?

Where did all the vulnerable people go? Where did the homeless hang out? Lysa interrupted his train of thought.

"Look. Where's she going?"

Finn looked up to see Kelly walking towards a notice board. After scanning it for a couple of minutes, she walked back across to them and took the spare seat.

"No luck then?" asked Finn.

"Not a lot," Kelly answered. "But this Mark character's only been around a few days. Maybe he hasn't reached here yet."

"So, where to next?" Lysa asked. Turning to Finn she said, "Can't you contact the police down here and see if they have any idea where he'll go next?"

"They wouldn't tell me anything; they'd consider it their investigation. Besides, Needham would find out I'm still here."

"But Marchant contacted you. Seeing as you're still after him, you can legitimately say you think you may be able to catch up with him."

Finn considered this. One thing was true, he could use Marchant's call as a reason to stay undercover. Needham wanted Marchant. It was almost an obsession with him, and if he knew he'd contacted Finn, he would want him to pull out all the stops in order to catch him.

"Okay. But even if I tell Needham about Marchant, I can't say he's down here. I haven't got a clue where he is."

"Yes, you have," answered Lysa.

Finn raised his eyebrows.

Lysa continued. "He said he wanted you to leave the country with him. He's hardly going to hang around up North. He's more likely to head down this way—bigger airports, easier to pass through the crowds. Even the ferries to France are an option."

Finn had already worked that out, but hadn't mentioned it. One way or another, he didn't need to worry about finding Marchant because it was a certainty that before too long, Marchant would track him down. He didn't want to scare the girls, so it seemed a better idea to concentrate on finding Mark.

"Agreed. I'm not contacting the police here though. Needham doesn't have to know where I am just yet."

"I hate to say this," interrupted Kelly, "but how are we going to find the psycho? Seeing as how I've drawn a blank here?"

This did present a problem.

Lysa looked from Finn to Kelly, and then back to Finn.

"Why don't I go around the churches? He kidnapped me once and if he sees me again, he might come out into the open."

There was not a chance Finn would allow her to take such a risk. Kelly looked alarmed at the suggestion.

"No, Lysa," said Finn. "We already decided against the churches because they'll keep away from them now they know the police are checking."

"You can't have a police presence in every church in London," she replied.

"Even so, I'm not risking it. I'm not losing you again. Not after last time." Finn shook his head at her, "We'll find him some other way.

"You were prepared to let Kelly try and find him, why not me?"

No. He wouldn't go through losing her again. He could go fight the bad guys, get himself shot, banged up, even killed if it came to it, but if anything happened to her, he might as well let Marchant torture him to death because it wouldn't be more painful. "I didn't want Kelly to do it either," he replied. "And to be honest, the only reason I went along with it was because I thought we'd draw a blank here."

"Oh, really?" butted in Kelly. "What if I had found someone who knew about him? What would you have done then?"

Finn stared hard at her. There was no chance he'd have let her become involved with Mark either. Fixing a gaze of determination on her he said, "If you had found anything out, I would have taken over, and if you'd decided you didn't want to take my advice, then I'd have had the police take you into protective custody."

Both women shook their heads slightly at him and frowned. It didn't matter, they would not be put at risk. It was time to be tough, to push them away. "Apart from the fact that I don't want anything to happen to either of you, I can't allow you to become involved. You're not even supposed to know who I am," he said, forcing a harsh tone into his voice.

"But we do," stated Lysa.

"And I shouldn't have told you. I should have just got on with my job and not become involved with either of you. It was utterly stupid of me." His insensitive words would hurt Lysa, and it pained him to speak them. But on one level, what he said was right. He should have waited until his investigation was over before taking things further with her. It was unprofessional, and now he had to consider the both of them before he could proceed. Taking risks with his own life was one thing, but he should never have involved them. Never.

The distress in her eyes were like twin blades of hot steel driving through his chest. She stood to leave the table, ready to walk away, but he wasn't going to stop her. It's better to risk losing her now than losing her for good because some demon kid psycho killed her.

"Well, I'm sorry you became involved with me, but I thought it was what you wanted."

He could see she wanted to cry, but was holding back. She was waiting for him to apologize, to ask her to sit down, say he didn't mean it, but he resisted, even though the words were already in his throat, desperate to burst out.

"I'll reimburse you for the clothes as soon as I can, don't bother coming to the flat," she said.

"Don't worry about it; I can claim it on expenses." He had to do this; it would keep them safe. He couldn't have their deaths on his conscience.

"You really don't care, do you?" She backed away from him, but her eyes locked his, willing him to tell her he didn't mean it. But he would not give in to the hurt he saw in those eyes.

"I like you, Lysa, but you know, I don't think me and you are going to go anywhere so we might as well end things here." How he wasn't choking on his words, he didn't know. He pushed it further. "I have a bad guy to chase and you need to go stick band aids on people." Every word that scraped its way out of his throat was a stinking lie. But it worked. She turned her back on him and walked away.

Kelly leapt to her feet. "I thought you were alright. How can you sit there after what you've just said? I wish I'd never met you, you selfish pig."

Finn said nothing as they walked away. Lysa looked back as she reached the door, and he badly wanted to jump up and follow them, but he kept himself firmly planted on the plastic chair until they were out of the door and away from sight. Then, he headed outside and towards the car. Despite what he'd said, he thought the churches would be his best bet at finding Mark. He was acutely aware Marchant would be on his tail, and Marchant wasn't a man to give up easily. Lysa and Kelly could not be there when Marchant found him.

60 - RING RING

The air conditioning on the BMW hadn't worked for the last hour of the trip down to London. Marchant twisted the controls every way he could, but no cool air came from the vents. An expensive car like this shouldn't have any problems, even if it was stolen and re-registered to appear clean. Expensive items should perform the way they were intended to. Since he'd been in the city, he'd had the windows open, but it wasn't any better. The summer heat wasn't lifting, and the traffic fumes irritated him and made him feel ill. He resolved to fly somewhere where there were few cars, and little pollution.

Ringing in his ear alerted him to an incoming call and he answered with a voice command from his Bluetooth headset. The caller conveyed the information he'd been seeking, confirming his suspicions about Finn. A man who'd been arrested with Pete was no longer in custody. No one knew his name, but they knew for sure he was no longer there. Enquires were being made and should turn more information up soon.

Satisfaction replaced his previous agitation. By now, Finn would suspect he was onto him, and he hoped he would be worried. It would be far more to his liking if Finn was on his guard, it would be more of a challenge. There was no skill in stalking an unsuspecting victim.

A new bank account and a new identity would take care of a nice new life where no one knew who he was. As he pulled up outside the little café, he reveled in what he would do to Finn when he found him.

From the modest establishment, he had a good view of the surrounding shops. He watched the people come and go, playing with ideas of what kind of lives these people led. Customers emerged from the deli across the street. After re-energizing himself with a light lunch, it was time to put in another phone call.

"Hello, Finn. Still around then are we?"

"Where are you? I daren't show my face anywhere, I've been waiting for you to call me back. Your mobile doesn't answer."

Marchant was enjoying the conversation already. "Maybe I chose not to answer it."

"Are we getting out of the country soon?"

"It's all organized, Finn, but there's something I want to ask you."

The reply was instant. "What's that?"

Marchant looked up at the surrounding buildings, admiring the Victorian architecture. They knew what a building should be like in those days. He savored the moment before he asked the question. "Did you really think you could fool me?"

"What do you mean?"

He had to give him credit, Finn didn't sound at all rattled. Marchant liked that. "I know who you are. You did a good job on that dealer though. You nearly had me fooled."

"Come on, Boss, what are you talking about?"

Still trying to kid him. The undercover cop to the end. "You know what finally did it, Finn? What finally told me what you were?"

He didn't pause long enough for Finn to answer. "It was because you didn't make the papers. Not even a wanted item, or a line about a mystery man getting away."

"I told you, I hid in the rocks. They didn't see me; they probably wouldn't have even known I was there."

Marchant shook his head even though Finn couldn't see him. "You're forgetting something, Finn. If I could get to Jake and have him killed, don't you think I could get to Pete? It's so easy for me to find out anything I want to know. Anything."

The threat was in the tone of his voice, as he had intended it to be. There was a pause before Finn answered.

"I know that, Boss, but you know I'd not cross you."

"I do? I know nothing of the sort. What I do know is that Pete was in the back of a police van with a man who gave his name as Finn. Now, that man mysteriously vanished. No charges, no custody. Vanished. Gone in a puff of smoke as if he were never there."

"I don't know about that. I was in the water, I told you."

"And the water is getting hotter, Finn."

"Honest, Boss. I'm for real. I don't know anything about another guy getting thrown in the van."

"When the water gets too hot, it can cook people, Finn," continued Marchant, savoring every word like a gourmet meal. "Playing Jake with Kelly was a wonderful appetizer, but I like a challenge for the main course. You're proving to be a fine challenge."

"Come on, Boss. Stop fooling with me. Where do you want me to meet you?"

Marchant ignored his request. "Don't you find the traffic down here terrible, Finn? It's so difficult to get from one place to another isn't it?"

"Down here? Where are you?"

"London. Same place as you," he paused. "Are you driving right now, Finn?"

"Yeah. If you can call it driving," Finn confirmed. "Where do you want me to meet you? I figured it would be easier to hide in the big city."

Finn would almost sound convincing if Marchant hadn't known better. "And I figure that sometimes I like dessert before the main course," he replied.

"What's your point, Marchant?" Finn's vocal expression changed. His previous keen to please tone was replaced by a voice with a much harder edge.

Wonderful, he had inched himself under Finn's skin. Now he was worth the effort of tracking down. Killing him would be a pleasure.

For the second time, Marchant ignored Finn's questions. "Traffic's pretty hard to get through here. It might be speedier if you get out and run."

Before Finn could speak again, Marchant cut off the phone. He left the café and walked leisurely around the corner to the entrance of the flats. He knew he had the right address. As soon as he'd seen Kelly Winter come out of the deli, he knew the woman with her must be Dr. Lysa Warner.

How long it would take Finn to reach them?

61 - THE LIVES OF THE FEW

There weren't enough dead. Mark was able to look outside of the body; it seemed like an eternity since he'd seen anything but blackness. Monty was annoying him, too. Apparently, when Mark himself became more conscious, so did his nagging former mentor.

Grohah still controlled the body but Mark sensed he was weaker and needed more people to die, but now he couldn't use the churches because the police were watching them.

Mark detected desperation in the entity that hadn't been there before. Everyone they passed, it looked in the eyes, and Mark saw the trick it used to make them follow, like a demented pied piper leading the people to their doomed destiny.

They walked along concrete and tarmac streets staring at every person they passed, collecting a string of people behind them. The hands that once belonged to him each carried a drum of petrol, as did some of the followers.

The entity was angry because the little girl had been in the church. It was her fault he could no longer carry out his plan methodically as he had wanted to. They had forced him to take this course of action, now they would see how powerful he was.

A policeman tried to stop them. It stared hard at him until his heart froze and stopped.

The entity didn't know much about policemen, and it tried to learn about them through Mark and Monty. It was frustrated because it felt it should have been able to take their minds just as easily as anyone else, but it was only able to entrance some of them because they seemed more alert, resistant almost and now there were weapons that had not existed before. Mark suspected the entity couldn't risk damage to the young body by trying to control too many of these policemen. If this body were killed, he would be sent back to the void.

Mark was merely the host for Grohah, and the power he'd initially felt was always Grohah, changing him, tricking him, until enough had died that he could subdue Mark and take control of the body it craved. Once the total number was complete, Mark would be lost entirely, and even the small lucid moments he had now would be gone forever.

Mark needed the body alive as much as his captor, and told Grohah that policemen could easily shoot him, and to avoid them if possible. Grohah listened to his host on this point.

But the irritation of the demon vibrated through their body. Grohah needed the lives, the blood, and it needed many now. Mark glimpsed greenery up ahead. It would make an ideal place for the sacrifice.

They moved forward with purpose.

***   ***   ***

Finn hit the traffic jam, but he couldn't see what was causing it. Agitated, he tapped on the steering wheel. It was too far to Gail's flat to run, so he had to wait until the traffic cleared. He should have taken Gail's phone number, especially as Lysa and Kelly were without mobile phones but Gail's number was unlisted, and no matter what he said to the operator, she wouldn't give it to him.

If he called the police, they probably wouldn't make it there any faster than he could, and the arrival of the police might put them more at risk. It was Finn Marchant wanted.

The traffic started to crawl slowly along the road, and Finn moved with it, willing it to move faster. He tried to work out a plan for when he arrived at the flat. The hidden gun weighed on his leg. Lysa had never seen it, but chances were she would see it soon. Marchant would expect nothing less.

Seconds turned into minutes, and each minute was an eternity preventing him from reaching Lysa and Kelly. A dread filled his stomach that he couldn't shift. He tried not to imagine what was happening back at the flat. If he did, he would leap out of the car and start running, no matter how illogical it was.

Chewing his lip, he finally saw what was causing the hold up. A mass of people, young and old, were crossing the road. At the head of the mass was a young slightly scruffy lad carrying two metal drums. They walked as one, all following the boy. From what Finn could see, at least two more men carried similar barrels.

Immediately he was torn. The boy at the front matched the photo-fit of Mark, yet Lysa and Kelly were in danger.

The sun flashed off silver badges on a couple of black police helmets bobbing above the crowd. They appeared to be following, not controlling the crowd, as Finn would have expected.

Marchant undoubtedly held Lysa and Kelly and was awaiting his arrival. It was his duty to his job to catch him, and his love and affection for Lysa and Kelly to make sure they were safe.

But the spectacle in front of him would result in mass loss of life. Some people stood and watched and others moved forward to join in the silent procession, as if pulled by an invisible force. Something else seemed strange. Apart from the rumble of slow moving vehicles, there was no sound in the street at all. He felt like a fish trapped in a bowl, about to silently witness a catastrophe unfolding. None of the spectators knew that unless he did something-- and he didn't know what he could do — all of the people in the procession would, without doubt, soon be dead.

But if he didn't go to Marchant, then Lysa and Kelly might die.

The lives of the few or the many?

He gained a little more speed as the throng moved nearer to the park, clearing the road. Then, he obeyed his instinct and pressed on the accelerator to head towards the flat. For the second time that day, he did something he shouldn't—he used the phone while driving.

After three attempts, the police were alerted to the location of Mark and possible forthcoming disaster, and Finn pushed on towards the flat.

62 - KNIVES

Nausea punched Kelly in the gut as Marchant walked through the door. Gail's living room faded from her sight. All she could see was the gym, his damp hand on her cheek, and the reptilian smile on his lips. Revulsion shook her body, making her want to puke on the carpet. She wanted to warn Lysa, but fear of the blade in his hand silenced her. Her friend's voice sounded distant although Lysa was only a few feet away.

Lysa looked from Kelly to Marchant, realization slapped her in the face. "You're not the landlord, are you?"

Marchant smirked the way he had when he told her he'd had Jake murdered.

"No, dear. I'm not the landlord," he said to Lysa. Turning to Kelly he sneered, "Why don't you tell your friend who I am, Kelly?"

Kelly sank down in the chair, the cup of coffee in her hand dropping to the carpet with a thud, the brown liquid oozing onto the red carpet, staining it black.

"Well, Kelly. Lost your tongue?"

Kelly couldn't take her eyes from this ghoul. She thought she would never have to see him again, never have to hear his voice. She whispered. "He's Marchant. We should have known he would find us."

"That's right, Kelly you should. Didn't I tell you I'd come for you if you went to the police?"

"She didn't go to the police," Lysa snapped. She's here with me visiting a friend."

Marchant wore a dark blue suit that looked brand new. He reached into his pocket and brought out a small red book. Flipping over the pages over he said, "Yes, that's right, a Miss Gail Simmons. You must be Doctor Lysa Warner."

Dread flickered across her friend's face, but if she was as scared as Kelly, she tried not to show it. Marchant brought the knife up to Lysa's cheek. She didn't move an inch.

"What do you want?" she asked.

*** *** ***

As a reply, Marchant brought the thin Commando Dagger down to the buttons of her blouse. He carried a gun, but he preferred knives. Better to play with. Of all his knives, this was his favorite. The thin rounded handle fitted perfectly in his hand. The double edged blade had served so well for troops in the Second World War. If he had been a soldier in those days, this dagger would be his pride and joy. You could slice or twist, make delicate ribbons of blood appear on skin with just the lightest of touches. Alternately of course, you could stab them right through the heart or slit a throat open in seconds. It was a wonderful weapon of torture. People had begged, cried, pleaded, and pissed themselves when faced with this beautiful dagger. With a thing of beauty like this, one could take much more pleasure with the kill.

"How long do you think it will take Finn to get here?" he asked, removing the knife from her chest and twisting the blade in the air, catching the rays of sunlight that streamed through the window.

Marchant felt the nervous energy vibrating in the air. Lysa obviously knew how dangerous he was, and he repulsed her. That was nothing new, he had repulsed many women. Slimy was how one woman described him, but once he cut out her tongue, she could no longer yell how much she hated him.

"He's not coming back here," said Lysa.

"Of course he is, dear. He has to come back for you."

Lysa shook her head. "No. We had an argument and he's gone back to Liverpool. We're staying down here for a few days holiday."

Marchant motioned with the dagger for her to sit on the settee. She didn't move.

His sneer would have made a serpent jealous. "He'll be here. I've telephoned him to inform him of my arrival."

*** *** ***

Lysa had been terrified at Glastonbury, but the craziness there was nothing compared to the fear racing through her nerves now. A sense of evil seeped from his pores, infecting the room. They were in far more danger than anything she had faced in her life so far. He pushed the door he'd entered by slowly, as if to shut it, but ensured it did not click fully into the frame. That taken care of, he moved purposely towards Kelly. He pulled her up from her chair and terror claimed the young girls face.

"Leave her alone. Don't you think you've done enough already?"

Marchant's eyes fixed on Lysa's, as turning, he pulled Kelly across the room and stopped in front of the settee. "And just what do you know about anything, Doctor Warner?"

His voice was steady, but anger lurked beneath the surface. This was a man who enjoyed causing discomfort to others. She wanted Finn to come, but she dreaded it also.

"I only know that Kelly's boyfriend was killed, and that she's very frightened of you, so maybe you killed him."

"I'm sure Finn's told you more than that, much more. Though I must say I was surprised to find Kelly here. I thought I would only have you to keep me company. It's a bonus to meet up with her again." He turned to Kelly, bringing his face close to hers.

"Sit on the couch, Doctor," he instructed.

Lysa calculated how fast she could go for help if she ran out of the door now. But that would mean leaving Kelly. It was too risky. She sat on the left of the settee, trying to think of how to get them out of this, and away from their tormentor.

Marchant sat next to Lysa, and pulled Kelly with him to sit on his right side. "Isn't this cozy? Do you think Finn will join the party, girls? Or, will he try to kill me?"

Kelly stayed silent, obviously too frightened of this man to be any use if they tried to escape. Her new found bravery had dissolved with his arrival. Lysa cursed herself for letting him in, but his identification had said Frederick Crowther. Cold steel scraped up her thigh, and her body tensed automatically. But, she had come through the massacre at Glastonbury, killing her own brother, and being kidnapped by a madman. She would survive whatever came next.

"How much does our Finn love you, Doctor? And why has he brought my little red haired friend along. Into threesomes, is he?"

Lysa didn't answer. She wanted to be sure that when she spoke, she wouldn't show fear. The man knew he had Kelly terrified and now he was trying to achieve the same with her. She would try not to give him the satisfaction. If he was going to kill her, he would do it without knowing how scared she was.

The knife moved further up her leg, leaving a red line on her skin, moving the hem of her shorts higher.

"Do you know it's a long time since I've killed anyone? I usually have other people do my work for me, so I'm a little out of practice." His lips curved into a sickening smile, "I hope I don't hurt you *too* much."

Lysa spoke the words as they entered her head. "The last person I killed was my brother, but at least I did it fast." The blade stopped, but indented her skin. A little more pressure would break it open as easily as tissue paper. She didn't look down, but turned her head to look him in the face.

"I'm impressed," he replied, inclining his body toward her, his back sideways to Kelly. Lysa willed the other girl to pick something up and hit him over the head, but she seemed frozen with terror. He stood, giving Lysa a reprieve. It was only temporary. He walked around the back of the settee and stood behind Kelly. He caressed Kelly's hair and then slid his left hand over her shoulder and down to her breast, his fingers sliding under her clothing. With his right hand, he brought the knife to her throat. Kelly was immobile as he caressed her and pinched her nipple between his fingers. "Nice tits. Jake must have loved fucking you. Maybe I'll have a real taste of you before I kill you." The smell of urine was strong as Kelly lost control of her bladder. He smiled at her distress and kissed her ear whispering, "Maybe you can piss yourself for me again later." Taking his hand away, he moved to stand behind Lysa.

He brought the point of the blade to Lysa's neck. "Move over next to her. Now!"

"Why?"

"Because I said so, and you will do what I say. I already made your pretty little friend here make a mess of herself. I can do the same to you."

"I'd not give you the satisfaction," Lysa said, and moved next to Kelly.

"Good girl. I can see why Finn likes you, you're tough like him. Has he told you some of the things he's done? How he helped torture a man? Kneecap him? I bet his friends in the police don't know about half of the things he's capable of. Then again, it wouldn't matter if they did. All in the line of duty."

She clung to what she knew. Whatever Finn had done, it had been because he had no choice. Even though his words in the bar had hurt her, she held fast to the things he'd said before.

"Now to set the rest of the scene for Finn," he said. "He'll have a wonderful view of you both on the couch as he comes through the door. He should be here shortly". He removed the dagger, but Lysa didn't allow herself the luxury of relief yet; relief would be her enemy and she needed to be aware of everything. Seconds later, he brought his hand up to Kelly's head at the same time she felt the blade on her neck.

Marchant traced up her throat and over her jaw with the knife-edge. Terror crept into her veins and she fought for control as the hostile steel moved to the corner of her mouth. Warm blood spilled over her lip as the tip of the blade scraped on her teeth.

"I think you're a bit too talkative, Doctor. Maybe I should cut out your tongue and present it to Finn in a nice little gift box?"

Lysa didn't lose her composure, though panic now reached into her body, grasping and twisting every nerve, electrifying her skin, making the fine hairs point skywards.

He was relishing every second.

"Do you know I haven't enjoyed myself so much in a long time? It seems I do have something to thank Finn for after all."

Her blood tasted like iron as it ran back down into her throat.

*** *** ***

At least two hundred. That would provide the release, but then it would have to move on. Although Grohah could control the police as they came into direct contact with, he couldn't control those he couldn't see, and that presented a problem he hadn't accounted for.

They were all sitting now, happy in the midday sun; drinking in its warmth as he talked to them. Speaking now not in words, but through the light-waves of the mind which reached out to each individual, controlling them, making them worship him, as was right. Petrol vapors rose in the heat as his workers doused the followers. The perfume which would release these people to him was new, and would do the job quickly and efficiently. He opened the small matchbox. So small, yet so powerful.

*** *** ***

Finn didn't bother to lock the car, but ran into the building and up the stairs, tense and alert. Stopping outside the door he pulled the gun from its hiding place on his leg. Marchant was waiting for him. The most evil man he'd ever met, with no care for human life was with the woman he loved, and another he was responsible for.

He drew a breath and pushed on the open door with his foot. It swung in slowly. What he glimpsed through the narrow opening pumped blood through his veins so fast, he almost heard it. The couch faced the open door. Marchant stood behind it, the two women sat in front of him. In his left hand a knife, pressed between Lysa's lips. A trickle of blood ran out of her mouth and down her chin. In his right hand, a gun, aimed at Kelly's head.

Images of Amy leapt into his mind. Pictures he had managed to blank out for the last seven months. The truth he'd not been able to tell Lysa. His Amy, lying naked in a tangle of mud and bracken. Butchered.

Until the death of a murdered policewoman hit the headlines, Marchant had thought she was a police informant; he hadn't guessed she was undercover. The thought of the same thing happening to Lysa shook him. He was about to take a shot at Marchant when the man spoke.

"I wouldn't try anything, Finn. If you do, the blade goes right through to the cushions behind her head. How long do you think she'll last?"

Finn couldn't risk it. It was a trap, but his only hope had been to creep in on Marchant and take him by surprise. The man was too smart for that.

Finn waited, looking hastily around the entrance for anything he might be able to use as a weapon. The wall at his left, nearest the door opening, contained a coat rack with an umbrella in the stand. A couple of telephone directories rested on the small table, and tucked underneath sat Lysa's holdall. The bag would be just out of Marchant's view from the couch. Finn dipped his hand inside and found something sharp. He quickly pocketed his find, pushing his gun into one of the coat pockets.

He walked into the room.

"Pleased you could make it, Finn. Come and join the party."

"It's me you want. You don't have to bring them into it. It's our argument."

"And what argument is that? The fact that you're a double crossing, stinking policeman? I should have known really, when they kept Jake inside, but let you out."

Finn glanced at Lysa and Kelly. Marchant could kill them both in an instant, but he probably had much more in mind, or he wouldn't have gone to such trouble to set this up.

"All right, Marchant. What's the deal?"

"I don't make deals with the likes of you. You should have learned that. I have my reputation to uphold. I'm afraid I'll have to kill these two, but I wanted an audience."

"Why not just kill me, Marchant? You could shoot me clean through the head in a second. I wouldn't even see it coming."

"Where's your gun, Finn? In the leg holster?"

Finn pulled his trouser leg up to show the empty holder, and then pulled up the other to show nothing was concealed.

"So where is it then? Hidden outside somewhere, ready for you to pick up?" His tone turned from calculated to the vocal equivalent of granite. "Go get it now, or I spill her blood first." He nodded down at Lysa.

"I don't have it. I left it in the car so I would come up here unarmed." Finn stopped as the blade pushed further into Lysa's mouth. She gagged and a fresh stream of ruby liquid spilled over her lips.

"Get it, Finn. Now!"

He couldn't take the chance. Walking backwards he pulled his gun out of its hiding place. If he tried to shoot Marchant, he would cause Lysa and Kelly's deaths.

"Walk over here. Drop it on the window-ledge, and walk back."

Lysa's eyes followed him as Finn did as instructed. "Sit down there on the carpet," Marchant instructed.

Finn sat cautiously, keeping his eyes trained on his adversary. A chance had to present itself soon. He couldn't let them down. Kelly looked terrified, taking him back to the day he'd dragged her out of the car. It seemed a lifetime ago. He'd been trying to protect her. If he'd left her alone, she wouldn't be here now.

Marchant brought the knife out of Lysa's mouth. She sagged down into the settee, rubbing her lips with her hands, her palms streaked red.

"I like your taste in women, Finn. The Doctor here has been keeping me amused. Tells me she killed her own brother. Maybe she could kill you just as easily." He turned his attention to Kelly. "Or maybe I could get her to kill our little redhead first. After they pleasure me first, of course. That could prove quite enjoyable."

Alarm lit Lysa's face. He was grateful Marchant couldn't see, he would only revel in her fear.

"She's a doctor, for God's sake. You can't expect her to kill people."

"But she killed her brother. She should have a taste for it now. It doesn't take long. It gets easier each time." Marchant paused as if in thought. "Maybe I should keep her alive, and then when I need someone disposed of, she could do it quite cleanly for me. That would be a novelty for a while, don't you think?"

"She killed her brother in self-defense. She was at Glastonbury. He was a drug addict."

Marchant turned his attention to the two women. "Stand up. Both of you."

They stood; Kelly, a little shakier than Lysa. Finn was maybe three feet in front of them.

"Face each other."

Marchant sprang over the back of the settee and stood on the cushions. Looking at Finn he said, "You. Move back, but stay on your arse. Don't get up." After Finn had complied, he turned back to the women. "Now, you both step sideways toward him. Just two steps, enough for me to stand next to you." As soon as they moved, he stood next to them on the carpet. Finn noticed Lysa was very slightly taller than Marchant, though Kelly was a couple of inches shorter.

He held out the knife to Lysa. "Here. Take this, but don't even consider going for me. I'll shoot you and your friend before you even make a scratch."

She took the knife. Dread sagged her face and dimmed her eyes. Marchant would make her do something terrible, something she wouldn't want to do.

*** *** ***

Lysa felt sick as her friends white lacy bra came into view as Marchant unbuttoned Kelly's blouse. Her red curls draped over her breasts. He took Lysa's hand, the one that held the knife, and moved it toward Kelly, placing it just above the lace on her right breast.

Lysa felt Kelly tremble. The girl's eyes pleaded with her, until finally she could hold back no more and the tears spilled out over the lids. Kelly turned her head to Marchant.

"Please don't make her do anything. Please. We won't tell anyone, we won't say a word. Just let us go."

Marchant grinned like a Halloween lantern, laced with promises of darkness and evil. Wicked eyes shone with anticipation.

"Don't worry, Kelly. She's a doctor. You can trust her, can't you? We can all trust doctors."

"Is this for my benefit, Marchant?" asked Finn.

Marchant ignored his question, turning his attention instead to Lysa. "I'm going to show you what I want you to do. I'm going to let go of your hand, but you have to keep the blade pressed to her skin. Watch what I do, because then I want you to make an incision along the same line."

Lysa caught her breath as she watched him trace his finger from Kelly's right breast up towards her throat, stopping at her collar bone. He then moved back down to her cleavage. He then traced the same path on her left breast, finally going back down to rest above the lace, parallel to where she held the knife.

He wanted her to carve a letter 'M' on Kelly's chest.

"Do it," he ordered.

Kelly's green eyes pleaded with her.

"I said, do it!" Marchant ordered. "I want to see the blood drip down her skin. I want him to see it."

Kelly glanced at Finn, who sat motionless on the carpet, his gaze fixed firmly on Marchant.

Lysa still held the blade. Marchant put the gun to Kelly's ear. "If you don't do it, I'll blow her brains all over this room."

Lysa summoned up as much courage as she could. "I can't, she's my friend."

"She'll be a dead friend if you don't."

"Well at least she'd be dead quicker if you just shot her now, you're going to kill us all anyway."

"Would you rather cut her now, or should I rape her instead?" He looked over to Finn. "He can't do anything to save either of you. Your only chance is to do as I say. I might not kill you after all. I might just slice you up a bit instead."

Lysa's heart pounded through her body. He meant every word.

"You'd better start now, before I get tired waiting and take things into my own hands."

Kelly sobbed. Lysa couldn't believe what she was about to do. She pressed the blade into the girl's skin, moving it upwards to form the first line of the 'M'. Kelly fainted, the blade nicking her chin as she fell to the floor.

*** *** ***

Finn moved quickly. As soon as he saw Kelly's legs buckle he knew it might be his only opportunity.

For only a second, Marchant's gun pointed at the air, and Finn used the moment to go for his legs, making Lysa lose her balance and fall into the settee as he moved. The force of hitting the wooden arm made her drop the knife. He didn't notice the instrument he'd taken from the hold-all fall out of his pocket to the floor.

Marchant swung the barrel around and fired, but Finn had already knocked him over and the bullet whizzed past, shattering a mirror before embedding itself in the plasterwork. Shards of glass showered the carpet with brilliant rays that danced manic reflections on the wallpaper.

Finn landed on top of Marchant, but he still held the gun, and now he pointed it at Finn's head, his finger squeezed on the trigger. Finn's hand moved to his pocket, but the scalpel wasn't there.

*** *** ***

Something deep inside Mark tried to make it stop, tried to explain that it was wrong, but you can't reason with a demon.

Police cars raced over the grass, the engine in the sky roared, but the entity wasn't worried. He sent a coil of thought up to the helicopter pilot, making him drive the machine to the ground. It crashed into the trees before exploding into flames on impact.

The few police that weren't in his control looked on, horrified. Grohah didn't care. They couldn't stop him taking his petrol-doused followers into the abyss.

*** *** ***

The shot filled the room. The scream of pain was almost as loud. Marchant's hand flew halfway across the room.

Finn looked up. Lysa stood by the window, Finn's gun in her hands, her body shaking.

"Who taught you to shoot like that?" Finn asked.

Her voice trembled. "I was aiming for his head."

Before he could reply, Marchant brought his left fist up and struck Finn a blow to the side of his skull. It knocked him sideways, and Marchant got up from the floor, grasping for the dagger. Blood sprayed from the stump on his arm, but he ignored it and lunged at Finn with the blade. He caught his leg, digging the knife into his calf muscle.

Lysa turned her attention to Kelly, who was kneeling on the carpet reaching out for something, but an animal like howl erupted from Marchant and Lysa turned to Finn to see Marchant had landed on him, pinning him against the settee. She squeezed the trigger again, scared that she would hit Finn instead of Marchant. The bullet missed both of them, but destroyed Gail's antique grandfather clock.

Her ears vibrated with the explosion of the gunfire, the smell of sulphur filled the room. Through the fog, Lysa saw Kelly climb onto the couch. But Marchant didn't.

"This is for Jake you bastard."

She plunged the triangular section of mirror through the back of his neck and straight out the front of his throat. Her hands bled from the sharp edges, but it was nothing compared to the geyser that sprang from Marchant's severed gullet. If he'd been able to look down, he would have seen his own frozen refection of terror in the blood smeared silvered glass, but she'd plunged the mirror in with such force she'd severed the spinal cord.

Kelly fell back to the cushions, the skin on her hands shredded. When she looked down, she saw the blood and screamed, and then it seemed she couldn't stop screaming. Even when Lysa and Finn tried to comfort her, with Lysa wrapping towels around her ruined hands, she still didn't stop. Finn turned as the police burst into the flat.

"It's okay. I'm undercover," he said holding his hands in the air. He nodded towards the still howling Kelly. "Get her an ambulance." Indicating Marchant he said, "You'll only need a bag for him."

*** *** ***

After hasty explanations and phone calls between the London police and Needham, the police let Finn and Lysa go. They promised to call in later and give a statement. Lysa made a makeshift bandage for his leg. He could walk on it, but it would have to be stitched up later.

Injured or not, they had to reach Mark.

63 - PETROL

Grohah wouldn't listen. Even though he was becoming weaker and Mark felt stronger, Mark still couldn't stop what was about to happen. Monty chipped away at him, telling him that he was wasting his time and to just let Grohah get on with it, but still Mark had to try. Even if he could never regain his body, he didn't want to be responsible in any way for any more deaths. His fingers took the matches from the box.

He concentrated hard, willing his fingers not to strike the first match, but they did, and the flame burst into life, ready to snuff out the lives of others.

He blew it out.

Elated with his small victory, Mark tried to climb further into his body, but Grohah retaliated by pushing him back. It was too difficult. He was going down, back to the blackness.

"Mark!"

Hearing his name gave him a surge back. Who could know his name? Nobody here knew him.

He struggled to see out of his eyes. It was the doctor. Why was she here—especially after what he'd done to her?

"Mark, look at me."

He looked, but as he did, Grohah grabbed her mind, and wrapped it up in a thousand tiny tendrils. She looked at him with dull eyes as she walked across the grass, taking the drum he offered her. She poured the remains of the petrol over herself.

*** *** ***

Finn couldn't believe what he was seeing; couldn't comprehend what Lysa was doing. Maybe she was trying to fool Mark? Once she was near enough, she would take the matches from him surely? She'd raced on ahead when she'd recognized the youth. He cursed Marchant for cutting his leg up, preventing him from running forward with her as swiftly.

A sigh escaped with relief as she took the box. It was just as he'd thought, now she'd run back. No. She couldn't be taking the matches out of the box. She looked as though she was about to strike one.

"No!" He heard himself cry out as he tried to rush toward her, but his injury slowed him so much he'd never make it. Police dogs barked as they raced past him, toward Lysa and Mark.

They reached her before he did, knocking her down and fixing her to the ground. An enormous black Alsatian pinned down Mark. As he fell down by her side, paramedics and a doctor jabbed a syringe into Mark. Finn snatched the matches as the park filled with police and ambulance crews.

He hugged her close. She looked up at him, her body shaking.

"I was going to do it, Finn. I was going to set all those people on fire, including myself."

"Good thing I called the police earlier then."

She looked questioningly at him. "You didn't tell them about the demon stuff."

He shook his head. "You must be joking. If I'd told them about that, they'd never have turned up. I told them their murderer was in the park ready to aid a mass suicide, or murder, whichever way you want to look at it."

"Can we go home now? Saturday night in casualty is tamer than all this."

"As soon as the paperwork is sorted out, we're on our way."

She sighed. "There's always the paperwork."

60 - EPILOGUE

Mark would never escape. The voices chipped away constantly. Monty griping about how stupid and weak he was, and Grohah complaining about dogs. Why couldn't he control animals as well as humans?

Mark could never shut them out, except by screaming until the wardens came and shot him full of drugs. Then, he could drift away and dream his own dreams, where he lived in his body alone, with no tormentors caught up in his mind.

They called it a multiple personality disorder. Huh, if only. Sometimes he showed them by taking their minds and controlling them for a few minutes, but the medication dulled his senses, and he could only do that now and again. It was a concession from Grohah for at least being half alive. Anyway, it scared him to control people. He only did it to the crueler wardens, just to make them wary.

Without the required number of deaths, Grohah was weaker, but he would never go away completely until Mark died. Mark feared the continual battle between him and the demon would never end. It scared him that the demon could so easily creep up on him and make him kill. If that happened, he would be out of control again.

*** **** ***

Grohah waited in the recesses of Mark's mind. He had waited many years to reach this far, and he had learnt by his mistakes.

Next time, he would be wary of animals.

Next time, he would win.

ABOUT THE AUTHOR

Lorraine McLeod has been writing for many years, first taking creative writing classes at Liverpool University. Through these classes she was inspired to write her first two novels and was featured in two anthologies. Later, she worked with the artist Gino d'Artali and was published with him in Bordersenses in 2001.

Her short story 'Parasite' won the July 2010 Story Slam event which was sponsored that month by On Spec Magazine.

Lorraine's day job involves working on the web but at home she finds time for writing and photography and painting.

Mr.Neon Blue – A short story available on Amazon.
Mr. Neon Blue has revenge on his mind. His best friend Roger is the cause of the accident Mr. Blue had in his racing car and he's out to make Roger pay.

On his way to track down his former friend he meets Erin, a lonely but bright child whose abusive parents don't let her mix with other children.

With Erin in danger and time running out to find Roger, Mr. Blue has to make a choice. Will he stay to help Erin or move on to find Roger?

http://www.amazon.com/Mr-Neon-Blue-Lorraine-McLeod-ebook/dp/B006W429E8